THE BREAKWATER

THE BREAKWATER

A TALE OF OLD PORTHCAWL

BY

ALUN MORGAN

COWBRIDGE

D. BROWN & SONS

1975

ISBN 9500789 8 0

Printed in Wales by
D. Brown and Sons Ltd.
Cowbridge and Bridgend
Glamorgan

TO THE MEMORY OF MY FATHER

AUTHOR'S FOREWORD

The difficulty in writing this book has been that so little is known about the men who built the Porthcawl breakwater, yet it has withstood the battering of tides and storms on one of the most exposed parts of the Glamorgan coast for over a hundred years and will probably continue to do so for another hundred, if not for ever.

My basic information comes from a diary written by John Vaughan, one of the workers on the breakwater. Although semi-literate until the age of thirty he kept spasmodic accounts of his day-to-day activities, later re-writing them in note form. Then a failing memory allowed one or two inaccuracies to creep in as, for example, in his description of events in Sea Bank House, which James Brogden did not occupy until his second marriage.

Nevertheless the notes contained vivid insights into Vaughan's working life, his endeavours to find happiness in marriage and his successful rise to fame in the industrious, brawling but God-fearing community of an embryo Porthcawl.

In an attempt to pay tribute to one, at least, of the forgotten men who laboured so long to create a structure taken for granted by townsfolk and holiday makers alike, I have expanded Vaughan's original notes into a story, not hesitating to fill the void with events and characters of a purely fictitious nature. I make no apologies for this, for the object of an historical novel is entertainment, not instruction; and those who prefer the latter may read works of scholarship on the subject.

ALUN MORGAN

June, 1975

CHAPTER ONE

FOR ONE WHO could not read until his thirtieth year, and then only with difficulty and hesitation, it is doubtless presumptuous of me to pen this story; especially now that the young people of today, fortified with compulsory education until the age of eleven and in possession of an artisan's vote, have a disinclination to listen to the advice of their elders. But it is a story that I, John Vaughan, late of Her Majesty's Royal Regiment of Artillery, must tell; for is it not unusual for a man who has served in many foreign lands and seen much evil therein (and stood up manfully against both) to return to his native soil and there meet an evil more destructive than any he had witnessed before? And when that evil has been compounded not only by his own countrymen but by that section of humanity referred to as the weaker sex, namely women, is there not a lesson to be learned by those who would endeavour to listen?

There is no bitterness in my soul over the events that befell me, for I faced adversity from the very beginning. At the age of eighteen months my mother died of the cholera in Merthyr; and, before another year was out, my father and two brothers were reduced to ash by a licking tongue of flame that escaped from a furnace at Crawshay's Cyfarthfa ironworks. So I, a penniless orphan, possessing no more than the rags I wore, still filthy from the slag tips that surrounded the town of Merthyr, was dispatched by neighbours to an aunt living in a village called Newton, close by the mouth of the Ogmore river in the county of Glamorgan.

No braver and more kindly a soul than my Aunt Sarah ever existed. She took me and nurtured me, although the task was hard, for she had five children of her own and a drunken, brawling husband who shunned all employment save that of poaching in the grounds of Tythegston Manor and Blundell's Court. My aunt's kindness, which shone constantly through her clear blue eyes, softened the hammer blow of my misfortune; and the mild

1

air of Newton strengthened and revived me. I grew to love the little cottage with its view of the ancient Norman church silhouetted against the background of the Bristol Channel, and I remember how on summer days the sea would beckon with flashes of blue and silver and off I would go to explore the long, empty beaches that stretched as far as the vast sand warren of Merthyr Mawr; or else I would take a crust of bread and make for Sker, there to lie on the soft turf near the old house, listening to the roll of the surf and the plaintive cries of seagulls, peewits and lapwings.

The children of the village became my friends, too; and many were the happy days spent playing hide and seek, leap frog or cattie and doggie on the village green. Sometimes we would dare each other to go barefoot into the mystifying darkness of St John's well, there to stand petrified as the strange water, low when the tide was in, high when it was out, bubbled and gurgled in the sand between our naked toes. But, all too soon, my childhood was over and I was again faced with the harsh realities of life; for my aunt, with a suddenness and speed that was astonishing, succumbed to a disease all too prevalent at the time: diphtheria. I watched, terrified and awe-stricken, as her plump frame was rapidly reduced to skeleton proportions, and ached to see her pump out her life in long, throttling gasps. Almost before she was cold my uncle was amongst the mattress and cupboard drawers to find what little money there was, and spent it within a week at the Ancient Briton, with the result that my aunt had to have a pauper's funeral. Soon the bailiffs were in, the children scattered—some to the workhouse in Bridgend—and my uncle built himself a driftwood hut on Newton Beach where he remained for the rest of his life.

When this further calamity occurred I was seventeen years old. I had already tried to find employment at a small dock which had been built a mile distant at a place called Port Call, but the Company was in difficulties, for the port was entirely dependent on the coal trade, most of the ships returning with profitless ballast. The old sailors of Newton prophesied doom for the undertaking for the port was open to the terrible gales that torment us in the Bristol Channel; and lying in wait for unwary ships were the Tuskar Rocks, which even the Vikings feared, and the treacherous shifting sands known as the Scarweathers. I myself had stood on Port Call Point, fearing for my life as the giant fingers of wind tore at my clothes, listening to the dreadful shrieking known to sailors as the Cyhiraeth, and seeing with my own eyes even four-masted giants smashed to tinder by the deadly waves. I had counted the cost of such storms, too, having seen the nave of Newton Church full to overflowing with the dead and the kitchen floor of Sker House crammed with the corpses of sailors.

Had I the wit then to have foreseen that one day a great and far-seeing man would, by the creation of a massive, sheltering breakwater, mitigate the effect of that deadly wind, and transform the port into a viable undertaking and by his genius create a large town around it, I would never have left the region. But I was young, not gifted then with foresight, and so I decided to seek my fortune elsewhere.

Before the year was out I packed my few belongings in a scarf, joined a drover at Cowbridge, and walked all the way to London.

CHAPTER TWO

BUT THERE WAS no fortune to be found in London, nor even regular employment; and in order to gain a roof over my head and food in my stomach I joined the Royal Regiment of Artillery which one day was recruiting at Woolwich. This period of my life I shall pass over lightly, for war has little meaning for those who have not taken part in it, save for the soldier's loved ones who fear for his safety; but as my service in the Queen's army had some bearing on my future life I must touch on it, however briefly.

As a gunner I quickly made the transition from a youth to a man. The handling of big guns—particularly the cumbersome eighteen-pounders—developed my shoulder muscles to the full, making my appearance in the dark blue uniform attractive to womenfolk, as I knew from their glances. But I had little time for dalliance, for no sooner had I mastered the intricacies of laying a gun correctly than the battery was posted to the Crimea.

3

There I learned the even greater art of showing no fear when all around was death and destruction. It was there, too, that I had my first glimpse of the extremes of goodness and evil of which men are capable in moments of adversity; a lesson which stood me in good stead for the rest of my life: that is, never to judge a man by his appearance. For some men who seemed unbecoming and diffident on the first meeting were the first to come to your aid in moments of peril; whereas those who were of a swashbuckling nature often cringed in the trenches in mortal fear for their lives. And during the time of the bitter cold and the ravages of typhus and dysentry I witnessed on many occasions how the elements of fear and self-preservation tore the masks off men's faces, revealing them for what they really were.

The war with the Russians over we were transferred to the baking, disease-ridden plains of India there to quell the turmoil in that great continent after the Mutiny. There I progressed in the art of gunnery being promoted to Bombardier at the rate of one shilling and eightpence a day, with a special allowance for training Punjabi Mussalmans in the art of mountain warfare. I was, therefore, pleased with my lot and looking forward to a long and honourable career, but in the eighth year of my service the bad luck that had dogged me from childhood returned in greater force; for when traversing a valley with a mountain train of smooth-bore twelve-pounders in the North-West frontier we were ambushed and I received a ball from a tribesman's musket in the upper leg, with a force that all but carried it away.

The moment the ball struck I experienced not only pain but a sense of foreboding, for I knew immediately that the bone was shattered; and having left a Britain in which the maimed and crippled received no sustenance of any kind, save that which their families gave them or could be obtained by begging, I did not rate my prospects highly: a frame of mind made worse by being carried, strapped to a mule, a distance of two hundred miles back to base. But I had reckoned without the skilful devotion of an Indian orderly at the hospital who, by means of poultices made from leaves (I know not of what kind) repaired both wound and bone so that I was again able to walk, albeit with a limp. And neither did I realise the protection afforded by the Royal Regiment to its invalided members, for when I had

4

recovered sufficiently I was shipped, in a fast sloop of the navy's, to Plymouth and there offered a post for life with the coastal artillery. Once a gunner, they say, always a gunner; and I very nearly remained one, but now two other considerations entered my life.

In the first place I had been abroad nearly nine years and the *hiraeth* to return to my native Glamorgan had grown strong within me. I wanted again to see the sea glittering between the sandhills, to hear the cry of the sea birds and to feel the soft turf of Newton Green beneath my feet. In short, I was homesick, a matter of import to all Welshmen. Secondly—and this was now a matter of even greater significane in my mind—I wanted once more to set my eyes on Miss Arabella Dinwiddy.

Miss Dinwiddy had, in a manner of speaking, been my childhood sweetheart: not a real one, for I had muffed my chances through the inexperience of youth, as the following episode will relate. One hot summer's day, just before leaving Newton, I had accompanied Arabella on a walk as far as Merthyr Mawr Warren and there, in the loneliness of that great expanse, had protested my love for her. Whereupon the young lady, being of a capricious nature, had given me a shove that sent me reeling, and then run away. Being well versed in the ways of village children I knew that such an action indicated a chase, with all that that implied; and I caught up with her just as she reached the top of a large dune. There we struggled together, laughing, until we missed our footing and fell, tumbling over each other until we ended up at the bottom of the dell. There Arabella, her cheap little cotton dress in disarray about her, sticking up slightly because of the voluminous petticoat underneath, lay on the sand in mock faint. Had I been of a quick mind I would have dropped down beside her and kissed her, for the invitation was obvious, but my senses began to reel at the sight of her bare legs, encompassed from the knees up in pantalettes. I did not know then what I know now: that pantalettes, however prettily edged with lace, were for ladies in reduced circumstances, a substitute for the full pantaloons of richer women. So taken aback was I that I just stood and gaped, my mouth completely ajar. In a flash Arabella, who saw the direction of my staring eyes and knew that I had detected her embarrassing secret, was on her feet and away off home.

Later that day I met her again, behind the tower of Newton Church and, to make amends for my lack of endeavour, I seized her and kissed her; whereupon she raised her dainty hand and smote me such a blow on my cheek that even today, when I think of it, I can feel the skin rise. I did not see her again for another week and when we eventually met she ignored me as though I was the village debt collector. All of which taught me my first lesson about women, namely that you can never tell your exact position in relation to them; for they must always keep their composure as a weapon against our greater strength.

Imagine my surprise, therefore, when, in the middle of a cannonade in the Crimea, I received a letter from Miss Dinwiddy. I immediately replied, enlisting the aid of a soldier friend who could write, for I was then still illiterate, and a correspondence developed between us; and by the time I embarked from India I had received no less than six letters, all of them precious for Arabella was then my only link with what I regarded as home. Moreover, in the letters I detected more than a hint of fondness; perhaps Arabella remembered that day on the dunes and her treatment of me, and accordingly my own dictated efforts became more and more impregnated with expressions of devotion.

When we eventually docked at Plymouth in May 1863, I therefore naturally found it difficult to curb my impatience; and immediately I was released from the service I took a night coach to Gloucester and there caught an early morning train to Bridgend, travelling in an open carriage to conserve my savings. It was as well that I was still wearing my artillery trousers and a leather jerkin, for the line had opened but ten years previously, and I swear that the tall-stacked engine, which never ceased enveloping me in a cloud of smoke and ashes, must have been Mr Stephenson's original Rocket. But I cared little, for in my valise was a silk shirt, the latest narrow trousers and a frock coat, purchased inexpensively in the Barbican; and around my waist was a body belt containing twenty gold sovereigns, the result of arrears of pay and a generous grant from the Artillery Benevolent Fund —enough, I imagined to keep me from starvation for a year.

But some kind of work I would have to find, for I would have to support Arabella if she consented to marry me; and there was every possibility of that, judging by her most recent letter. I had

6

no qualms about finding suitable employment for, in spite of my limp, I was agile and stronger than most men. And had I not seen much of the world and become wiser because of it? If any man could fight the Russians and Indian tribesmen and have seen all that I had seen, surely, I adjudged at the time, the future need have no fears for a man such as I had become.

Little did I know what lay ahead and that at twenty-five one is only at the threshold of wisdom: for there was about to begin a period of excitement and calamity greater than I had ever known before, with all the evils and pitfalls that I have alluded to at the beginning of this story.

CHAPTER THREE

I TARRIED AT Bridgend just long enough to sluice myself down at a horse trough and partake of a meal of ale, cheese and bread, then set off on the six mile walk to Newton. I savoured to the full the sight of the green fields and hedgerows, a pleasing contrast after the arid earth of India, and made good time until I reached the top of a hill called Three Steps; there my leg began to trouble me and I was obliged to sit down and rest. After twenty minutes or so I heard the clip-clop of hooves on the stony surface of the lane and looked up to see a donkey approaching, pulling a diminutive cart. Sitting on one of the shafts, his legs dangling in the dust, was a small, wiry figure of a man. He reined in the donkey as he came level with me, took a clay pipe out of his mouth and grinned.

'Travelling down, Mister?'

'As far as Newton,' I said, rising.

He jerked his head in the direction of the other shaft.

'Put your clobber in the back and I'll be glad of your company.'

I threw my valise into the cart amongst a conglomeration of old sacks and bits of metal and perched myself precariously on the vacant shaft. The little donkey made a complaining movement with its shoulders, but after a moment or two set off down the slope towards Dan-y-graig. My companion glanced sideways at me.

'Been travelling far?' His accent was one I could not quite fathom.

'All the way from Plymouth.'

'I see you're a soldier. On furlough or finished with the service?'

'Finished.'

'Wounded?'

I studied the stranger. He was aged about thirty, with thin, straggling hair, a long nose, merry, dancing eyes and a wide, flexible mouth. He looked for all the world like a benign pixie and I found myself liking him immediately, but with the reserve that had now become part of my character I resolved not to be too communicative.

'Wounded. How did you know?'

'Your leg,' he said. 'I can see that one is thinner than the other.'

'In India,' I replied. 'A tribesman got me with a musket.'

He was silent for a while, then:

'Foreign parts! I wish I'd been to foreign parts. Cornwall is the furthest I've been to.'

'Are you Cornish?'

'I am, but now I'm almost a Welshman. Mark Treseder is my name—Mark the Tin they call me round here, for my main trade is tinkering, but there are better things to do now with the docks developing as they are.'

'What better things?' I asked.

'Trade. I do a little trading with the sailors. Many of the ships come from Devon and Cornwall and I have one or two connections there—they send me apples and cider and other things which I sell in Bridgend market. In return I ship them stockings and woollens. It's a better living than tinkering. If I had a boat of my own I'd do well at it. I'll get one one day.'

'I shall have to obtain employment myself,' I said. 'What are the possibilities nowadays?'

The tinker glanced again at my leg.

'Plenty if you're strong. There's stevedoring at the docks —humping the coal and iron off the trams. Then there's building the inner dock walls and the breakwater, but that's heavy work. Some of the stones is as big as four of these carts. It's dangerous, too. Get one of those on your good leg and you'll be finished. Ain't you got no education of any kind, mister, or trade?'

I shook my head. Ever since receiving Arabella's first letter I had tried to educate myself in the art of reading and writing, but without proper instruction I had found it hard going.

'Pity,' said Treseder. 'That's what Brodgen's short of, I hear. Time-keepers and book-keepers he wants. Anyone with a knowledge of arithmetic or ledger work is hard to find around here and he's crying out for them.'

This information created some apprehension within me and, to make things worse, Treseder followed it up with:

'All the best jobs is going to them as has education these days. Mark my words. In a few years time there'll have to be schools for ordinary folk—there's got to be. It's not just around here there's developments going on but all over the country. There'll be a time coming when no job will be worth the having without a man being able to letter and number; and it's the children of today who'll be lucky. Older folks like us will be left behind—out in the cold: labourers for the rest of our lives. See if what I say don't come true.'

'I agree,' I replied, for it was a theme I had heard discussed in the barrack room and I myself had often envied the self-confidence and easy acceptance of responsibility which my officers displayed, stemming no doubt from their superior education at public school. I added, wistfully, 'But for the time being I will have to take what work is offered me.'

By this time we were approaching Dan-y-graig woods and, as the gradient steepened, Treseder applied a hand brake. The little cart pushed hard against the hind quarters of the donkey, making it stumble occasionally, but it continued its sure-footed progress. Suddenly around a bend, the sea came into view, framed by tall trees on either side. I caught my breath. It was my first glimpse of my childhood home for nine years.

Treseder waved an arm in the direction of the green coastal plain, now only half a mile distant.

'You can see what they're doing even from here. See them puffs of smoke? Them's engines—dozens of them. There's railway tracks all over the place. And see that tall thing on the edge of the water—that's Brodgen's breakwater, the start of it. I hear tell they're going to build it out for a quarter of a mile to shelter the dock entrance. Then the ships'll be able to wait for berthing in calm water.'

9

I strained my eyes into the distance. I could see a dark area of what appeared to be a small forest but which, on closer examination, revealed itself as a mass of swaying masts; and beyond that, in the open water, more masts. The sea itself was blue—not as blue as the Mediterranean but blue enough—and in the intervening fields I could pick out the white blobs of cottages, more than I had ever seen before. There were bigger buildings, too and what looked like whole rows of houses.

'There's been a lot happening since I've been away,' I said.

That man Brogden's a hard task-master,' said Treseder, 'but he's fair and honest—the men like him. That's more than you can say of his wife. She's one of them aristocrats—connected with the army and should have been a soldier herself. Look out if you meet her. She'll walk right through you. But James Brogden —he's a gentleman! Good at everything, not just building docks. He's got coal mines and iron works but he can still find time to paint pictures; and he can sing—and turn his hand to carpentry and stone masoning! What's more, he's never too busy to see you. Knows all his workmen by name.'

'He sounds a remarkable person.'

'He's got big plans for Porthcawl—they're calling it that now, after the Welsh; and when he's finished it will be some place, believe me. I've heard talk of a big town behind the docks with hotels and a promenade. He'll do it, too! He's got more energy than any other ten men I've met—but that wife of his . . .'

He stopped suddenly and eyed me beadily.

'Are you married by the way, mister ?'

'No, but I hope to be so in the near future.'

After the implication of his previous remarks I thought Treseder was going to warn me off entering the state of matrimony, but he said abruptly:

'Will you be wanting lodgings ? I've got a room for a single man. If you're interested, that is.'

'I shall certainly want lodgings,' I said. 'For the time being, anyway.'

'Then you won't want better than I've got. It's next door to Myrtle Cottage. Do you know where that is ? It's the one with the figure-head in the front garden.'

I knew Myrtle Cottage very well. I had often climbed up the gaudily painted wooden figure-head of the ill-fated "*William Miles*" and perched myself on its head. The cottage was only two hundred yards from the sea and the prospect of staying near there pleased me.

'Come there this evening,' said Treseder, 'and we can talk over terms.'

With that we entered Newton and I noticed with surprise that several large and imposing houses had been built on Clevis Hill. But the village itself seemed unchanged: the church was its usual quiet, battlemented self, the cottages were still there and the green turf of the common glistened in the strong sunlight. In the distance the sea sparkled invitingly as of old. I breathed a sigh of satisfaction and reached for my valise.

'I'll see you tonight then, Mr Treseder.'

'Tonight or sooner. Come when you want to. My wife will be pleased to meet you.'

He jerked the rein and the donkey clip-clopped off down the lane. I turned to survey the familiar scene.

Then, as I looked, I became aware that something was amiss. For a moment I could not fathom the reason. The village was exactly as I had left it, there was no doubt of that; but now there was something mystifying that eluded me. Gradually it dawned on me: there was no one to be seen. Except for two children playing in the distance near St John's Well the village was completely deserted. The cottages had a quiet, shut-up look and even the Ancient Briton, usually noisy at any time with beer drinkers, was strangely silent. I walked over to my aunt's old cottage and knocked on the door, but the sound re-echoed emptily back to me and I was left standing, fingering a valerian bush that grew out of the wall. Disconsolately I turned and was just in time to see an old woman disappear behind the lychgate of the church. She was, I remembered, old Ma Perkins, the church cleaner, who used to belabour us children if we as much as disturbed a flower in the graveyard. I hurried over and caught here just as she was about to enter the porch.

'Hullo, Mrs Perkins. How are you?'

The old crone shielded her eyes from the sun with a bony hand and stared at me. At last recognition came to her.

11

'Why, if it isn't John Vaughan after all these years. Have you returned from the wars, John?'

I nodded and for a few minutes we conversed, she asking about where I had been and I answering to the best of my ability; but as soon as I could I asked the two questions now uppermost in my mind.

'Mrs Perkins, where is everybody?'

The old woman gave a toothless grin and waved her arms in the air.

'All over at Porthcawl, of course, working at the new docks. All the men and most of the women—a lot of the children too. There's jobs for anyone who can use a shovel or a hammer.'

I breathed a sigh of relief, for I had been suspecting an epidemic of some sort. Then I asked the second question.

'Can you tell me where I will find Miss Arabella Dinwiddy?'

There was a sudden and marked change in Ma Perkins. She stared at me for a moment, speechless, then became flustered.

'Down at Porthcawl like the others I expect.'

She nodded several times, gave a cackle and retreated into the dark interior of the church. I heard her voice again from a distance.

'You'll find her down there somewhere. You go and look.'

Somewhat taken aback at her demeanour and the sudden end to our conversation, I made my way to the lychgate and stood there, pondering. Ma Perkins had given the impression of someone who possessed a secret she did not wish to divulge, but I shrugged off a feeling of unease and decided to take Tredeser's room as quickly as possible so that I could spend the rest of the day searching for Arabella.

With this in mind I set off for Porthcawl, but had gone only half a mile when there occurred an event so traumatic that I remember it vividly even today, and so must describe it in detail.

I had reached the gorse- and bramble-clad area of Back's Common when I heard a sound that stopped me short in my tracks. It was a girl's laughter and there was no mistaking it—it was Arabella's. I looked in the direction from whence it had come and there, sure enough, was the object of my childhood dreams. Only her head was visible for she was partly hidden by a hummock of sand.

I decided to surprise her and made a small detour to come up behind the hummock, all the while keeping the back of her head in view. I was delighted to see that her hair was as golden as ever and still set in carefully arranged ringlets. I reached the top of the slope and for the second time within seconds froze into immobility.

For Arabella was not alone. She was sitting astride the prone figure of a man, her dress bunched up around her like a tea cosy. She was not wearing pantalettes or even pantaloons, as far as I could see, evidently much to the enjoyment of her willing captive. As I watched, her merry laughter was joined by the deeper guffaws of the man and they both had a little wrestling match, in which Arabella contrived to stay on top. Suddenly the man saw me and stopped his gyrations. Arabella paused, too, sensing an intrusion and turned her head, her blue eyes full upon me. Slowly her mouth dropped open and a flush came into her cheeks.

I paused just long enough for our eyes to meet and then turned and walked away. The hurt I felt was not caused just by Arabella's infidelity—although that was hard enough to bear—but by the fact that her companion was none other than Jeremiah Meredith, an arch enemy of mine, a bully and as nasty and vindictive a character as it would be anyone's misfortune to meet.

CHAPTER FOUR

I SAT ON THE BED, my head between my hands and my elbows on my knees. That Arabella had forsaken me was a blow to my pride but understandable. Who was I, absent for nine years, to expect a young girl to remain constant all that time? There had not even been a formal engagement between us. But that she had aligned herself with a man like Jeremiah Meredith turned my stomach. Anyone other than Meredith would, after due thought, have been acceptable; but not him.

This Meredith had been the bane of my youth. Always big for his age, he had lorded it over us children with spleen and vindictiveness, using his weight and size to intimidate and exact retribution. Of objectionable appearance with his big bulging eyes and snotty nose, he was the bully par excellence. His favourite pastime had been plucking the wings off butterflies, smashing birds' nest and torturing small animals; and once, when I had remonstrated with him over these malpractices, he had raised his fist and smashed my nose to pulp. Later, when I had grown big enough to tangle again with him, I succeeded in giving him such a blow that he had stumbled backwards into St John's well, there to slide down the steps and be saved from a broken neck only by the presence of the holy water, which unfortunately was particularly high that day. Thereafter we treated each other with respect, but never far below the surface there was malice and hatred on both sides. Think as hard as I could I could see no valid reason why Arabella should have been intimate with such a man.

After brooding thus for a while I went to the window. Mrs Treseder, forewarned by her husband, had given me a friendly welcome and leased the room at a weekly rental. It had a pleasant aspect, being comfortable and facing south. All the time I had been there distant sounds were reaching my ears: spasmodic shouts, the whistle of steam engines and a continual roaring sound which I could not fathom. Now and again, from just up the road, came the dull throb of a machine and the sudden shrill scream of a mechanical saw. When I stuck my head out of the window the sound became more audible, but I could see nothing, for a ridge of sand was interposed between me and the dock area. Curiosity gained the upper hand over my morose mood and I decided to see what was going on. I retreated back into the room, filled the wash hand basin with water, cleaned myself thoroughly and then set out to examine for myself the changes that had taken place whilst I had been away.

I made straight for the ridge from the top of which, I reasoned, I would have a good view of all that was going on. I was not disappointed, for from my vantage point I could see in all directions. To my left was a long line of trams from which men were hurling boulders and shovels-full of soil; and a small army of people were spreading the resulting debris over a large area which I remembered as once nothing but a coney-infested warren. Immediately in front of me was a muddy incline, one hundred yards wide and two hundred long, sloping gradually away from me until it ended in an earthen wall twenty feet high and bounded on the seaward side by a long causeway of rubble and stones. In the deepest part of this incline men were toiling, filling trams and horse-drawn wagons with a glutinous mud. The work was obviously hard for in parts horses and men were struggling up to their fetlocks and knees in quagmire.

Wishing to examine these activities at close quarters I descended from the ridge and picked my way across intersecting tramlines until I reached the main railway sidings. There I had to be careful for several locomotives were shunting long lines of wagons filled with coal. I then passed through an equally dangerous area of lime pits interspersed with mounds of sand, until I came to a large pyramid of faced limestone blocks at which a score or more boys were chipping with chisels and hammers. Not one block, I estimated, weighed less than five hundredweight. Finally I reached the dock itself—the original dock which I had known as a boy. Six ships were berthed at the wharves and the continuous roaring sound I had heard was being made by the coal tumbling down chutes into the holds. The tide was ebbing and it was apparent from the activity on board that the vessels were preparing to depart. At the harbour entrance three more ships were awaiting their turn, one of them with its sails still full rigged. All this was of such absorbing interest that I had a mind to sit down on a bollard and study everything in detail, but the air was full of coal-dust which made my eyes smart and so I decided to move to the lee of higher ground.

There I received another surprise. On the rocky promontory of Porthcawl Point where the old stumpy breakwater had been was a tall wall carefully and meticulously mortised into the craggy undulations of the headland. It was the size of the base of the wall that astonished me for it was at least sixty yards across. The pyramids of Egypt, I reckoned, could not have had more care and preparation lavished on their foundations; but having seen what the wind and sea could do in that exposed place I understood the reason behind such an undertaking. Whether the breakwater (which then had only just been started and ended in a series of irregular steps into the water) would withstand the elements when extended to its fullest length was something about which I had grave doubts.

As there was no one working in the vicinity of the wall (the tide was too high to permit that) I turned to look at the sun setting over Hartland Point but my attention was distracted by the sight of another tramroad undulating across the rocky ground towards a quarry some quarter of a mile distant. I was of half a mind to go and examine that as well; but just then I caught sight of the Anchor public house and, my throat being parched from the coal-dust, I decided to refresh myself instead with a jug of ale. Accordingly I crossed the rails, avoided a wagon being trundled by a train of horses and entered the tap room. Save for a surly looking fellow behind the serving counter the place was empty.

I ordered my ale and, in an attempt to start a conversation, said:

'Very quiet here this evening.'

'They'll be in shortly when the tide drops.' The inn keeper placed my ale on the counter and turned his back on me. With my attempt at pleasantries at an end I trudged through the none-too-clean sawdust to a corner and sat down.

Through the open doorway I could still hear the multitudinous sounds of the docks and I marvelled at what I had seen. Not since leaving India, where I had once witnessed a teeming mass of natives building a water tank had I received such an impression of concentrated human endeavour. Another fact that struck me, too, was that out of all the people I had seen there was not a single one that I had recognised. It was as though my old world of the small parish of Newton-Nottage had disappeared without trace and in its place was a new and larger community of strangers, into which I now somehow had to fit.

It was whilst I was occupied with these thoughts that three men entered the room and, schooled though I was to shocks and sudden happenings, I felt my heart miss a beat; for one of the men was my enemy, Jeremiah Meredith. At first he did not see me and he and his companions went to the counter to order a quart each of ale. At last his eyes became used to the gloom and he turned towards me. He said something in a low voice and his friends turned too. There was some sniggering and then a loud guffaw. I pretended not to hear and sat staring straight in front of me.

Then Meredith said, loud enough for me to hear:

'That's him, lads. That's the one who fancied himself with Arabella.'

I glanced at Meredith but pretended not to recognise him. In reality I was weighing up the situation. Meredith was even bigger than he had been as a youth, a good six feet tall and heavy with it, although he had a paunch about his stomach. I recognised one of his companions also, one Mog Williams, who had been a toady of his and still was by the look of it. If things got rough it was going to be difficult to deal with all three, especially as my leg precluded rapid movement; but knowing Meredith as I did I resolved to prepare for any eventuality.

At last Meredith, tiring of my studied indifference, nudged his companions in the ribs and called out:

'How did you like what you saw today, Vaughan?'

They sniggered again.

'Fancied your chances there, didn't you? But it's me who's had her. I've been having her ever since you were in India.'

I continued to stare silently at Meredith. No Welshman can stand being made a fool of and the fire was coursing through my veins, but I contrived to remain outwardly calm. We Celts are brave fighters, as our history shows, but we have one weakness: when upset we lose our self control and tend to fight wildly, without science. The army had taught me how to retain my composure and yet destroy the enemy with cold, calculated fury. That was what I now proposed to do, if necessary.

I drained my jug and carefully replaced it on the table.

'Meredith,' I said quietly, 'you always were a bully and a bully you'll remain.'

This seemed to take them aback a little and I saw a look of apprehension cross Meredith's face. He remembered that fall down the well.

Don't take that from him,' shrilled Mog, just as he used to in the old days. 'Give him one, Jeremiah.'

'I will if he don't look out,' said Meredith, without sounding too sure of himself.

With unhurried movements I got to my feet, picked up the jug, went to the counter and ordered another ale. All three of them watched me, no doubt surprised by my boldness. But I had reckoned without an old, childish trick that Meredith and his

17

cronies were adroit at. Unknown to me one of the trio got down on all fours behind me and, just as I was turning away from the counter, Meredith gave me a shove. The back of my knees caught the recumbent figure and I went sprawling, landing on the floor with a thump that jarred my spine.

Fighting to keep my self control I got up and carefully dusted the sawdust from my clothes. Shaking inwardly, but determined to do what had to be done, I moved nearer the three of them. Carefully I placed myself so that Meredith was on my left and Mog in front of me. I then addressed the latter.

'Mog,' I said, 'you always were a creeping little toad. Still doing what your master tells you, I see.'

This set them laughing again, for the memory of my fall was still amusing to them and they no doubt thought they had the measure of me; but this was what I wanted, to lull them into a sense of false security. I addressed myself once more to Mog Williams.

'It's time you became a man, Mog. You haven't changed much since we were children. How about growing up? You might even find a woman who'll like you then, but as you are . . .'

I paused, for the muscles of my right arm and shoulder were poised ready and, just as Mog thought I was going to go on with my little speech, I brought my fist around with as much force as I was capable of. It buried itself up to the wrist in Meredith's fat stomach and he doubled up, a long drawn out hiss of air escaping from his mouth. As he fell I tapped him with my left, just to straighten him and let fly again with my right, catching him on the nose with as much force as before. Meredith went down as though pole-axed and lay on the floor, moaning.

'Now then, Mog,' I said, 'it's your turn.'

But with a speed that would have done credit to a mountain goat Mog was out of harm's way.

'It was only a joke, Johnny bach. We didn't mean no harm.'

'I'll do you harm if you cross my path again. Where's the other one?'

The third fellow was already up against the far wall, a look of awe on his face. I flicked a few more spots of sawdust from my jerkin and stepped across the prone figure of Meredith, now bleeding like a pig.

'Tell him,' I said, 'when he comes to, that he's welcome to any woman he wants, but if he mocks me again I'll kill him.'

In a leisurely fashion I crossed the room and went out into the cool, evening air. I am not a vindictive man and it is impossible for me to harbour a grudge for long, but I must admit that at that moment, in spite of my still-pounding heart, I felt a surge of elation at having put Meredith in his place.

CHAPTER FIVE

AT BREAKFAST next morning Mark Treseder listened to my account of the event in the Anchor with a gradually darkening countenance; and when I had finished he said:

'You know who Meredith is, don't you?'

'Why, yes,' I replied, mystified by his demeanour and lack of amusement at what I thought was a good story. 'The biggest bully this side of Offa's Dyke.'

Treseder shook his head impatiently.

'He's the son of Ezekiel Meredith.'

'I know that, too. I remember the family from the old days.'

'Then you obviously don't know that Ezekiel Meredith is the chief gaffer down at the docks.'

At first the full implication of Tredeser's words did not sink in, but after a few moments I began to see the reason for his gravity.

'Is he now?' was all I could say.

'I can tell you this,' Treseder went on, 'Brogden's foreman is away in London—will be for a few weeks—and Ezekiel has been given the responsibility of hiring labour. I can't see him taking you on now that you've bashed his son's nose in.

'I had no alternative,' I said defensively. 'There was no way out of it, except by being a coward.'

'I grant that, but you see the difficulties we're in, don't you?'

I was somewhat ameliorated by the use of the word "we": in time of trouble it is always good to know that one has allies.

'Then what's to do?' I said. 'I must obtain employment and there seems precious little chance of that except at the docks.'

Mrs Treseder now joined us. She was small, like her husband, with the same straggling hair, dancing eyes and thin, mobile lips. They looked more like brother and sister than husband and wife. She stood behind Treseder stirring a bowl of oatmeal porridge.

'Go down to the docks with Mr Vaughan, Mark. Ezekiel owes you a favour after you sold him them shirts cheap. Tell him Mr Vaughan has been serving his country and wants a job. He'll listen to you.'

'I doubt it,' said Treseder uneasily. 'Ezekiel's as nasty as his son, They both harbour grudges till doomsday. He won't listen to me.'

'But you must try,' said Mrs Treseder sharply.

'Very well, I'll try. But don't expect anything to come out of it.'

'Take Dafydd Hopkins with you.' In explanation to me, Mrs Treseder added: 'Dafydd Hopkins is the strongest man around these parts. If there's any trouble he'll help the both of you.'

'All right,' said Treseder, 'we'll take Dafydd with us but it won't make any difference to Ezekiel.'

Mrs Treseder nudged her husband sharply with the bowl.

'Then tell Mr Vaughan what you were talking to me about last night.'

Treseder looked sheepish for a moment and received another nudge for his pains.

'Go on, tell him. He might be glad to hear of it now, after what's happened.'

Treseder began slowly:

'Mr Vaughan—'

'Call me John,' I said, trying to put him more at ease.

'Very well, John. When I got home last night I told Annie about you and how much I'd taken a liking to you and we fell to talking. I've told you of how I do some trading—well, if I could find a partner there's the making of a very good business. I can't do it on my own. Between seeing the ships' crews to arrange for the goods to be brought across and then collecting them and taking them to Bridgend market, it's more than one man can do. Now if I had a partner who could look after the shipping side I could do the selling. And when I met you I said to myself, "Now here's a man too good to use a pick and shovel for the rest of his

20

life—perhaps he'd come with us." We'd make a success of it, believe me. If you accept you'll never regret it.'

He paused to see the effect of his words and I spent a moment or two in thought before replying.

'Thank you for your trust in me. It is a honour to be offered a partnership, but I have no knowledge of trading, and what little I know may be a handicap to you rather than an asset.'

'I can teach you all you need to know,' said Treseder eagerly. 'You'll soon get the hang of things. What I need is a good honest man who is not afraid of hard work. The knowledge will come later.'

'I do know one thing,' I said, and it is this: all business undertakings require capital and I would be dishonest if I failed to inform you now, at the very start, that I have very little of my own.'

'How much could you put up?'

'Twenty pounds—that's all I've got in the world.'

'We need a hundred to get a good boat. Dafydd Hopkins is coming in on it—he'll be skipper. Between us we've got sixty. With your twenty we'd need twenty more, plus a bit extra for stock.'

'There's no hurry,' said Mrs Treseder quickly, 'Mark wasn't thinking of starting till next spring. Perhaps between now and then you could save the other twenty.'

'How can I save?' I said. 'No job—no money. Perhaps I could get work on a farm.'

'On a farm! at fourteen shillings a week! You'd get more as a deck hand.'

'If only,' said Mark, 'you'd not clobbered Jeremiah. I know they want men on the breakwater. It's good money, to. A pound a week.'

'What's the good of talking if you don't think Ezekiel will give me a job.'

'Then stop talking and go and see Ezekiel,' said Mrs Treseder sharply. 'Both of you go and see him now. If he refuses because of what Mr Vaughan has done to Jeremiah then at least we'll know where we stand. Then we can think again.'

Mark and I saw the truth of this female logic and we finished our buttermilk in thoughtful silence. For my part I was pleased with the offer of a partnership from two people like the Treseders, whom I now adjudged as friends; and it was a comforting feeling to be liked and wanted in a strange environment. But the immediate cloud on the horizon was Ezekiel Meredith and the possibility of his preventing me from obtaining employment; and so I felt relieved when Mark said at last:

'Come, John, let's go down to the docks and get it over with.'

We left the cottage and made our way along the causeway on the eastern side of the embryo harbour. I noticed that the ships' masts, which previously had been upright and swaying gently to and fro, were now pointing drunkenly in all directions; and when we reached the old dock we could see the reason why. The tide was out and every vessel was lying askew on the thick, slimy mud. One, a large schooner, had been trapped at the harbour entrance, looking for all the world like a stranded whale, conveying instantly the reason behind the building of a new harbour.

When we reached the edge of the basin Mark halted, placed his fingers to his lips and gave a piercing whistle. In response a head appeared at the cabin door of a small coaster.

'Dafydd!' yelled Mark. 'Come ashore. I want to speak to you on urgent business.'

A great lumbering figure detached itself from the ship and came wading through the mud. A few moments later, with a puffing and grunting, Dafydd Hopkin appeared at the top of the steep harbour steps. He was not exceptionally tall but of immense girth, with long arms and a chest like a barrel; but although he gave the impression of almost limitless strength one thing belied his ferocious appearance and that was his face. Across a countenance burned almost black by sun and salt wind a beaming smile played, heightened by gleaming white teeth and eyes as blue as the sea. Once I had recovered from the shock of being confronted by such a bear-like creature I saw that here was a man of affability and good humour; and, as with Mark Treseder I found myself taking an instant liking to him.

'Dafydd,' said Mark, 'this is John Vaughan. He may come into partnership with us. Don't shake hands with him like you do ordinarily—he might need his fist later.'

Dafydd's grin became even wider and he proffered a hand like an iron shovel, but the grip was gentle as he had been instructed.

22

Mark then spent a few minutes appraising him of our difficulties, ending with:

'So that's how it is, Dafydd. To set up business we all need more money and John here can't lay his hands on any more until he gets work.'

Dafydd scratched his head but the beam never left his face.

'Never did like them Merediths much. Can't do no harm to go and ask Ezekiel though, is it?'

'That's what we think,' said Mark. 'Any idea where he might be?'

'Over at the breakwater, I'd say,' said Dafydd. 'I hear tell they're having trouble with the bedding stones.'

'Come on then,' said Mark. 'Let me do the talking.'

He led the way across the earthen dyke to the promontory where we paused and looked down. A group of men were standing on the jagged rocks beneath us and thirty or forty more were straining at ropes and winches in an attempt to drag a particularly large limestone block into position on the steeply sloping ramp. As we watched one of the ropes unravelled and the block ran backwards a few yards, nearly crushing a man who foolishly tried to impede its progress with an iron bar. There was a groan of dismay from the men and some of them sat down in an attitude of despairing resignation. From a commanding position on the highest point of the rock a big man started cursing. His back was towards us but I knew from his bulging neck that it was Ezekiel Meredith.

'Get a chain!' I heard him shout. 'A rope's no bloody good for that thing. You should have had more sense, Evans. The rest of you men hold fast till the chain's attached.'

I felt Mark take my arm.

'Come on. Now's our chance.'

We clambered down a flight of rough hewn steps to the razor-sharp rocks below and made our way to a large salt pool, on the other side of which stood Ezekiel, his back towards us. I heard Mark take breath.

'Ezekiel. Can you spare a moment?'

Ezekiel swung round and immediately his eyes took us all in. They dwelt on me and a glower spread across his face.

23

'What d'you want, tinker?' he asked, not taking his eyes off me for a moment.

'Mr Vaughan here had just returned from abroad,' piped Mark, 'and is desirous of obtaining employment. I have advised him of your position in the docks and we were wondering if there's a vacancy he can fill.'

'Is that so?' Meredith levered himself down from his rocky pulpit and walked around the pool until he was but a yard or two away. There was a glimpse of malicious enjoyment on his face and he was as I remembered him: a bigger version of his son, with the same bulging eyes and pugnacious, snub nose; but his mouth was larger, drooping at the corners in a way that reminded me of a shark's. When he spoke it was with a sarcastic, mocking tone.

'So Master Vaughan would like work, would he? Hey, lads! Come over and listen to this.'

Sensing that something was afoot, and glad of the opportunity to rest, the workmen gathered around us, effectively blocking our retreat to the steps. They formed a close semi-circle, making me feel uneasy, for the unevenness of the ground precluded rapid movement, especially for me with a lame leg. I took comfort from the sight of Mark on my left and Dafydd still smiling, on my right.

'Well, now,' said Ezekiel. 'This is rich! And what might you be doing, Mark Treseder, asking on account of this fellow? Has he no tongue of his own?'

'I am his friend,' said Mark too quickly for me to reply. 'He is lodging with me. He had been away so long that he does not yet know many people hereabouts. If you could offer him a position we would be obliged.'

For a moment Ezekiel's shark mouth lifted at the corners in the glimmer of a smile.

'Oh!' So that's the position, is it? He should have thought about that last night before he picked a quarrel with my son.'

'Your son asked for it,' I said quietly.

'Oh! did he now?' Ezekiel's mouth reverted to its inverted 'u'. 'Well, then, no one can say that Ezekiel Meredith is not fair in the granting of jobs, but know this! Anybody who asks for employment from me must do it in the proper manner: on his knees. So down on your knees, Vaughan, and ask away. I'll consider your application right now.'

24

There was a sniggering from the men and I shook my head.

'I get down on my knees for no man. If you cannot give me work I shall not beg for it.'

'Then that's unfortunate for you,' said Meredith. 'Hey, lads! This upstart knocks my son about and then comes asking a favour. What shall I do? Give him a favour right now?'

'Aye,' somebody shouted. 'Give him a favour, Ezekiel. Give it 'im hot.'

'Now we want no trouble,' cried Mark quickly. 'Either you give him a job or not. If not we will go in peace.'

'You'll not leave here in peace,' said Meredith, bending down and seizing a crowbar. 'Stand aside, tinker—and you Dafydd Hopkins. I've no quarrel with you, but I want Vaughan for myself.'

'Ezekiel, 'machgen i,' said Dafydd, speaking for the first time. 'You try anything on Mr Vaughan and I'll stove your head in for you, see if I don't.'

This statement halted proceedings momentarily, with Meredith obviously thinking things out. Then he turned to the men.

'Listen, lads. You heard what I said. I've no quarrel with the tinker or Hopkins. Hold them both while I deal with this upstart.'

But this was easier said than done, for Dafydd's reputation as a strong man was widely known. There was a murmuring but no movement forward.

'Do as I say,' yelled Meredith. 'If any man fails me it will be his last day of work here.'

Such a threat was bound to have some effect, for in those days dismissal from employment meant starvation or beggary. One or two of the braver fellows edged forward but Dafydd swung round and they shrank back again.

'Hold them!' screamed Meredith, now beside himself with rage. 'Hold them, I say, or you'll answer for it.' He took a pace forward himself, crowbar raised high.

What happened then occurred with such speed that I have difficulty remembering the exact sequence of events. First two men made a rush for Mark and bore him to the ground. In a flash Dafydd was across to them. He seized the attackers by their shirts, bumped their heads together with a crack that echoed back from the rock face, lifted them bodily and flung them into the pool. They landed with a splash that sent water cascading in all directions. But almost immediately a swarm of men were at Dafydd, some taking him by the knees and some from behind in an effort to hold his arms. He still kept his feet and I remember men flying from him like ninepins. Mark was felled by a blow on the head and before I could go to the rescue, Meredith was upon me, his bloodshot eyes blazing, crowbar raised high. Suddenly there was a shout like the crack of a pistol and, with a speed that was astonishing, everything came to a halt. Even Ezekiel, his bar about to come down, froze into immobility.

'Meredith! Put that iron down!'

Everyone turned to look up at the high wall behind us, from whence the voice had come. Standing there was a tall, commanding figure of a man, immaculately dressed in a frock coat and top hat. Behind him was another man, similarly dressed but much older. Holding on to the older man was one of the most beautiful women I have ever seen, wearing the latest in crinolines with the bustle at the rear.

The voice cracked again.

'Put that bar down, Meredith. This moment, I say.'

There was a clatter as Ezekiel dropped his weapon. A short silence followed and then my would-be destroyer began to whine.

'No harm meant, Mr Brogden. We wasn't in earnest.'

'It looked earnest enough to me,' snapped Brogden. 'I've told you before: I'll have no fighting among the men.'

Meredith looked so contrite that I was of half a mind to smite him there and then just to knock the hypocrisy out of him, but thought better of it.

Mr Brogden spoke again.

'I've heard bad reports about you recently, Meredith. I don't much care for your methods. Kindly be at the dock office in one hour precisely.'

Meredith touched his forelock and Mark got to his feet, grinning. The men began to slink away and I heard one whisper to Dafydd, 'No harm meant, Dafydd. We wouldn't have hurt you.' My eyes were still on Brogden but occasionally darting to his female companion, who appeared to be regarding me with a great deal of interest, a faint smile hovering about her dainty lips. Then, to my surprise, Mr Brogden addressed me.

'You there, man! What's your name?'

'John Vaughan, sir,' I replied. 'Late of Her Majesty's Royal Regiment of Artillery.'

'I can see that.' Brogden's face softened a little and a hint of amusement came into his eyes. 'Well, John Vaughan, I would like to see you, too. I want to know why you are involved in a fight with my foreman. Be at my house tomorrow at noon sharp.'

And without further ado all three of them disappeared behind the parapet. Mark, Dafydd and I looked at each other.

'Pity,' said Dafydd. 'I was just beginning to enjoy that.'

CHAPTER SIX

As I HAD several hours to spare before the appointment with James Brogden I decided to emulate a childhood practice and go for a walk to Sker. Before setting off I placed my best clothes ready on the bed for I had decided that, whatever the reason Mr Brogden wanted to see me, I would endeavour to make a good impression upon him, and therefore intended getting back early to wash and change. As it was pointless to ponder any more, I put the interview out of my mind and set out for the walk.

I crossed the ploughed fields to Lock's common, enjoying every footstep in the soft, yielding turf and paused at the edge of the cliffs to savour the salty freshness of the air. There was not a soul to be seen on either the common or the beaches, and I felt a singular lightness of spirit. This was the Porthcawl I remembered as a boy: working its magic and making me feel vital and alive again. In great good humour I traversed the undulations of the cliff edge and made my way to the moorland of Sker and when the old, rambling house came into view I recalled the stories I had heard about the place: of the luckless maid and her love-lorn suitor; of her ghost which is said to haunt the room in which she was imprisoned by an irate father; and of the Gwrach y Rhibyn, or Hag of the Mists, a lost soul which wanders about the dunes uttering cries which are a portent of death. I remembered, too, the stories of the Cyhiraeth, a ghostly wailing or shrieking sound which the country folk fear, for it is the certain sign of a ship-wreck to come; and of the White Horse, a frightening spectre, always the harbinger of a dreadful calamity.

But on that fine morning the thought of ghosts and the supernatural had no fear for me, for the moorlands of Sker, although intimidating on a dark winter's evening, are beautiful when the sun is shining. The hummocks of heather are interspersed with hosts of rare flowers and the constantly moving sand dunes provide a home for many strange birds. For one seeking solitude from the clamour of the world there is no better place; and I know of no one who would not benefit by a walk there at any time of the year.

Soon I reached Kenfig Pool, a quiet and mystifying expanse of fresh water under which, some say, a whole city lies buried, although I myself have never heard the bells of the submerged church ringing, as local people maintain. There I was glad of a rest and so I ascended one of the larger sandhills and sat down to admire the view across to Maudlam church.

The warmth of the sun and the murmur of the sea must have lulled me to sleep, for the next thing I knew was being suddenly awakened by the sound of a horse at the canter. I twisted my head and saw in the distance a fine chestnut being ridden by a woman in black riding habit. I watched, fascinated, as the rider, sitting side-saddle, managed her mount with consummate ease; for having been an artilleryman I could appreciate good horsemanship at any time, especially by a woman sitting in such an unnatural position. But, as I looked, the pair disappeared behind a mound and I heard the horse's hooves falter. Almost immediately the horse reappeared, but this time without its rider. Startled, I got to my feet.

At first I was undecided whether to go for the horse, now quietly cropping the grass not far away, or search for the woman. I went for the woman and soon found her, a crumpled figure lying at the foot of a ridge of sand. One glance was enough to tell me that she was the same person that I had seen the day previous with James Brogden. She appeared to be breathing normally so I got down on my knees and began rubbing her hands. After a few moments she opened her eyes.

'Where am I?'

'At Kenfig Burrows,' I replied. 'You've fallen from your horse.'

She struggled into a sitting position but gave a gasp of pain. 'My leg! I think I've hurt my leg.'

'Let me see.' I began straightening her left limb which was bent under her dress. The woollen stocking was torn but there was no sign of a break. I felt carefully along the tall riding boot and when I came to her ankle she gave a sharp cry.

'That's where it hurts. Have I broken it?'

'I don't know.' I studied the pain-wracked face. Aged about twenty-five, the woman was even more beautiful than I had first thought, with exquisite lips, a finely chiselled nose and eyes of a startling blue-green colour. A flawless complexion and a halo of rich, copper coloured hair completed the picture, making her one of the most striking women I had ever seen; and suddenly I felt in awe of her. But there was no recognition for me in her eyes, which surprised me not at all, for I am not conceited enough to think that I have a memorable face.

'Could you try standing up,' I said, 'and see if the ankle will hold your weight. However bad the pain you must not unlace your boot. If the bone is broken the boot will sustain it until you get home.'

'Very well, I'll try.'

Helped by me she got to her feet and leaned heavily against me. Through my jerkin I could feel her breasts boring into me, soft and yet firm and pointed; and her hair, deliciously scented, tickled my cheek; all of which made me feel suddenly weak at the knees, for I had never been in close proximity to such beauty before; and when my arm encircled her small, corsetted waist to steady her I felt the strange magnetism of her flesh even through the thick material of the habit.

'It was a rabbit,' she said. 'A rabbit startled the horse and it swerved.'

'No matter, Do you think you can stand whilst I get your horse?'

The blue-green eyes smiled their thanks.

'I will try. I am indebted to you for your help.'

'It's nothing,' I replied. 'Keep your weight off your injured foot until I get the horse. It will take only a minute.'

I retrieved the chestnut, still munching happily at the grass and led him to the woman who grimaced as she put her injured leg forward. Holding the rein with one hand I helped her into the saddle, experiencing yet another thrill as I held her thigh to settle her. Once mounted she smiled down at me.

'I think I shall be all right now.'

'I will come with you and lead the horse. If he shies again you will be in trouble.'

'Very well. I will reward you when we get home.'

'I want no reward. It is a pleasure to help you.'

And so it was. I enjoyed the three mile walk back to Porthcawl, the horse plodding along obediently, knowing that a firm hand was on the bridle. The lady and I spoke little, just enough for me to ascertain that she was a niece of James Brogden, spending a holiday away from London at Sea Bank House with her husband; and with a few questions she gleaned who I was and what my career had been. I glanced up occasionally to see that all was well and now and again she smiled back at me, but for the most part kept staring straight in front of her, her lustrous hair blowing back in the breeze. I fell to wondering about her husband. If he was the old man I had seen at the breakwater I did not envy his task in keeping the love of such a woman. With her looks alone she could make a man deliriously happy or sick with despair, probably both at the same time. I could visualise her in a ballroom, attracting the men around her, making all other women green with envy. Glad that I had no such problem to contend with I contented myself with hoping that James Brogden would hear of my good deed, with results favourable to myself.

After an hour's sedate walking we reached Sea Bank House and I led the horse up the drive to the front door. Standing there was a tall, buxom woman with commanding, aristocratic features. She eyed me with distaste and addressed herself to my charge.

'You're back early, Catherine!'

'I had a fall, Aunt Helen. I think I've broken my ankle. This kind gentleman helped me.'

'A fall! Broken!' Mrs. Brogden went into action like the soldier's daughter she was. 'Jenkins! Phillips! Smithson! Come at once.'

Servants and groomsmen appeared from all directions. Catherine was helped down from the horse and carried into the house, the horse led away, and within moments I was left standing on my own. I looked at the sun, for I had no watch, and was relieved to realise that I had about an hour before my appointment. I began walking down the drive but had only reached halfway when a familiar voice rang out.

'John Vaughan! Will you come here please?'

I turned to see James Brogden advancing upon me, arm outstretched. He was shorter that I had imagined when I had seen him on the parapet, being of little more than medium height, but his body was strong and robust. He was dressed in knickerbockers and a short worsted jacket edged with yellow piping. He seized my hand and shook it warmly.

'I am indeed grateful to you, Mr Vaughan, for helping my niece. She is very dear to me—it would have been terrible if anything had happened to her. And this on the last day of her vacation, too.'

'I am sure she will be all right,' I replied. 'I do not really think a bone is broken. More than likely it's a bad sprain.'

'I hope so. I hope so. Will you come indoors?'

'I'm not dressed properly,' I said. 'I intended returning home to change before seeing you.'

'Nonsense! No need of that. I don't judge people by their clothes. Come in and I'll see you now—and by the time you leave we'll have news of Catherine. You'll want to know how she is after looking after her, won't you?'

He led the way back up the drive, through a spacious hall to an oak-lined room which I adjudged to be his study. He sat down at a large desk strewn with plans and documents and motioned to me to sit in a chair.

'Well now, Mr Vaughan, I'm glad of this opportunity to speak to you. I know all about you—very little goes on around here without my finding out. I also know why you were involved in that fracas at the breakwater yesterday, but I won't say anything about that. You were in the Royal Artillery, I understand. Tell me about it.'

I told him the story of my service life and he listened with interest. Whilst I was talking I studied his face and I began to realise why James Brogden was both respected and liked. It was a strong face and yet a kindly one, with dancing, alert grey eyes and a fine mouth partly hidden by a large moustache joined at the ends to very long sideburns. He gave the impression of being both compassionate and powerful, a man who could make up his mind quickly and give concise, clear orders; but one who had a deep understanding of humanity. I felt that I could serve such a man for the rest of my life with the utmost loyalty; and I was pleased to think that Brogden seemed to like me, for when I had finished he smiled and said:

'Well, now! I believe you are the man I am looking for. I take it you know all about the different types of explosives?'

'I do sir. Muzzle-loading guns and breech loaders require different charges, and a Cohorn mortar is different again. I have had a great deal of experience of them.'

'Good! And you have seen the new dock and the breakwater?'

'I have, sir, and very remarkable they are. I remember the old dock with horse-drawn trams pulling the coal all the way from Maesteg. Eight hours it took each tram, I believe, and the ships were very small.'

'Small they were. That is why I am building a large inner dock. Then we can have bigger vessels—steam ships even—which can load and unload at leisure, independent of the tide. Porthcawl will become the principal coal port next to Cardiff, mark my words! It will also become a main railway terminal area, using the new gauge. Porthcawl has a great future, John Vaughan—a great future.'

'I am very glad,' I said, 'for I intend to settle here and obtain employment.'

'And that you shall if you can handle gunpowder as well as you say. But first let me acquaint you of the position. An act of parliament has been applied for to build the new docks. That is a mere formality. My friends in the House assure me so. I have already started, as you can see, and the outline of what is to be is already discernible. Around the docks a large new town will grow, bringing prosperity to all in a wide area. But the town will depend on the docks and the docks will depend on one thing—the breakwater. The breakwater is the key to the whole concept, for ships must have shelter from the gales. Without the breakwater there will be nothing. Do you understand that?'

I replied that I did and Brogden got up and began pacing around the room, his hands behind his back.

'The breakwater must be right. You have seen the start of it but I am not satisfied. As an engineer I am worried about the foundations. Mortar and large stones are not enough. I have seen blocks weighing ten tons or more tossed around like matchwood in a rough sea and can you imagine the pressure of a wave on the slightest crack? It can prise bedded stones apart like a giant's chisel.'

He glanced at me to see if I was taking all this in. Satisfied, he went on:

'So far there is not a great deal of danger. The ramp facing south-west is sufficient to break the force of waves but the further we extend to sea the trickier it becomes. The breakwater will have three terraces, each supporting the other and the tallest one must be at least sixty feet high to be effective. Also we intend placing a beacon on the furthest point for the protection of ships at night. Such a structure requires an immense foundation. Each block at the base must be keyed into the existing rock at low water—not just mortared in, but keyed in. If that is not done the whole edifice will tumble. That must not happen—I will not let it happen. Whatever else may come about I intend the breakwater to be the greatest thing I have ever done—my memorial, if you like. I want people a hundred years hence to look at it and remember that I, James Brogden, built it. Does that sound conceited of me?'

'No,' I replied with sincerity. 'If a man is in a position to do something great then he must make it last, otherwise there is no point in doing it.'

'Thank you.' Brogden took one more trip around the room then sat down. 'Now then! Could you, with your knowledge of explosives, blow holes in the rocks? Not any holes—I mean holes of varying sizes: some small, some large; yet do the work quickly for the tides will give you little time and mistakes will be difficult to rectify. And could you, on top of that, work with a team of experts in stone walling led by a North Walian who is—er—not easy to get on with, to say the least?'

I had an urge to say that I could get on with anyone save the Merediths but thought that facetiousness would endanger my position, so I said instead:

'I am of a fairly easy nature, Mr Brogden. I have had plenty of practice in team work on the guns.'

'Good! Team work is important. You will blow the holes, the men will alter the shape of the cavities to suit the blocks and Mr Owen will do the laying. Done properly the foundation will be secure. I shall inspect your work frequently. Do not be offended by that; it is something I must do.'

'I understand that, sir.'

'Very well. Your starting salary will be three guineas a fortnight —equivalent to that of a foreman, for the work is dangerous. Is that acceptable to you?'

I stifled a gasp of surprise. Three guineas a fortnight was wealth to me, a salary on which I could easily save. I tried to make my voice sound normal.

'Thank you, sir. That is entirely acceptable.'

'Excellent. Make that foundation into a real jig-saw, one on which the waves and currents will make no impression and you and I will get along very well together.'

Brogden then went on to outline his future plans for the port as a whole and he spoke so animatedly that I, too, became fired with his enthusiasm. I believe that he would have gone on talking for hours, but a knock at the door interrupted him. The elderly gentleman I had seen at the breakwater hurried into the room.

'I am sorry to intrude, James,' he said, in a high-pitched, quavering voice, 'but I thought you'd like to know that Catherine is better. No bones broken—merely a sprain.'

'Good! Good! Charles, come and meet the young man who helped her. Mr Vaughan—Sir Charles Whitney-Browne. Sir Charles is Catherine's husband.

I took the hand proffered and found the grasp feeble, which set me wondering again why such a pulse-quickening woman should have married a man old enough to be her father. I came to the conclusion that it must have been for wealth and position, but I did not condemn for I did not know the full circumstances behind the matter, and in any case I was now in the presence of my betters whose mode of life was very different from my own.

Sir Charles did not stay long, for he was obviously excited by the event. He patted me on my shoulder, expressed his thanks once more and then doddered from the room. Brogden also thought it was time to conclude the interview, for he took me by the arm and gently led me through the hall to the front door. At the top of the steps he shook hands again.

'Come to the dock office tomorrow. We will go into matters further then."

'Very good, sir,' I said. 'And thank you for the trust you have shown in me. I will not let you down.'

'I know that, John—I shall call you John now. That is why I have chosen you. You realise, of course, that the work will not last for ever. Once the foundation is completed I have competent masons who will carry on. Have you any skills in that direction?'

'None, sir, I am afraid.'

'Then we must think of something else for you. Your leg may be good for a year or two yet, but when middle age comes it may let you down. General labouring will aggravate it. What is your standard of education like?'

'Poor, sir, I am sorry to say.'

'Then I shall help you. Would you like to attend school?'

'I would indeed, but are there any schools for grown men?' Brogden frowned.

'No, not for grown men. There are two small Church of England schools here, but they are for children; and it is a disappointment to me that only half the children go there. There is a private school, however—perhaps you could go there. At my expense, of course. I will look into the matter and let you know. But enough of that for now. Go off and enjoy the rest of the day, for tomorrow you will be hard at work.'

He smiled and disappeared into the house. I walked down the steps to the drive then turned and looked at the imposing house. I could not help feeling some envy, for I had glimpsed a mode of life to which I could never aspire. There was no malice in my thoughts, however, for I had been received by two men who, although far above me in station of life, had treated me with nothing but kindness.

But at that moment I made a decision. Short of dishonesty and malpractice I resolved to do everything in my power to better my lot. No longer would I be content with a rented room in a cottage. I wanted a house, too, albeit not a large one; and if I could find a good-looking woman to go with it, so much the better.

CHAPTER SEVEN

MY WORK on the breakwater proved to be both exacting and demanding and, as James Brogden had said, dangerous. At low water I carried out surveys, closely examining the rock structure and making my plans accordingly, always in close consultation with Owain ap Owen, the North Walian in charge of the team. Then I prepared my charges, some large but some so small that they were nothing more than gun cotton. Fissures and holes were blown in the rocks, the size of the aperture depending on the shape of the slab to be slotted in. The workmen used their chisels and picks to ensure a good fit and finally Owain, with an uncanny intuition for the right size of block, would complete the laying and mortaring.

It was slow work, being entirely dependent on the tide and Owain's insistence upon exactness of detail. He supervised the chipping away of every limpet, arguing correctly that the existence of even the smallest shell fish would upset the balance of the blocks. I was troubled, too, with the inconsistency of the gunpowder and some of the fuses, which burned irregularly, making retirement from the explosion a chancy affair; but was pleased that my demand for better products was instantly and generously met.

I made it my duty to get on well with Owain ap Owen. He was a short, bow-legged man with long greasy hair, a hooked nose and darting, suspicious, heavy-lidded brown eyes. He spoke with the hissing accent of the north and was unpopular with the men, partly because of his speech, which was difficult to understand, and partly because of his attitude, which varied between dislike and open contempt. It is a pity that there is this antipathy between south Walians and the men from Snowdonia, for we are all Welshmen at heart, but it does exist. Whether it is because the mountains divide us, making communication difficult, or whether we southerners are jealous because they held out so much longer against the English, I know not. It has to do with a sense of humour, too, for we in Glamorgan are much more light-hearted in our approach to life, often teasing each other and playing practical jokes, but rarely taking offence. Owain, on the other hand, took offence very easily. He never became angry but he brooded and the man who offended him was never forgiven. I made sure that I, at any rate, did not aggravate his touchy nature; and we managed to work together with passable harmony.

James Brogden—as good as his word—visited us often, always in the company of his clerk, to whom he continually dictated a stream of instructions and memoranda. He seemed pleased with our slow and painstaking work, never showing impatience or uttering an admonition. On one occasion he pleased me by telling me that Lady Catherine Whitney-Browne was now fully recovered and was looking forward to holidaying in Porthcawl next year, which news exicted me a little for I could still feel the touch of my hands on that warm, vibrant body and had on one occasion even gone as far as dreaming of her, an experience which did me no good at all, when I woke up and realised the trick my subconscious had played on me.

One aspect of my work, however, caused me some amusement. In my position of explosives expert I was empowered to give orders to Ezekiel Meredith, who had to fetch and carry the exact size of block that we required. He did his duty with a glower and I often caught him eyeing me with hatred. I knew that, if ever the opportunity arose, he would try and get his own back; and accordingly I kept myself on the alert, but some time was to elapse before he tried it. Mark Treseder visited me frequently at the breakwater, in between his tinkering and trading activities, sometimes bringing tit-bits from Mrs Treseder's larder to keep up my strength. Both of them were delighted at my appointment and many were the evenings we spent together planning for the future, for we were all determined to go on with our business venture. Dafydd came, too, when his ship was in dock; and I was always pleased to see his cheerful face appearing on the parapet above me. On one occasion, on my way home from work, I glimpsed Arabella Dinwiddy, but she merely blushed and hurried away. I had no feelings of regret about her, however, for my sights were now set on higher things—at least that is how I consoled myself, for I still felt the smart deep down inside me.

At the end of my first week's work Mr Brogden's clerk drew me aside and informed me that arrangements had been made for me to present myself on the following Monday at the school of Mr Thomas Thomas of 5, Lias Cottages. This delighted me for Mr Thomas, known as Tom Tom, and his wife Charlotte, had been respected teachers even before I had left Porthcawl. Unkind people said that they could not speak English correctly, but they had a long list of successes with scholars even in the days when they had just one room above a blacksmith's shop at the dockside; and so I regarded my enrolment with them as being the first rung in my advancement, an opportunity I did not intend to miss.

Accordingly I ensured that I was prompt for my appointment and was outside 5, Lias Cottages with ten minutes to spare, which also helped me to boost my courage, for it is not an easy matter for a man of twenty-five to go to school. The cottage appeared to be too small for a place of learning, in spite of the sign in the garden which read 'Old School House', but at the appropriate time I walked up the short path between the rose bushes and, after a glance at the sea to encourage me, knocked on the open door. A stout, rubicund, balding man wearing a shabby, green, fustian suit and a pince-nez appeared immediately and welcomed me.

'Ah! Mr Vaughan, I've been expecting you. Please to come in.'

He led the way along a narrow passage on either side of which was a low, open door leading directly into two small rooms which did duty as classrooms. In one a group of children aged between ten and sixteen were busily reading books on their laps. In the other were several smaller children mostly boys one of whom stuck his tongue out at me as I passed, whereupon I responded in like manner. After nearly bumping my head on a low lintel I found myself in a small kitchen. Mr Thomas motioned me to sit down at a bare table and did likewise opposite me.

'Now then, Mr Vaughan, how much schooling have you had?'

'None—none at all, Mr Thomas. I have tried to teach myself but I've never had proper tuition.'

'No matter, Can you read that?' He pushed a book towards me.

' "Cat" ,' I read, 'and "hat" .'

'Good! That's a start.'

'It wasn't difficult,' I replied. 'The pictures are under the words.'

'Really?' Thomas snatched the book away. 'Of course, now stupid of me. Try this one.' He handed me another book open at the middle.

' "Dear" and "deer" .'

'Good! And the next one.'

I hesitated.

' "Bore", I think, and "boar" .'

'Do you know the difference between them?'

'I'm not sure. I know one is an animal, but I'm not sure which.'

'Ah! Turn over the page and read what's there.'

The print was large but I was non-plussed.

'I cannot do this.'

' "Wait" and "weight". Try the next.'

I mouthed the first letter but could not get the word out.

' "Write" and "right",' said Thomas. 'Never mind. That is what you are here for—to learn to read. Mr Brogden thinks you will prove an apt pupil. We do the three R's here—reading, writing and 'rithmetic—and of course we use the Holy Bible as a text book. Do you know your multiplication tables?'

'I can get as far as the five times,' I said, 'but I am not sure of the rest.'

'What is five sixes?'

'Thirty.'

'Six eights?'

'Forty-eight—I think.'

'Eight nines?'

'Seventy-three.'

'Eight twelves?'

'Ninety—ninety something.'

'Hm! I see,' said Thomas, looking as though he could see very little. 'Well, now! We have work to do. I think it best for you to join the seniors. I will put you to sit by Sally Martin. She is one of my best scholars—a monitor, in fact. She will help you if you are in difficulties. Sally!'

In response to his shout a thin, gawky girl of about fourteen entered the room. She had freckles and pig-tails that stuck out at the side and was dressed in a clean but much-darned pinafore dress. She looked apprehensively at me and no doubt she was as frightened of me as I was of her.

'Sally!' said Thomas. 'This is Mr. Vaughan. I want you to help him as much as possible.'

Sally curtsied and, not knowing quite what to do, I held out my hand. She took it and I noticed that her own hand was trembling.

'Well, now,' said Thomas. 'Allow me to take you to meet your class.'

He led the way back down the corridor and when he entered the classroom all the pupils got to their feet. There were about a dozen of them, half of them girls who looked at each other and then giggled with great amusement.

'Quiet!' roared Thomas. 'Please to get a chair for Mr Vaughan, Sally.'

Sally did as she was told and I was thankful when she placed it at the back of the room. She sat in another chair beside me, her head down, afraid or too embarrassed to look at me.

'Now, then,' said Thomas. 'Take up your slates. Sally, get Mr Vaughan a slate. I want you to copy this from the blackboard.' He turned, adjusted the easel, and with a piece of chalk that squeaked every inch of the way wrote 'Aesop's Fables'.

'Mr Vaughan, can you make anything of that?'

'Aesop's Fables,' said Sally in a voice just loud enough for me to hear.

'Aesop's Fables,' I repeated and Thomas looked startled.

'Sally! Did you help Mr Vaughan then?'

Sally hesitated.

'Yes, Mr Thomas.'

'I am glad of that. But do not do it too often. Give him the opportunity to try for himself.'

'Yes, Mr Thomas.'

Thomas turned again to his blackboard and wrote 'The Story of Brer Fox'. Sally and I looked at each other. She laughed and I laughed. The ice was broken between us and straight away I forgot the sense of inferiority I felt at being helped by a girl half my age; and from that moment on Sally helped me in every way possible. It is to her, rather than to Mr Thomas, that I owe the birth of my love of learning, which has remained with me to this day.

CHAPTER EIGHT

MY WORK on the breakwater and my schooling still left me time to partake in the activities of the community, and on Mid-Summer's Day there occurred an event which, although innocuous in itself, led to important consequences for myself.

It began when the elders of Newton decided to revive an old custom called Beltane, which had its origins in the Druidical worship of the sun-god, Beli, with the object of ensuring good harvests. Mark Treseder, like the good Cornish Celt that he was, had got to hear of it and intended to witness it. He asked Dafydd and me to accompany him and so, at the appointed time, we made our way to the village green.

The ceremony, we learned, had strict rules which must faithfully be carried out, otherwise the object is lost. Nine men had to turn their pockets inside out and divest themselves of all money and metal objects, including buckles, braces and belts. From the woods they gathered timber from nine different trees, which was made into a bonfire on a site near St John's Well. They then had to kindle a flame by rubbing two sticks of oak together and set light to the bonfire. Meanwhile the ladies of the village baked cakes of oatmeal and brownmeal, cut them up and placed the resulting pieces in a bag. Everyone present drew out a piece. Those who obtained brown meal portions had to leap three times over the fire, but those who had drawn oatmeal had to remain as bystanders. After the jumping, the charred logs were carefully preserved to start the next year's Beltane, so that good luck would follow from one year to another; and ashes placed in the participants' shoes also ensured happiness.

Eager to see this old custom, which had been discontinued for thirty years or more, we arrived in what we thought was good time, only to find that a goodly crowd had already gathered. The wood had been stacked ready and the nine men were busy rubbing their pieces of oak together. They seemed to be having little success, which was understandable for, as is usual with mid-summer day in this country, it had rained all the morning and the sticks were wet, as was the bonfire and the grass surrounding it. But at last one of the men got his wood to smoulder and, after blowing carefully at it for a few moments, he leaped to his feet with a whoop of joy and held aloft the burning brand.

There then began a series of events the like of which I have not witnessed since, which turned what was intended to be a solemn and semi-religious occasion into one of hilarity and ribaldry, for the successful brand-lighter had forgotten that he had been divested of all metals, which included his belt buckle, with the result that, the moment he jumped up, his breeches slid to the ground with a speed that would have done justice to a monkey on a stick. At first there was a stunned silence, with every eye riveted on the poor fellow's bare anatomy; then there was a laugh followed quickly by a roar of merriment. The man dropped his brand, which immediately went out on the wet grass, hoisted up his breeches and ran off into the anonymity of the crowd, which continued to rock with laughter.

The next act in the drama, or farce as it turned out to be, was introduced by no less a person than old Ma Perkins herself. She hurried forward, seized the brand with a gnarled fist and, after announcing that she was 'damned' if she was going to wait another half hour for the fire to be lit, stated her intention of re-kindling the wood at the hearth of her own cottage. This was not strictly according to custom; and, to forestall her, the remaining eight men went to work with a will with their rubbing, but to no avail for Ma Perkins soon reappeared shielding a merrily burning brand with her apron. She hurried over to the bonfire but just as she reached it her apron caught alight and Ma Perkins disappeared behind a pall of smoke. Without hesitation a youth standing nearby seized a pail of water, placed there for just such a purpose, and flung its contents over the old woman. Ma Perkins came to a sudden and unexpected halt, her hair, face and dress streaming with water. Instead of being grateful she shook her fist at the boy.

'What did you do that for, you fool? It was only my apron. Now look at me! I'm soaked.'

'Sorry, Ma,' said the youth, grinning. 'I thought you were on fire.'

Weeping with rage and frustration Ma Perkins made her way back to her cottage, leaving behind a piece of oak so sodden that there was no hope from that direction. The crowd turned expectantly again to the bonfire, which seemed to be as damp and uncooperative as before. Suddenly there was a shout and one of the men ran to the wood pile with a burning stick. After what seemed ages, during which time all those present held their breath, the bracken caught alight There was an outburst of clapping.

But the Celtic gods were not smiling on their fire that day. The wood spluttered and sent up a few lugubrious flames, but that was all. With great optimism the elders went around holding out flour bags, into which various people dipped their hands, expressing delight or disappointment according to what they drew out. We expected them to come to us but Fred Walsh, the chief elder, passed us by.

'Fred!' called out Mark. 'Ain't we having any?'

'You'm from Porthcawl, ain't you?' said Fred, who was of Devon stock. 'And you'm from Nottage, Dafydd Hopkin. These here cakes is only for us villagers.'

'But we're all one village,' protested Mark. 'The parish of Newton-Nottage, that's what we are. You can't leave us out.'

'I can and I will,' said Fred and went on to other people.

'Mean sod!' muttered Mark. 'Favouritism, that's what it is— favouritism! Look! He's going round all his bloody relatives.'

'I didn't know you were so keen to jump,' I said laconically.

'Of course I want to jump,' said Mark. 'This is an historic occasion. I'd like to be able to say I jumped over a Beltane fire. Wouldn't you?'

'Me too,' said Dafydd, 'and I don't see how they can stop us if we want to.'

In the meantime one or two people, after holding up their authorised brown meal bits, had taken a leap across the meagre little fire. Not much effort was required for there were no tall flames to make it dangerous. A few girls tried it also, showing a dainty ankle and a flurry of lace; and Mark interposed his opinion that that was why the gods had ordained the ceremony: to see girls' ankles. As the fire slowly took hold more men jumped, some of them travelling prodigious distances; and the event approached something of a competition, each good leap drawing a round of applause. I could sense that Mark and Dafydd were becoming restless.

'I'm going to have a go,' whispered Dafydd. 'To hell with rules.'

43

'Me, too,' said Mark.

'Now wait!' I said. 'The elders won't like it. You'll be very unpopular round here if you go out of turn.'

But to no avail. Dafydd's eyes were measuring the distance to the fire. He rocked to and fro for a moment as though to gain mental and physical strength and then he was off, covering the ground very quickly for such a big man. But just as he got to the fire he slipped and went skidding along the grass, one leg high in the air. His backside hit the ground but his momentum was such that he went sailing through the bonfire like a knife through butter, scattering ashes and embers in all directions. He picked himself up on the other side and ruefully surveyed the damage. The Beltane fire, or what was left of it, was past redemption.

Everyone present was so surprised, not to say dumbfounded, that at first not a sound could be heard. Then a hubbub arose above which rang Fred Walsh's voice.

'Look what the big bastard's done! He's ruined the fire.'

'Sorry,' said Dafydd, looking sheepish. 'I didn't mean to smash it up like that.'

'I'll give you sorry!' screamed Fred, hopping about in his anger. 'I'll teach you to disobey the rules!'

He searched frantically in his flour bag, drew out a piece of oatmeal and flung it at Dafydd, who ducked instinctively. The oatmeal flew through the air and struck, of all people, Owain ap Owen, who was standing at the edge of the crowd, minding his own business. The cake must have been baked at the last Beltane thirty years ago judging by the effect it had, for it struck Owain on the forehead with a thud and he fell backwards, collapsing on a large sack he had been carrying. The sack slowly deflated, exuding a peculiar squelching and popping noise.

'Get them out of it,' screamed Fred, now past himself with rage. 'Get them off the Green. They've ruined everything.'

I ran to Owain's aid, who was still lying on his back, a dazed expression on his face.

'Come on, Mr Owen,' I said. 'Allow me to help you.'

As I got him to his feet I could see that the crowd was pelting Dafydd and Mark with meal cakes and I did not know whether to remain with Owain or go to the aid of my friends. But the throwing was done in a good-natured way, for the majority saw the humour of the situation and so I thought it best to help my superior. I had reckoned without the elders, however, who began using language for which, if the great god Beli had heard it, he would have descended and smitten them for their blasphemy; and when sticks and stones were added to the armoury I decided it was time to beat a retreat.

'Over to the "Ancient Briton"!' I yelled and, trundling Owain on front of me, made for the public house, for I knew that once inside we would be comparatively safe, the landlord not allowing fisticuffs on his premises. Propelling Owain, who was still tightly gripping his sack, I joined the other two and we made a dash across the common for the inn. Once inside Dafydd slammed the door and slid the bolt.

'Phew! Who said Newtonians are a peaceful lot?'

'They normally are!' said Mark, 'but now, thanks to you, they're not.'

'I couldn't help it,' said Dafydd defensively. 'It's not my fault I slipped.'

I sat Owain down on a chair. He still seemed dazed.

'Where am I?' he muttered faintly.

'In the Ancient Briton,' I replied. You're quite safe now but you've had a bump on the head.'

Owain began to struggle up again but I held him back.

'I must get out,' he cried. 'I can't stay here. This is a public house—a house of sin. I've never been in one in my life. What would Marged say?'

'Well, you'd better stay a while,' said Mark, looking through the window. 'Porthcawlians aren't too popular right now.'

'But I've done nothing wrong,' whined Owain. 'I was struck by some hooligan with a stone.'

'That was no stone,' I said. 'That was a piece of bread.'

'Bread! Bread! Was that bread?'

'Never mind, Mr Owen,' said Dafydd consolingly. 'You must have something to make you better. I'm going to have a quart myself.'

'Of what? Ale! I've never tasted the devil's brew. Elderberry wine is the only thing I've ever permitted myself.'

'Well, they sell that, too,' said Dafydd hopefully. 'Would you like some, Mr Owen?'

45

Owain's heavy-lidded eyes flickered. Always tight with his money, he could not resist the temptation to have something for nothing, sinner's place or not. He nodded and Dafydd was soon back with three foaming jugs and a glass of dark liquid.

'Are you sure this is elderberry wine?' asked Owain, sniffing it suspiciously.

'Of course it is. Try it and see.'

Owain raised the glass to his lips and took a small sip.

'It doesn't taste like the wine Marged makes but it is passable. Diolch.' He drained the glass and rose to go.

'Sit down, Owain,' said Mark, putting a restraining hand on his shoulder. 'Go out now and you'll get lynched.'

Owain quickly sat down again.

'Stay a while, Owain,' said Dafydd. 'Another ten minutes won't make any difference to Marged. Bottoms up lads. Let's join Owain in another drink.'

We drained our jugs, feeling better for the effort.

'That was good,' said Dafydd, smacking his lips. 'I wouldn't mind having another go at that fire now.'

'Like hell you will!' I said quickly. 'Here, Dafydd, take this money and buy us all another round.'

Dafydd did as he was told and we all sat around the table eyeing our replenished vessels. Then I noticed that Owain kept feeling down to see if his sack was safe and curiosity got the better of me.

'Please tell me, Mr Owen,' I said, 'what you have in that sack. I can't help being interested, for it made some funny noises when you fell on it.'

'Did I fall on it?'

'You did,' said Mark. 'And funny noises it certainly made. What have you got in it—fish?'

'Well I never!' said Owain. 'I remember now. A good thing I had it with me, isn't it? It broke my fall. I might have been injured otherwise. They say that God looks after his own.'

'I'll look after you,' muttered Mark, 'if you don't tell us what's in it. It stinks to high heaven.'

But Owain, like the good North Walian that he was, was enjoying his little secret, and I doubt if he would have told us then but that a copious swig of wine began to loosen his tongue.

His face took on an infuriating owlish look.

Well, now! So you want to know what's in the sack. I was round Ogmore bay today collecting it. Very good it is, too.'

'Collecting what?' asked Mark, rolling his eyes in despair.

'Seaweed, of course. For the garden. Didn't you know that the Ancient Britons used it as fertilizer for their crops?'

'Is that so?' said Mark. Disinterested now that the secret was out, we fell to drinking our ale in silence. An occasional glance through the window told us that the crowd had regathered around the bonfire, their rapt attention indicating that they were about to have a second attempt.

'I wonder if they'll have another Beltane next year?' ruminated Dafydd.

'Not after what you've done,' I said.

'Did you notice how wet everything was? Typical for mid-summer's day. It always rains on mid-summer's day.'

'It wasn't the wet that dowsed the damn thing,' said Mark. 'It was your fat arse.'

'The way you're going on,' said Dafydd, grinning, 'anyone would think I did it on purpose. Anyway, you wanted to jump. Didn't he, John?'

But I was staring at Owain. A remarkable change had come over his swarthy countenance. Instead of the usual dolorous expression there were signs of alcoholic animation.

'I think,' I whispered, 'that Owain's getting drunk.'

'Whoosh drunk?' said Owain. 'Don't you shay I'm drunk.'

'Of course not,' I responded soothingly.

'Mind you,' said Owain, 'I feel funny.'

'It was that knock on the head, I expect.'

'Yesh. I mean yes. Funny! I can hear my voice from far away.'

'Dafydd!' I said reproachfully. 'Have you been up to your tricks with that elderberry?'

'Who, me?' said Dafydd, grinning. 'I wouldn't do a thing like that.'

'I see you have,' I said, 'your face gives you away.'

Then Owain started singing, softly at first, but gradually with a mounting crescendo. To us it sounded like a cross between the Marseillaise and 'Men of Harlech'.

47

'Strewth!' exclaimed Mark. 'You wouldn't think he's the terror of the breakwater now, would you?'

The singing stopped as suddenly as it had started. Owain's owlish expression returned and he bared his yellow teeth in a leer.

'I can tell you lot where you can lay your hands on five pounds.'

We sat forward.

'Where?' asked Mark.

Owain's cunning eyes showed enjoyment at another secret.

'I thought that would interest you! I heard you three were saving up to buy a boat.'

'Where, Owain?' repeated Mark. 'Tell us where we can get five pounds.'

'Will you give me half if I do?'

'Willingly,' said Mark without hesitation.

'Can I have another elderberry first?'

'Dafydd!' said Mark. 'Get this—get Owain another drink. Here's the money.'

Dafydd was back in a flash.

Owain sipped carefully before replacing his glass on the table.

'Listen! I heard about another old custom today—over at the Ogmore. They're having a race there. The quickest man across the stepping stones wins five pounds.'

'I've heard of them races,' said Mark. 'They started with the congregation of Merthyr Mawr church seeing who could be quickest across to the "Pelican" after Sunday services.'

'I don't know about that,' said Owain, 'but I do know that this year the lord of the manor is giving five pounds to the man who makes the best time across the stones. Each parish is entering a runner. Ewenny, Ogmore and Merthyr Mawr have put in for it but there's no one from Porthcawl.'

'How do you know?' asked Mark.

'Because I was there this afternoon. I saw the entries pinned on the door of the Pelican. There's no Porthcawl name there. If you ask me they're keeping quiet about it.'

'Now let's get this straight,' said Mark. 'Are you suggesting that we enter for the race?'

'Wrth gwrs! How else can we get the money?'

'But we're not runners! I'm too old, Dafydd is too slow and Mark here has a gammy leg.'

'What about Guto Bach Dwl?'

Immediately we saw what Owain was getting at. Guto Bach Dwl was a deck hand on Dafydd's ship, a notable runner. In English his name means Stupid Little Guto, but he was not stupid: he merely looked so, having been born with a congenital defect that made him look like a village idiot; and if I have any quarrel with my fellow Welshmen it is that they are too quick at giving nick-names to people because of their physical appearance. Poor Guto had borne his unfortunate name since puberty, but with equanimity and good humour, and had made up for his defect by athletic prowess.

'Owain's right!' said Dafydd, slapping his knee. 'Guto can cross the Tuskars like a deer when he's after conger. Them stepping stones would be easy for him. When's this race?'

'Saturday.'

'That doesn't give us much time.'

'No matter,' said Owain. 'The important thing is to enter a man. I know how we can win.'

'Oh!' exclaimed Mark. 'What are you getting at now, Owain?'

'Don't forget! Half the money's mine. You promised.'

'You'll get your money. What did you mean by saying you know how we can win?'

For reply Owain reached into his sack and drew out a long length of bladder wrack. He placed a piece of the seaweed on the table, thumped it with his fist and spread the slimy ooze over the wooden surface.

'You don't have to use much. Just a piece or two's sufficient on a stone.'

'Well!' Mark leaned back and eyed the North Walian with admiration. 'You crafty old devil. I think I know what you're getting at.'

Owain tapped the side of his nose with a forefinger.

'I have a friend the other side. It was Hopkins slipping on the Green that reminded me.'

'How do we put the seaweed on the stones?' asked Dafydd.

'Simple. The runner's assistant does that. Each runner has an assistant whose job it is to wet the stones. That's to give everyone a fair chance, for if one runner falls into the water he can splash the stones, making it difficult for the next man. So the assistants stay in the water making sure the stones remain wet. A bit of seaweed here and there won't be noticed. See what I mean?'

'One thing,' said Mark. 'What's to stop our man slipping?'

'Easy! You splash away the slime before it's his turn.'

'Uffern!' exploded Dafydd. 'Do you think it's possible?'

'It's been done before,' said Owain, winking.

'It's dishonest,' I said. 'I'll have nothing to do with it.'

But I did and, against my better judgement, embarked on a venture which had dire consequences, both for me and my friends. All because Dafydd, as he admitted afterwards, had laced Owain's elderberry with bootleg brandy.

CHAPTER NINE

Guto Bach Dwl, enticed by the offer of first-mate's position on our intended boat, readily consented to run in the Ogmore race, and went into immediate training. I still had my doubts about the shady method to be employed but was over-ruled, Mark reiterating that any slips by our adversaries would be into harmless water. Accordingly I became an accomplice and, on the evening prior to the event, went with Guto to survey the scene of the encounter.

It was a pleasant spot, with the ruined castle and the undulating, dark green hills a striking background to the shallow, gently-moving river. The stepping stones were irregularly spaced but on the whole fairly close together. The majority had flat, even surfaces but a few were out of true because of the constant pressure of the water and therefore likely candidates for the machinations of Mark who, although he had appointed himself as assistant, was that evening busy with his tinkering commitments. Guto made a few practice runs and then we conferred as to the most likely sites for depositing the seaweed. I drew up a plan for Mark's benefit, carefully numbering the stones, and when Guto expressed himself as satisfied, we made our way home again.

When we emerged from the Merthyr Mawr dunes into the plain of Newton Burrows I was suddenly struck by the appearance of a small valley which I knew as Wig Fach. This valley had always been densely wooded and void of habitation, but now I could see that many trees had been cut down to make clearings and that wisps of smoke were emerging from the topmost branches. I drew Guto's attention to this and his usually vacant face took on an expression of deep concern.

'Keep away from there, Mr Vaughan. Squatters, that's what they are. Plenty of thieves and robbers among them.'

'Thieves and robbers! Surely not these days, Guto.'

'They are all right. Some folks say they're descendants of the Cefn Riders.'

'Cefn Riders! Nonsense! They disappeared years ago.' But Guto was adamant.

'Anything stolen from Newton or Porthcawl ends up there, but folks is afeared to do anything about it. Some have been there but had their heads split open for their trouble. Stay away, Mr Vaughan. Them's Cefn Riders all right.'

'How many of them are there?'

'Nigh on a hundred I would say, men, women and children.'

'How long have they been there?'

'Ever since the docks started. Some of the men work there but most poach off the land. There's no proper houses there, just huts and tents.'

'Very interesting,' I said.

By now Guto was hopping up and down, intent upon getting his leg muscles into shape for the morrow's event. I was obviously slowing him down, so I made a pretext of having to rest my leg and urged him to go ahead. Guto required no second bidding and raced off, leaving me to own devices. I waited until he was out of sight then stared at the valley. A sense of adventure urged me to see the place for myself and, aided by a confidence in my ability to look after myself (now largely modified by age) I hesitated only to assess whether I had enough time to make a detour. Deciding that I had I cut across the dunes and made for the valley entrance.

The first sight that greeted my eyes was a group of children playing in a sand hollow at the fringe of the trees. They were filthy, with matted hair and bare feet. Their clothes were in tatters and three or four of the youngest were completely naked.

51

As I approached they stared at me with silent hostility and, in order to appear friendly, I ventured a salutation.

'Good evening, children. Do you live here?'

There was no response. The oldest of them, a boy aged about twelve, began to shepherd the others away from me and they did not stop until they were in another hollow, a good fifty yards away.

Chagrined at the rebuff but not unduly perturbed at that stage, I entered the wood by a well-trodden track and almost immediately came to a small clearing in which were half a dozen crude habitations. They were nothing more than shelters built from branches and twigs and one was merely a tent made of rotting sail cloth. A wood fire was burning in the middle of the clearing around which three or four women were squatting. When they saw me their mouths gaped in surprise and they stared silently at me. Remembering my experience with the children I said nothing but merely smiled pleasantly; but as I walked past I could feel their eyes boring resentfully into my back.

Further along the path opened out into another, much larger clearing about fifty yards long. Here there were more dwellings, better constructed than the others, being real huts with turf roofs. I saw no sign of life until I came to the end of the clearing, when four women and a very old man leaped out from a hut and formed a line across the path. I came to an abrupt halt.

'Where are you going, mister?' demanded one of the women, a huge Amazon with dark, gipsy features.

'Merely walking,' I replied. 'I am a stranger here enjoying an evening stroll.'

'Then turn around, stranger, and stroll back where you came from. We want none of your likes around here.'

'I mean no harm,' I said mildly. I understood this valley to be empty and I am surprised to find people here.'

'Well there are. Be on your way.'

The old man raised his stick and brandished it an inch or two from my nose.

'Get down out of it or you'll have a taste of this.'

I acknowledged defeat and went back down the path, but when I thought I was out of sight I forced my way through the thickets until I came to a second path, running parallel with the other and going upwards in the same direction. This I followed until I emerged from the wood and could see the sea. There I paused to breathe a sigh of relief, for I had found the little valley claustrophobic and my reception unsettling. I was glad, however, that I had met no younger men and surmised that they must have been away on some expedition or other—no doubt dishonest. But when I continued up the path I saw that my troubles were not yet over. Coming towards me around a bend were three men, unkempt and wild-looking, carrying bundles and oak clubs. They were as surprised to see me as I was to see them, but whereas they stopped I kept going on towards them, for I knew that it was not wise to show fear in such a place. They remained on the path, however; and, like their womenfolk, blocked my progress.

'Good evening, gentlemen,' I said, showing my now well-practised smile. 'Allow me to pass, please.'

They glowered at me and then at each other. One, the biggest of the three, dropped his bundle and fingered his club.

'What do you want here?'

'Nothing of import,' I replied. 'I am merely walking and I take it this path is a right of way.'

'It's no right of way,' growled the man. 'Not for the likes of you, anyway. You've no business here. This is private property.'

'Private property! I was not aware of that.'

'Are you arguing with me?'

'No,' I replied. 'But I assure you I thought this was common land. If, however, I am wrong, I stand corrected, but as far as I am aware—'

'He's a spy!' cried a fellow with squint eyes and brown, tusk-like teeth. 'Give him a stroke, Matt.'

'I ask you again,' said Matt. 'What are you doing here?'

'And I tell you again, merely walking. I am no spy.'

Matt eyed me up and down, taking in my height and size. He snarled round at the others.

'I'll give him a chance. We don't want the authorities down on us. You!' He pointed his club at me. 'Give us your word you won't come here again and we'll let you go, otherwise I'll break your pate here and now. Do you understand?'

'I understand very well' I replied. 'And I can assure you I have no wish to return here, not after the reception I have had from your fellows down in the valley. Now kindly let me pass.'

They made way for me but once past them I turned and walked backwards, still facing them, for experience has taught me never to turn my back on an enemy. When I thought I was of a sufficient distance between us for safety I turned again and resumed normal walking. I had meant what I said about not wishing to return. I had not enjoyed my visit to Wig Fach.

But as I surmounted a rise in the path I was in for another surprise. Coming through a gateway some distance away was a tall, beautifully proportioned girl. She was dressed completely in black and had long black hair. She did not see me for she turned up the path and began walking in front of me, some twenty yards distant. I followed behind her, admiring the graceful gait and the hair, which was as black and glossy as a raven's plumage and extended down to her waist. She was, I imagined, about twenty years old.

I followed her for some distance, wondering where she was going. Then she startled me by suddenly stopping and sitting down on the grass verge. I slowed my pace and, when I drew level with her, she glanced at me but turned her head quickly away again, but not before I had noticed that she had a sun-burnt complexion, coal-black eyes and a red, shapely mouth.

After my encounters in the valley it was doubtless foolish of me to stop, but my curiosity was still uppermost, for I wanted to know what such a striking girl was doing in so lawless a place. Also, when she had glanced at me she had tossed her head, which is a sure indication of interest. All women do this, whether they have long hair or short, when they want to attract a man's attention, although they will not admit to such a weakness. So I stopped and, although I knew the way perfectly well, I bade her good evening and enquired as to the best route for Porthcawl. She remained silent, still looking away from me, and I was about to give up and move on when she spoke.

'From which direction have you come?'

'From down there.' I indicated the valley and surprise flooded the dark eyes.

'Then I advise you not to return that way. Go to the top of the lane and there you will meet the main road to Porthcawl. Turn left and you cannot go wrong.'

I proffered my thanks but remained where I was, pretending to admire the countryside. After a while I said:

'It is a beautiful evening, is it not?'

No reply.

'Do you live hereabouts?' I persisted

There was a long pause but at last she deigned to answer

'I do, Why do you wish to know?'

'Because I have just passed through yonder valley and met some very hostile people. You are the first civil person I have spoken to '

'There is no harm in being civil but it would be wise of you not to come here again '

'Why not? Why are the people here so afraid of strangers? I meant no harm yet I was threatened on more than one occasion.'

'You cannot blame them. They are afraid.'

'Afraid of what?'

'Losing what little they have.'

'But I will not rob them of anything.'

'Probably not. Perhaps they thought you were a bailiff or an agent of the land owners.'

'That I am not, but if they go on as they are they will attract animosity and it will be worse for them.'

The girl shook her head angrily, sending the black tresses flying.

'We are here because we have nowhere else to go.'

'Why is that?'

'Enclosures chiefly. All the people you have met have been dispossessed, mostly by greedy landowners.'

'I am sorry. I did not know that.'

'Have you ever heard of tŷ-un-nos?'

I nodded. Tŷ-un-nos was an old Welsh belief that if a man could erect a hut on open ground in the space of one night the hut and the land around it were his by right. It was a fallacious belief and had no right in law, but I did not think it opportune to say so.

'That is why we are in this valley,' the girl said hotly. 'We have erected our dwellings and now the land is ours. No one else wants it, anyway. It is no good for cattle or sheep. But they—we—are still afraid that someone will come and drive us out. Does that explain why you are unwelcome here?'

'It does, and I trust all goes well with you. But the people I met will give you all a bad name, I fear.'

'We have that already. Everyone speaks ill of us. They say we are thieves, but that is not so. There may be a few who are, but most of us are law abiding. All we wish is to be left in peace.'

'How do you manage in the winter?' I asked. 'Surely it must be cold in those huts.'

'It's not easy but it's better than the work house. There we would be separated—fathers from mothers, children from parents. We manage tolerably well and it is a warm valley, facing south.'

'What is your name?'

This was too sudden a question. The dark eyes became suspicious again.

'Why do you wish to know?'

'I like you. You have explained things to me about your folk that I did not know before. I would like the opportunity to know you better.'

'Bethan Rowlands. But you must not talk to me again.'

'Why not?'

'It is dangerous for you. If some of the men saw you talking to me now they would be angry.'

'Let them. I should be angry if they tried to stop me.'

'What is your name?'

'John Vaughan. I am in charge of the explosives at the docks.'

'Then you work for James Brogden. It is thanks to him that my family is here.'

This non-plussed me, for I could see no connection between James Brogden and Bethan Rowlands living in Wig Fach. The girl saw my disbelief and added:

'My father was a miner in one of Brogden's collieries at Maesteg. Now he can hardly breathe for the coal dust. We had to leave our cottage when he could no longer work. Brogden's like all the others—once you cannot work for him, out you go.'

'I am sorry,' I said. 'But you cannot blame James Brogden for that. Coal dust is a danger all miners must face. I know from personal experience that Mr Brogden is a very kind man. There must have been some mistake. He would not turn anybody out.'

'Well, he turned us out. At least his overseer did.'

56

'Ah! That's different. You can hardly expect Mr Brogden to know everything that goes on in his undertakings. I am sure that if he had known himself—'

Bethan shot me a scathing look and got to her feet.

'You are a Brogden employee. You will support him come what may.'

I could find no answer to that. In the meantime Bethan began walking down the lane in the direction of Wig Fach.

'Bethan,' I called. 'Wait. I would like to ask you something.' Bethan's pace slowed but she did not stop.

'What is it ?' she flung over her shoulder.

'Can I see you again ?'

'No.'

'Why not ?'

'It is impossible.'

By now she was ten paces away. I raised my voice.

'Please let me see you again. I shall be going to the Ogmore races tomorrow. Come with me,'

'No.'

'Be at the valley entrance at two o'clock. I will meet you there.'

This time there was no answer. I watched the retreating figure, noticing how the hem of her skirt eddied the dust with her speed. Soon she was out of sight, so I turned and made my way up the path to the main road. Within me I felt a strange excitement. That I would see Bethan again I had no doubt, for I would make it my business to do so, even if it meant returning once more to the forbidding valley.

But when I got home to the Treseders I said nothing about my encounter and ate my flummery in silence.

CHAPTER TEN

IT WAS Mark Treseder's idea to take Guto Bach Dwl to the Ogmore stepping stones in the donkey cart. The object was to save Guto's legs for the race, but the idea was misconceived for the cart became bogged down in the sand and the donkey refused to co-operate. It ended with us all pushing cart and donkey, with the result that Guto was not in the best frame of mind when we arrived, a mood made worse by the cavilling of Owain, who insisted upon accompanying us to keep an eye on the prize money, if won.

I, too, kept an eye open when we neared Wig Fach, hoping to see Bethan, but there was no sign of her. I was not too disappointed at that stage for I had not really set my heart on the matter; but I again made my leg an excuse to dawdle, telling the others to go on without me. I hung about for half an hour but caught no glimpse of her, so I went on to the Ogmore river, where I found that so many people had assembled that I had to force my way through the throng and search for the others. I found Dafydd and Owain eventually, standing on the turf slope of the castle bailey. From that position we could see well nigh everything that might transpire.

There was movement everywhere. The roadway above us was filled with carriages, many of the well-to-do coming from Bridgend to watch. There were well-dressed men in abundance, and ladies in beautiful dresses, making me feel out of place in my work-worn clothes. On a specially constructed stand at the upper end of the castle a group of superior-looking gentlemen had gathered; and at three o'clock precisely one of them called for order. He held up a large watch and, above the noise which abated only a little, we heard him say something about time-keeping and starting. Then four men lined up in front of him, among them Mark, and so we knew that these were the runners' assistants. They drew straws and Mark looked around, saw us and held up four fingers.

The route of the race had been carefully marked out with white-washed ropes. It ran from the starting post about one hundred yards on the Porthcawl side of the river, across the stones and up a steep lane leading to the door of the Pelican Inn. There an official was standing whose task it was to raise a flag when the runner reached the door. The total distance was, we estimated, just over a furlong and from our elevated position we had a good view of every yard, including the all-important stepping stones.

The runners then appeared and were introduced in the order in which they had to race. First came the Ewenny man, a tall, athletic figure with a large waxed moustache and hair parted in the middle. When his name was called he bowed to the spectators and flexed his biceps, although what biceps had to do with racing I failed to see. Next came the Merthyr Mawr champion, a squat man with flame-coloured hair, a striped shirt and tight-fitting breeches which accentuated his enormous thighs. He did a little running on the spot for our benefit, at the same time waving to his supporters.

Third for presentation was the Ogmore candidate; and Dafydd, Owain and I stared at each other in consternation. If any man was going to win the race, barring accidents and Mark's foul play, it was he; for the fellow looked every inch a runner, with a beautifully proportioned body and long, striding legs. There was no nonsense about him either; he merely stood there looking cool and completely at ease.

'I hope Mark knows what he's about,' hissed Owain. 'I don't like the looks of that one.'

Finally came Guto. Standing beside the Ogmore champion he appeared puny and insignificant; and I heard a few unkind remarks in the crowd about his unfortunate face. It was noteworthy, also, that, whereas the previous runners were loudly cheered by their supporters, Guto drew only a thin round of applause, mostly from we three. We tried, however, to make up in noise what we lost in numbers and Guto smiled gratefully at us.

Next the assistants entered the water, Mark among them, and began splashing the stones. When the wetting had been carried out to everybody's satisfaction they inspected each other's work and took up positions. Mark was second away from us and I noticed that he was standing by two medium sized stones which I had indicated to him as likely candidates for his attention. I was almost too ashamed to look, so conscious was I of the subterfuge about to be committed.

Everything was now ready for the race to begin. The starter raised his flag and the first runner took up position, one hand on the starting post. The crowd hushed and I found my eyes darting between the tall Ewenny competitor and Mark, who by now was surveying the river, apparently disinterested in all around him. The distance was too great for me to see anything on the stones but I had no doubt that the nefarious deed had been done.

The flag dropped and the Ewenny man was, away springing from the post like a deer out of cover. He came across the open ground at a great pace, his arms and legs pumping like pistons. He leaped on the first stone and then went striding across, missing out every other. Then he came to Mark's stone and when his foot struck one his leg went up into the air as though some giant force had struck him from behind. So sudden was the slip, and so fast was he moving, that he entered the water head first: one moment he was there, in full view of all, the next he had disappeared. There was a stunned silence followed by a long-drawn-out groan. The runner resurfaced, climbed gallantly back on the stone, grinned sheepishly and resumed the race, exuding water like a sponge; but it was a lost cause and both runner and crowd knew it. I heard Owain hissing excitedly beside me.

'Diawch! One or two more like that and the money's ours.'

I watched Mark move to another position further out in the river and begin splashing the stones. He did it with great thoroughness, rubbing with such intensity that I felt sure the judges would tumble to his trickery; but apparently not for the red-headed Merthyr Mawr champion went to the starting point and stood there, acknowledging the applause of his supporters. He spent a few minutes doing his running-on-the-spot exercise then signalled confidently that he was ready. Once more the crowd became silent and I noticed that Mark had lit his pipe, a bored expression on his face.

Down went the flag and away went the runner. Being smaller that the first man his strides were shorter, but his powerful legs moved like lightning and he seemed to cover the ground just as quickly. When he reached the first stone it was obvious that he had a different ploy for crossing, for he took them one at a time, like a ballerina making sure of each step. Across he went with a graceful, rhythmic action until he came opposite Mark. There he seemed to pause in mid-leap and when his feet struck a stone they did a rapid tattoo, as though he had resumed his running-on-the-spot exercise, except that he was slowly falling backwards. Miraculously he recovered his balance and bravely tackled the remaining stones but now with circumspection, which slowed him down; and when he reached the bank he was limping badly. Grimacing with pain he hobbled up the slope and managed to reach the Pelican, where he was received by a sympathetic handclap. By now many people in the crowd were murmuring and I saw the judges in deep and earnest conversation. I thought again that Mark had been rumbled, but after a long parley and a few shrugs they indicated that the race should go on, and so I breathed freely once more.

Beside me Owain was hugging himself with excitement and, in spite of myself, I felt the same; for the magnificent Ogmore runner was now standing nonchalantly by the starting post, apparently untroubled by the previous mishaps.

'Uffern!' said Owain. 'This one will want watching.'

But now I could see something strange happening in the river.

'He's not the only one,' I said. 'I think Mark's having trouble.'

Owain's eyes followed my gaze. Mark, obviously angry, was having a heated argument with a man I recognised as the Ogmore runner's assistant. We could see Mark gesticulating and, with an expression of disgust, wade to the bank, but the man followed; and Mark, after waving him away, returned to his original position. Again the man went with him and it was obvious that wherever Mark went the other fellow intended going also. I could not refrain from chuckling.

'Mark's been discovered,' I said. 'This should be interesting.'

'Diawch!' said Dafydd. 'I hope not.'

But there was no time to think more about it for the starter's flag was raised and the formidable Ogmore athlete was crouching ready at the post. He shot off like a cannon ball, covering the ground with great, loping strides; and so light was he on his feet that he hardly seemed to touch the ground. Across the stones he went, taking them two or three at a time, each step sure and fleeting. From the last stone he took a prodigious leap, landing half way up the bank, and then tore up the lane, scattering dust and pebbles like a meteorite. Before you could say Llewelyn Fawr he was hammering on the door of the Pelican. Hardly out of breath he gracefully acknowledged the roar of the crowd. I doubt if he had taken more than thirty seconds from start to finish.

'Duw!' groaned Dafydd. 'Guto'll never beat that! Not in a hundred years!'

'Why didn't Mark stop him?' shrilled Owain, almost beside himself with frustration.

'Keep quiet,' I ordered, 'or we'll all be in for it.'

'But why—?'

'I told you! Mark's been rumbled.'

The applause went on for along time and subsided only when the crowd saw Guto standing at the post. Again there were a few titters at his appearance, quickly stopped by Dafydd glaring at the offending scoffers; and eventually silence reigned as our champion, left foot forward, a do-or-die expression on his face, prepared to achieve the impossible.

'Fly, Guto bach, breathed Dafydd. 'Fly like the wind.'

And indeed Guto did fly. I have never seen a man run so fast. He was at the first stone before we could blink, and four strides took him to the middle of the river. Then trouble struck. After one great leap Guto began to slither, not once but several times; and it appeared to us that no sooner did his feet touch a stone than they shot out from underneath him, first one way and then the other. Somehow he kept his balance and went from perch to perch, but at a gradually diminishing speed for he was obviously not in command of his own equilibrium. Eventually he ended up on a particularly small stone, swaying dangerously and thrashing his arms in a vain attempt to remain upright. The crowd held its breath, but the end came quickly. His arms still flailing he hit the water with a flat, resounding smack. Almost immediately he was back on the stone and resumed the race, but it was obvious that so much time had been lost that he could not be the winner.

Dafydd, Owain and I stared after his retreating figure as it disappeared up the lane, then we were jostled forward by the excited throng rushing for positions to view the prize-giving. As we had no wish to partake in that we made our way to the stepping stones but were prevented from crossing by a long line of spectators returning from the opposite bank, a slow process for the ladies in their crinolines were unsure of themselves. Whilst we were waiting a disconsolate Guto joined us, still dripping water.

'What happened?' shouted Owain. 'Why did you fall and not that Ogmore man?'

Guto shrugged.

'Don't ask me. Them stones was like blocks of ice. I couldn't stay upright, leave alone run.'

'Mark will know the answer,' I said, grinning, for I saw the funny side; and an old childhood saying kept going through my head: 'cheatings come to provings, cheatings come to provings'.

After ten minutes or so there was a break in the procession across the stepping stones and we managed to slip across. We found Mark sitting on the bank, wringing out his trousers. Owain could contain himself no longer.

'Well! What went wrong?'

Mark shook his head ruefully.

'I couldn't do anything. That Ogmore bastard had his eye on me the whole time.'

'But why did Guto slip?'

'If I knew the answer to that,' said Mark bitterly, 'we'd be up there getting the prize, wouldn't we?'

'Five pounds!' hissed Owain. 'Five pounds gone west!'

'Them stones was like blocks of ice,' repeated Guto. 'Blocks of bloody ice—all of them.'

'Oh go to hell!' said Mark. 'I did my best.'

We made for the donkey cart which had been entrusted to a small boy for a fee of one farthing, but had gone only a short distance when we found ourselves walking through a gauntlet of grinning men. I recognised one of them as the Ogmore runner's assistant who had plagued Mark. Something about their demeanour puzzled me.

'Better luck next year, boyos,' said the Ogmorian, his grin nearly splitting his face. 'A good race. Sorry you lost.'

'Bugger off,' responded Mark. 'You're not sorry we lost.'

'Well, no, come to think of it we're not, not now we've got the prize. A good race all the same—a very good race.' And with that they all burst out laughing.

'What's so funny?' snapped Mark.

'Funny?' said the Ogmore man. 'You, boyos, for thinking you could get the better of us. You've got to get up early to do that this side of the river.'

One of the men made a rude noise and I could see Mark's hackles rising; and indeed I began to feel annoyed myself, for no man likes to be made a fool of.

'Come on, Mark,' I said. 'Don't bother with these louts. They're all savages around here.'

'I know that,' said Mark, 'but I've got a score to settle with this one. You!' He pointed at the Ogmore assistant. 'What were you doing hanging around me in the water?'

'To stop your monkey tricks, boyo, that's why. We knew what you were up to when the first runner fell. Don't think we're ungrateful, though. You did our work for us.'

'Oh!' said Mark, taken aback a little. 'Is that so?'

'That's right. And very nicely you did it, too. Couldn't have done better myself.'

In spite of himself I could see Mark's eyes become curious.

'How come my man fell then? I made sure you didn't do anything.'

'Ah!' The fellow could hardly contain himself for glee. 'Now wouldn't you like to know. I'll tell you this, though. We from the Ogwr stick together when you Porthcawlians are around, whether we're from Ewenny or Merthyr Mawr. You won't get the better of us. You may have been watching me but you forgot about my butties, didn't you? That'll teach you to interfere with our races.'

Up until then Dafydd had been standing quietly by listening to the conversation. Suddenly he stepped forward and took a deep breath, expanding his enormous chest.

'What did you do to my Guto?' he asked quietly.

The Ogmorians looked with awe at Dafydd and then at each other. One or two of them stepped back a pace.

'Come on,' said Dafydd. 'I want to know. Nobody plays tricks on my Guto without accounting to me for it. What did you do to him?'

He took another pace forward and the men fell back in confusion. Suddenly Dafydd darted at them, but they were too quick and, scattering like rabbits, they ran for the safety of the stepping stones. There they paused to regroup, hurling insults at us. Another move from Dafydd and they streamed across, nearly knocking each other into the water. When they got to the other side the Ogmore assistant cupped his hands about his mouth and yelled out:

'Try Ewenny clay next year, boyos. It's better than seaweed.'

64

CHAPTER ELEVEN

ALL THE SUMMER work proceeded on the breakwater. We made the most of the unusually fine weather and, although daily progress seemed slow, the long finger of stone became more majestic with each week that passed. This was most noticeable from my working position at low water mark, from which I could see the blocks of limestone towering above me, ascending in giant steps to the foreland. Already it appeared impregnable; and the south-west escarpment, a huge apron of faced stone, was effective in its job of taking the sting out of the waves, although we all knew that the real test would come later when the autumnal gales arrived.

Owain, once he had recovered from the disappointment of losing fifty shillings, showed pleasure in the progress of the work and on one occasion I fancied I heard him singing softly to himself, but when he saw me regarding him he reassumed his old, dour, uncommunicative self; and in spite of our recent escapade I got no nearer to him. Some said his attitude was caused by a nagging wife who rarely allowed him to speak at home, and so I let it go at that, for who can judge a man until all his circumstances are known?

I still kept a weather eye open for Ezekiel Meredith and his son, who was working in one of the quarries, but as far as possible they kept out of my way; although one day I had a narrow escape when one of the heavy iron winches crashed down from the topmost tier, missing me by inches. On the surface it appeared to be an accident, for many men had been hurt—some badly maimed—by falling objects and I cannot swear to it being otherwise; but Meredith was nowhere to be seen when it happened and when he did reappear seemed disappointed that I was still in one piece. The incident sharpened my resolve to be on the alert at all times.

Tides permitting, I went regularly to school, working so hard and progressing so well that Mr Thomas expressed himself as delighted with me and informed Mr Brogden, who one day stopped to compliment me. Sally Martin gave me extra tuition, helping me greatly in the transition from nursery rhymes to Aesop's Fables; and with her help I eventually tackled Pilgrim's Progress and Robinson Crusoe. She saddened me when she told me that she was leaving at Christmas to take up an appointment as pupil teacher at a school in Gloucester; but this increased her resolve to do as much as she could for me in the time remaining, and I responded to the best of my ability.

Between work and schooling I went at every opportunity to Newton Burrows, hoping to see Bethan, but for two weeks I caught no glimpse of her. Then one day, on a blazing afternoon in July, I espied her leaving the valley and making for the beach. I cut across the dunes to head her off, but she saw me and began walking very quickly. I had to travel at a fair pace myself to catch up with her and when she saw that escape was impossible she stopped and waited for me with an expression that was both angry and frightened.

'Good afternoon,' I said. 'I have been hoping to meet you.'

'Please go away. I have told you before, I do not wish to see you.'

'And I told you before you cannot stop me.'

She turned in exasperation and continued her journey to the beach. I lengthened my stride and walked beside her.

'Please let me talk to you,' I said. 'Just a few words.'

'No. Go away.'

So we walked in silence until we came to the beach. There she looked fearfully around to see if anyone was near, but both the beach and the entire warren were deserted.

'What is it you want?' she asked petulantly.

'You did not turn up when I waited for you. I was afraid you were not well.'

'I was quite well. I told you I wouldn't be there.'

'I know, but I hoped you would change your mind. I was very disappointed not to have your company. You would have enjoyed the race at the Ogmore.'

'Maybe. Is that all you have to say?'

'No. I wish to speak to you on a certain matter.'

She looked around again then sat down suddenly in the sand,

'I have told you before—you are in danger by speaking to me but on your head be it. Sit here and then at least we will not be seen.'

This was a wise move, for when I sat down beside her I could see that we were sheltered from prying eyes by a bank of sand;

indeed we would not have been discovered except by someone blundering on top of us.

'Well?' she asked. 'What is this matter you wish to speak to me about?'

This non-plussed me for, although I knew what I wanted to say, I had reheared no opening gambit. I decided it was best to come straight to the point.

'I have not been able to forget you since we met. I would like to have the opportunity to know you better.'

'That's impossible, and you know it is.'

'Why is it impossible?'

'It is.'

'But why?'

'We live in different worlds.'

'Oh, come!' I exploded. 'I have been poor myself and know what it is. You are poor now through no fault of your own. I could help you.'

'Help me? How could you help me?'

'By making it possible for you to leave that dreadful valley.'

'And what makes you think I want to leave?'

'You would like to live in a nice house, surely?'

'A house! What are you talking about?'

'Just this. Give me the opportunity to know you better and then—perhaps—if we thought we were suited we could be married.'

'Married!' Bethan's dark eyes stared at me. Then she turned her head quickly and looked out to sea. 'Now you are playing with me—for your own ends.'

'That I am not! I will be honest with you. I am not married and have a good position at the docks. I am looking for a wife and have thought of nothing but you. So, why can't you give me the chance to know you better?'

For a long time Bethan did not answer, then she said:

'I cannot leave the valley. I have a father and mother dependent upon me.'

'You can bring them with you. They don't like it here, do they?'

'No.'

'And your father is ill. Living in a damp hut can't do him much good.'

'It's impossible, I have told you: if some men should see you now—'

'To hell with the men, I can deal with them.'

Another long silence, so long that I thought my pleading had been in vain. Then I heard a quiet, almost inaudible sob.

'Oh, come,' I said. 'Please don't cry.' I put a hand on her shoulder but she jerked it away.

'Go away! You are tormenting me.'

'That's the last thing I want,' I said, moving nearer. 'I will go if you wish me to, but please tell me you'll see me again.'

The shoulders began to shake so I tried again. This time there was no rebuff so, greatly daring, I slipped my arm around her waist and we sat there, with me enjoying myself immensely in spite of the sobs. But when I tried stroking her hair she leaped to her feet.

'I must go home.'

'Not before you promise to see me again.'

'How many times do I have to tell you? If you do not value your life, think of me.'

I rose and proffered her a handkerchief which, after some hesitation, she took, for she appeared to have none of her own.

'If you have trouble with any of the men,' I said, 'you must let me know.'

She thrust the handkerchief back and began walking in the direction of the valley.

'I will come with you,' I said, catching her up.

'No.'

'But I will. I cannot allow you to walk home unaccompanied.'

Seeing that she could not shake me off she walked by my side in silence, with myself afraid to say any more in case of a direct refusal, for I believed that I had made some progress in a short time. When we reached the gorse bushes at the entrance to the valley I halted.

'Tell me that I shall be allowed to see you again.'

But Bethan was staring straight in front of her, sudden, stark fear in her eyes. I turned and followed the direction of her gaze and saw three men, not twenty paces away. I recognised them immediately as the fellows who had impeded my progress at the head of the valley. This time only one, the fellow called Matt, was carrying a club. I heard Bethan cry out:

'Run! Run quickly before they catch you.'

'No,' I replied. 'Let us meet this here and now.'

I grasped her arm and propelled her gently towards the men. She was unwilling and petrified with fear but I persisted and we came face to face with the three ruffians. The man, Matt, twirled his club.

'So! We have caught you at last.'

'Caught me?' I replied. 'I fail to understand you. No one has caught me.'

Matt ignored me and pointed his club at Bethan.

'What are you doing with this man and you betrothed to my brother? It's lucky for you he knows nothing of this.'

'I am not betrothed to your brother, 'cried Bethan with more spirit that I thought possible a moment or two ago. 'To him or anyone else.'

'That I can understand,' I interjected. 'A more filthy and reprobate fellow than this I have not seen for many years and his brother can be no better.'

This was too much for Matt who stepped forward a pace, raising his club. I pushed Bethan away but she ran between us.

'Leave him alone, Matt Pugh, do you hear? He has done you no harm. Leave him alone, I say.'

'No harm?' said Matt. 'No harm you say? He's a trespasser. He's already had one warning and now he's taking you away from my brother. That's harm enough. Step aside, Bethan.'

But Bethan went at him, pummelling his chest with her arms. Matt seized her and flung her into the direction of his companions. They grabbed her and held her fast, still struggling.

'Keep hold of her, lads,' said Matt, licking his lips. 'This trespasser must be taught a lesson he won't forget.'

I was of an inclination to go to Bethan's rescue but Matt was already advancing upon me, feinting with his club; and I knew I would have to deal with him first. I retreated in front of him for a man with a weapon requires special treatment. Luckily I had studied the art of eastern men who have a scientific technique for dealing with armed opponents; and accordingly kept going backwards, biding my time and waiting for the rush I knew would come. We continued thus for half a minute or so.

Then, with a bellow, Matt hurled himself upon me. I waited until the last moment and went down before him, at the same time seizing his filthy shirt. As his momentum carried him forward I rolled over on my back, thrusting my good leg into his stomach and giving a mighty heave. Matt went sailing in the air, landing heavily a good six feet away on the grass, making me wish it had been solid rock.

But he was up in a flash, the club still in his hand, his face twisted with anger. I let him come on again, retreating as before just out of harm's way; but this time he was more circumspect, making several feints that had me guessing. Rush he had to however, to get me; and when he came I varied my tactics. Again I went down but this time I slewed sideways grabbing him by one shoulder and flinging him across my leg. He twisted as he fell, landing on his club arm; and the weapon fell from his grasp. I was on it like a flash and threw it with all my strength into a distant clump of gorse.

'Now then, Matt.' I said, grinning, 'we can fight as equals.'

To do the fellow justice he had courage and readily raised his fists; and so we circled each other like prize fighters. But he had no skill, whereas I had been reared in the hard school of the army; and when he came towards me, arms flailing, I stepped forward and shot out my left like a ram-rod, catching him between the eyes. He staggered back and, before he could recover, I drove in another left and then another. Four or five times I hit him in all, each time jerking his head back; and then, when I thought he was sufficiently bemused, I brought across a right that caught him clean on the mouth. He staggered, his legs buckling, but failed to go down, then stood back, spitting out teeth and blood.

I should have finished him off then, without mercy, but was foolish enough to look round at Bethan. This was my undoing, for Matt came at me like a windmill and I caught one of his thrashing blows on my eye, which made me see stars. To save myself I had to back away hard, but that was also Matt's undoing, for he thought he had me on the run; and when he made a mad, final rush I launched myself at him and sent a crashing right through his flailing arms. It struck him on the bridge of his nose and stopped him in his tracks; and before he could recover I stepped in close and uppercut him to the chin with all the force

I was capable of. I swear he lifted an inch or two before he fell to the ground; and to my relief remained there, the blood gurgling in his throat.

I turned immediately to Bethan who was still being held by the other two, but no action was required for when they saw me advancing they released her.

'Understand this,' I said, 'if this lady is molested in any way by you or anyone else, I will bring a hundred men from the docks and deal with you all. Is that understood?'

This was a lie, for I doubted if I had more than a dozen friends who would have joined me in such a venture and they would take some persuading; but the threat appeared effective for they nodded. I pointed at the prone figure of Matt.

'Take him away with you and when he comes to tell him what I have told you.'

They picked up their companion, one taking him by the shoulders and the other by the legs, and carted him off into the trees. I turned to Bethan, very conscious of my right eye which was now tight closed.

'You cannot stay here now. I shall find a house and you must marry me.'

She stared at me wide-eyed, her mouth hidden by two clenched hands. I thought for a moment she was going to say something but suddenly she gathered up her dress and ran off into the woods.

I was no wiser than before as to whether she wanted to meet me again, and merely had a black eye for my pains.

CHAPTER TWELVE

SOME WRITERS can prolong a story, stretching out the words and events to a prodigious extent, but such is not my nature. A superfluity of verbiage is irksome at all times, whether it be written or spoken; and so I will confine my relation of the events that followed my fight with Matt to the bare essentials, leaving out all unnecessary adornments, even if this offends the suscepti- bilities of my more delicate readers.

71

Truth to tell I became consumed with an unabating desire for Bethan. She rarely left my thoughts, especially during the hot summer nights spent in the stuffiness of my little room. I wanted nothing more than to marry and possess her and was prepared to do this even if it meant taking on the whole of Wig Fach.

This required allies and so I confided in the Treseders, which seemed a wise move, for they had already noted my black eye and knew that something was afoot. At first Mrs Treseder was horrified at the thought of my involvement with a girl from such a place. but when I explained the position fully to her and described Bethan, she relented. Being a woman she saw the romantic side of things and as a result became my abettor and accomplice. Mark, on the other hand, was antagonistic from the beginning; and even when his wife averred that there could be no harm in it if the girl loved me he remained dourly apprehensive. Being the good friend that he was, however, he did not harp on the fact, but I knew from his demeanour that he would remain unconvinced until events proved his fears groundless.

I also told the Treseders of my intentions of taking a house of my own; and this created even greater consternation until I explained that I would continue having my meals with them until the time of my marriage. This mollified them a little and Mark was further heartened by my firm promise that, come what may, I would enter partnership with him, the necessary capital being available in six months or a little under. In this way, therefore, we continued to live happily under the same roof.

The opportunity of acquiring a home came sooner than I expected, Tamarisk Cottage coming up for lease at a rental of five shillings and sixpence per week. This residence, set in the heart of Nottage, was a little grander than I had originally envisaged, being a thatched Tudor edifice with a large garden. But it had many advantages, among them several secret recesses where I could deposit my money. This was of major importance to me now, for the constant immersion in salt water, although beneficial to my leg, which seemed to grow stronger with each day that passed, played havoc with my clothing and body belt. The latter in particular suffered, for each soaking frayed and blistered it to such an extent that I was in constant fear of losing my accumulated wealth (which now amounted to twenty-five sovereigns) to the tender mercy of the Bristol Channel. One of the bedrooms possessed a false beam where this could be safely deposited; and I resolved to do this immediately I had taken possession. Above all, however, Tamarisk Cottage was a residence of character, a substantial place, which would aid me in my endeavour to obtain my desire; for what woman could resist the joy of setting up home there, especially one who had so little?

One way and another, therefore, the future seemed promising and I was optimistic enough to order some furniture from Mark who promised to get it for me cheap at Bridgend market. I even bought a fork and hoe, for I intended to make the large garden pay for itself; and was therefore delighted when legalities were completed and the cottage became mine, with an assurance from the landlord that I had the option of a further year's residence.

With all this completed I resumed my assault, if that is the right word, on the dark beauty of Wig Fach. In this I was successful for after only one further visit, when I again met her by chance, she at last consented to see me again. From then on I knew that, if I persevered, she would be mine, and when one evening she came running towards me with a smile I realised that my ambition had a fair chance of a successful conclusion. Towards the end of August she was kissing me goodnight and I adjudged it time to take her to see the cottage. For this eventful occasion I hired a trap and took her to Nottage in style, feeling very proud of the inquisitive and admiring glances I received on the way. Bethan's eyes opened wide when she saw the place and I heard her take in her breath with pleasure. I knew then that from that moment on there would be little competition from the males of Wig Fach.

I even got her to take me home one evening, leading me by a circuitous path to the family hut, for she was still apprehensive about Matt and his companions. We never as much as glimpsed the thugs, however, and I came to the conclusion that my warning had not been in vain. Bethan's home was much as I expected, being just a rough wooden edifice with a roof made of branches and turf. There were only two rooms and the minimum of crudely hewn furniture, but everything was spotless and meticulously swept. Bethan's mother entertained me to the best of her ability, giving me tea from the only china cup she possessed and oatmeal cake, which she had cooked herself in a decrepit iron charcoal stove situated at the door of the hut. Truth to tell I did not take to Mrs Rowlands, for she was dark to the point of being swarthy and immensely fat withal. She simpered rather than spoke and I came to the conclusion that she had an innate inferiority complex, for she kept making excuses for her predicament and pointing out how much better off she had been previously. I consoled myself with the thought that I was marrying the daughter, not the mother; although I had reservations about living with such a woman.

Mr Rowlands, on the other hand, I both admired and pitied. He was a handsome man with a shock of white hair and steady grey eyes. He was Welsh speaking and had difficulty with his English, with the result that he quickly withdrew from our conversation, although he followed it to the best of his ability, for he was constantly wracked with long bouts of coughing. Between these bouts he seemed to have difficulty with every breath and I realised for the first time the price miners have to pay in their dangerous craft. I did not fancy his chance of remaining long on this earth, but I did not let this depress me unduly for I continually caught Bethan's anxious glances upon me and I knew then that she wanted me as much as I wanted her, even if her reasons were economic rather than amorous. For in those early days of wooing she never spoke to me of love, although my protestations of affection were continuous and forceful; but I consoled myself that real love would come once we were married.

Then, one day in late September, there occured an event that was to seal my fate. It was the hottest September in living memory. All the old inhabitants said that they had never known anything like it; and I can well believe them, for I have never experienced such heat at that time of the year. It was as though the sun was loth to lose its power, the rays beating down day after day with a strength that burned the grass and fried the blackberries, filling the air with the scent of over-ripe fruit and hot gorse. Even Ffynnon Fawr ran dry and there was a constant procession of people armed with pans and buckets going to the much reduced spring at Ty Coch. We sweated in our clothes and it was a daily relief to me to get into the sea in pursuit of my work.

I had made my way to Wig Fach in the afternoon, the tide being then full in; and with the perspiration oozing from me had got as far as the entrance to the valley. There was no sign of Bethan which was understandable, for I had made no firm arrangement for an assignation at that time because Owain, with his North Walian intransigent attitude to work, had said that he wanted me to measure some particularly large limestone blocks; and then, because of the heat, had called it off at the last moment. I did not enter the valley for I had an arrangement with Bethan never to do so except in her presence; so instead I walked across the plain to the beach, which was her favourite place when she had an hour or two to spare.

I had reached the last ridge of sandbanks and was staring out to sea, noticing its steely-blue colour shimmering gently in the heat, when I happened to glance sideways and as a result saw a sight that all but stunned me.

For there, in the same burrow that I had first sat and spoken with Bethan, was the object of my dreams, save for this difference: she was lying on the sand completely naked. Her clothes were in a neat pile beside her with the exception of a chemise, which did duty as a ground-sheet to protect her hair from the sand. As I watched she sighed with contentment and turned her head towards me, but obviously remained unaware of my presence for she made not the slightest movement. It was as though she had given herself over so completely to the sensuality of the sun's rays that she was incapable of realising the impact of prying eyes such as mine; and I stood there for several moments not knowing what to do.

That Bethan had done such a thing on previous occasions was apparent to me immediately, for her lithe figure was sunburnt all over, with none of the tell-tale marks that the dock workers had after removing their shirts for the day's toil. I could not take my eyes off her, noticing the smooth rounded breasts, the slight curvature of the stomach and the long, shapely legs; and I was filled with amazement that one day soon I would be able to enjoy all those charms at my leisure.

I thought hard. Should I move away silently, keeping my presence a secret until such time arrived that I could tell her and make a joke of it? Or should I wake her and scold her for tempting fate at the hands of any Wig Fach lout who happened to pass by? As I pondered I saw her eyes flicker and she shielded them with her hand, but still there was no sign of awareness that I was there. In the meantime the sweat poured in increasing rivulets down my body and my eyes remained glued on the bronzed, recumbent figure.

Then I did what I suppose any virile man would do. I walked into the hollow and sat down beside her. At the last moment she heard my feet scrunching in the sand and started up, but I placed a hand on her shoulder and gently forced her back into the lying position.

'Do not move,' I said. 'I have been watching you for some time so it makes no difference now.'

Again she struggled upright but again I forced her back.

'Let me see you,' I whispered, my voice unrecognisable even to myself. 'This will be my joy when we are married. I love you and that makes it permissible.'

She relaxed a little under the pressure of my hand but crossed her arms modestly over her breasts and twisted her body away from me.

'No. It's wrong,' she cried. 'You should not see me like this before—before—'

'Lie still,' I commanded sternly. 'For a moment or two at least, and then I will allow you to dress.'

I was of a mind to lecture her there and then about her foolishness, but instead drew her shoulder back until she was half facing me. The sun beat down stronger than ever, making me bold; and I touched her breast. She made a moaning sound and her head fell back on the white chemise.

'Let me touch you,' I said. 'Just once.'

She remained still and tense while I fondled her soft, yielding flesh and I could not resist the temptation to bend down and kiss the red mound of her nipple. I heard her suck in her breath and so I transferred my lips to her open mouth and kissed her hard and fiercely, at the same time allowing my hand freedom to roam at will. Gradually she relaxed and began to respond hungrily to my kiss, which was a very long drawn out affair.

Then I could resist my impulses no longer. Still kissing I undid my clothes and, breathless with passion and excitement

76

mounted her gently but quickly in a manner which would permit no refusal. She resisted for a moment, but it was a token show of force, and with a deft movement of her body helped me in my endeavour. Suddenly I was in the warm haven of her body and drawing in my breath fit to burst.

But I had been celibate too long. Before I knew what was happening I felt the strength of my body gather its forces and, try as I would, I was unable to prevent their sudden outward explosion. There were great flashes of light—more than when Matt hit me—and a rushing noise in my brain. Then it was over and I lay quiet, cursing myself for having been so quick. The sun stabbed deep into my back, sapping what little energy I had left.

I looked down at the sunburnt face an inch or two from mine but Bethan's eyes were closed and she was lying stock-still. There was no way of telling what her thoughts were at that moment.

But I knew what mine were. There would be no turning back now. The siege of Wig Fach was at an end.

CHAPTER THIRTEEN

WHEN BETHAN TOLD ME she was with child the wedding was fixed for Boxing Day at Newton Church. This surprised me a little for it had not entered my mind that anyone from Wig Fach had connections with the established church, which was stupid of me for many good, God-fearing people lived there. I myself had no special thoughts on the matter for, although I am God-fearing myself and see His manifestations about me every day, I have always maintained that, if the man in the moon should visit this earth (and some say he will one day) he would be amazed at the way the various sects quarrel and assert that only they are right; and so it mattered little to me where we were married.

I was more concerned that Bethan was already with child but I consoled myself that this was not the first time such a thing had happened; and as Mrs Rowlands expressed a strong wish that it should be a church wedding the necessary arrangements were made and Bethan and I began attending sevice regularly. For my part I went on with my own quiet preparations. I dug the garden ready for the spring sowing of vegetables, painted the cottage door and white-washed its walls; and used my knowledge of carpentry to make many items of household furniture. I also bought a feather bed—a good one, costing all of three pounds, for many had told me that if a man and woman are happy in bed they will be happy in other things as well, a fact that I now know to be true.

All this was not plain sailing, however, for the weather broke in October and it rained unceasingly for two months. The basin of the new dock filled with water and it became a quagmire in which work for both men and animals became impossible. Mr Brogden, good man that he was, kept the men in his employ, making them quarry and face the stones until we had huge mountains of limestone blocks on our hands—more than I ever thought we would use. This strained his resources, for there was not work for all that many, and may have contributed to his eventual financial downfall. The weather did not affect me, however, for we kept on working at the breakwater in spite of the misery of getting soaked every day and going home like bedraggled scarecrows.

There were two pointers of what lay ahead for me. One day I cut down a large part of the ivy that clung to the walls of Tamarisk Cottage and was promptly informed by a neighbour that I had done away with my only sure safe-guard against bad luck and sorcery. As though this was not enough he then gleefully intimated that, as the chimney would not draw in a satisfactory manner, the devil was sitting atop the roof. I did all that I could to make that chimney smoke properly. I swept it, cleaned the flue crevices and even rebricked the reachable portions; but to no avail, for all the time I was there the fire never drew and the rooms frequently filled with smoke. I often think of that neighbour and wonder about his premonitions of dire events to come.

At that time, however, I was not unduly concerned and made arrangements for a lively pre-marital night of revelry, to be held on Christmas Eve. I invited, beside Bethan and her parents, all my friends and new-found acquaintances with a special invitation to Mr Brogden, which gave me the opportunity to put into writing my thanks for his generosity in paying for my schooling. He declined the invitation, as I expected of such a busy man, but couched his reply in such affectionate tones, and wishing me every luck in my marriage, that I still treasure the letter today. Mark Treseder, whatever his feelings about the forthcoming nuptials, was all for a party and procured a leg of ham, a huge keg of Devon cider and two bottles of contraband brandy. Mrs Treseder baked bread and a large fruit cake and Dafydd borrowed extra chairs and glasses. I hired the trap to fetch Bethan and her parents and paid in advance for the services of Ffelish Gunter, the fiddler from Newton. All was therefore ready for an evening of jollity.

Bethan and her mother arrived first and Mrs Rowlands, after looking around the place with evident approval (it was the first time she had been to the cottage), settled down on the only comfortable chair by the fireplace and remained there, to the best of my knowledge, throughout the entire evening, unmoved by the occasional cloud of smoke that enveloped her and drinking tea with her little finger extended in the manner of fashionable ladies. Mark and his wife came hot on their heels armed with a donkey cart-ful of victuals and then I dispatched the trap which had brought Bethan and her mother to Dafydd's place for the extra chairs. The other guests started arriving and soon the place was crowded with people, both the kitchen and main room seeming full to over-flowing.

Bethan was dressed in a red dress, somewhat reminiscent of those that Spanish ladies wear, which contrasted vividly with her black hair and making her more striking than ever. I felt very proud of her and glowed with satisfaction at the admiring glances of the men as they came to pay their compliments and wish us well. Soon Mark's cider (into which he had poured the brandy, making a very potent brew) loosened all our tongues and it was not long before the house was full of animated conversation and laughter. Ffelish Gunter produced his fiddle, all the furniture was pushed aside and we went on dancing until a halt was called for supper. I, of course, stayed as much as possible by Bethan's side, surreptitiously holding her hand and enjoying her close proximity. Then, just as everybody had eaten their fill and Ffelish was

79

reaching once more for his fiddle, there was a loud knocking on the front door and a voice from without shouted:

'Behold the Mari Lwyd, with simple friends to ask permission to sing.'

Immediately everyone looked at each other with consternation tinged with jubilation, for the Mari Lwyd is a Welsh custom which can be either happy or fearful, depending largely upon the reputation of those taking part. No one can say when the custom started for its origins are shrouded in mystery. It takes place at Christmas when a crowd of men visit houses and demand entrance for the Mari Lwyd, which is one of their number dressed in a white sheet with the skull of a horse on his head. The skull, which has been whitened by burial in lime, is bedecked with ribbons and streamers; and its appearance outside a door on a dark winter's night can be very frightening. The men are supposed to be chosen for their wit and singing qualities but of recent years there have been too many irresponsible youths among them, whose wild spirits have done harm to crockery and furniture; and so when the knock came we were anxious to find out who it was composed the party.

'It's all right,' said Dafydd who had, gone over to the window. 'It's only Sam Craddock. He's harmless enough.'

'How many of them are there?' asked Mrs Treseder sharply.

Dafydd drew the curtains again.

'About twenty, I would say.'

'Uffern!' exploded Owain. 'They'll eat us out of house and home. Put the food away, Mrs Treseder.'

'No,' I said. 'We must do as the custom demands, even if they eat everything here.'

I pretended not to see Owain stuff some ham into his pocket and went over to the door.

'Is that you, Sam Craddock?' I called.

'It is. Me and Mari and her followers.'

'Are you all responsible?'

Sam hiccupped.

'Of course we are! Hardly had a drop to drink all night.'

'It doesn't sound like it to me. Let's hear you sing.'

'Right, John Vaughan. You shall hear us sing like angels.'

I heard Sam call for order and then the party sang a lament about the fate of the poor in mid winter; and it was immediately obvious that some of the men were the worse for drink, for they slurred both words and notes. When it was over I called out:

'You'll have to do better than that if you want to come in here, Sam. You're not singing like true Welshmen.'

'You're right,' said Sam. 'Now lads, that was bloody terrible. Mr Vaughan won't let us in until we sing properly. We'll have "Ar Hyd y Nôs".'

There was a murmuring from the men and I heard somebody relieve himself on what was left of my ivy, which augured ill for the second attempt, but 'Ar Hyd y Nôs' is a hymn which all Welshmen can sing, drunk or sober; and they sang it melodiously and with such feeling that we all applauded.

'How's that, Mr Vaughan?' said Sam triumphantly. 'Now will you let Mari Lwyd in?'

'Not yet,' shouted Dafydd. 'You've got to ask a riddle first.'

This seemed to stump Sam for there was a long silence. Then:

'We can't do that. We lost Roger Ward in the Knight's Arms.'

'What's he got to do with it?'

'Roger's our englyn and riddle man. He was took ill in the Knight's.'

'I know from what,' said Dafydd. 'Sorry. No riddle, no entry. I suppose you've lost the bloody horse's head too, have you?'

'That we have not,' said Sam. 'Show him, Jenkin.'

There was a shuffling of feet and the awful skull appeared at the window. There were screams of simulated fear from the women.

'Right!' said Dafydd. 'We can see Mari. Let's have the riddle.'

Again there was a murmuring, then a voice piped out:

'Answer this one, Dafydd Hopkin. Why does it take a man quicker to get from Nottage to Newton than from Newton to Nottage?'

We all looked at each other. If we failed to answer we were in honour bound to unlock the door and let the party in.

'I know,' shouted Guto, who was sitting on the stone staircase. 'Because of the hill. It's easier to run down the hill.'

'Wrong,' said the voice. 'Is that you, Guto Bach Dwl? Trust you to think of that. Try again. Why is it quicker for a man to get from Nottage to Newton than from Newton to Nottage?'

81

We racked our brains but could think of no answer.

'We give up,' I called out. 'What is the answer?'

'Because the girls of Newton are prettier than the girls of Nottage.'

We burst out laughing and there were shouts of ribaldry from my Nottage guests. I walked over to the door, slid back the bolt. and revealed the swaying white figure of the Mari Lwyd.

'You are welcome,' I said. 'As long as you behave yourselves.'

'We'll behave ourselves,' said Sam, pushing the swaying Mari in front of him, forcing down the horse's skull so that it just cleared the lintel. 'We've got to. Our next call is at Sea Bank House. Mr Brogden wants to show the Mari Lwyd to his guests.'

And it was immediately obvious that, although one or two of the men were in great high spirits, the company would be well-behaved, for they were all employees of James Brogden and knew that to go to the master's house in a drunken condition would not augur well for their future. They drank moderately and ate less and so Owain's fears were unfounded; but this did not stop the horse-play for which the Mari is famous, although the man with the skull got as good as he gave, for every time he stooped to muzzle a woman's arms or breast someone would reach up under his white sheet and pinch his bottom, one doing it so hard that the skull fell off revealing the Mari to be Robert Evans, a labourer with twelve children, whereupon I slipped a shilling into his hand, a penny for each of his progeny for Christmas.

They were with us for only half an hour but that was long enough, for twenty men on top of the company already there made the cottage as full as a limpet shell. and I had great fear for the crockery and borrowed furniture. But everything went off without mishap and when they departed it was to the accompaniment of our thanks and best wishes, for some country people do not think Christmas complete without a visit by the Mari Lwyd. When they had gone we resumed our cider drinking, Ffelish launched us into a jig and we went on dancing until midnight, at which time the trap arrived to take Bethan, her mother and a few of the Newton guests home. I saw them off happily, knowing that the trap driver would look after Bethan safely until they got to Wig Fach, and then said goodnight to my guests who departed in various stages of intoxication. The only people left were Mark, his wife and one other woman who had volunteered to stay behind to clear up. While the women were busy at it Mark and I relaxed in the chairs before the fire. Mark pulled out his clay pipe, filled it with tobacco, lit it and eyed me through the cloud of smoke.

'A good night, John. I'm glad it went off well.'

'A good night indeed, Mark. Thank you for all the help you and Mrs Treseder have given me.'

Mark waved a hole in the smoke.

'It was nothing, I am glad that you are happy.'

'That I am. I have been very lucky, Mark. I have a good job, a nice cottage and a beautiful wife to go with it. No man could ask for more.'

'No. That's true.'

Mark puffed again on his pipe and I said nothing more for I knew that on the subject of Bethan we were still on dangerous ground. Then Mark said:

'Now about the future, John. Next month, weather permitting, I'm going with Dafydd to Appledore to inspect a ship for sale. If it's suitable would you be free to give your share of the capital —some time in the spring, say.'

'That I will. You shall have everything I possess.'

Mark eyed me beadily.

'I know you will give what you can, John, but you are nearly married now. You have commitments and this cottage. Will you be free to do as you wish?'

'Of course. I have told Bethan what I intend doing and she fully approves.'

'I am very glad to hear it. If we all pull together the venture will be a success. Now tell me, John, come the spring how much money will you have available?'

'At least thirty pounds,' I said, rising. 'And to put your mind at rest I will show you twenty-six gold sovereigns right now. You can have them now if you wish.'

Mark waved his arm in an expression that told me not to bother, but I knew how anxious he was about the venture, especially since my involvement with Bethan and the cottage and so I decided to reassure him. I went up the stone stairs to my bedroom, lit the candle and felt along the thick roof beam for the hidden cavity where I had deposited my money, complete with body belt. But as my fingers reached the hiding place I felt the chill hand of fear.

The wooden shutter that concealed the aperture had been torn away and inside it was quite empty. There was no sign of either the belt or the money.

CHAPTER FOURTEEN

To BE ROBBED of one's possessions is a miserable experience, but to lose one's entire life savings is nothing short of calamitous. My throat turned dry, my hands shook and I felt mentally and physically sick. I searched the room in despair and found the wooden lid of the aperture, painted black to simulate the beam, beside the bed. I knew then that I had lost all, with precious little chance of ever finding it again. I returned to Mark and told him. He stopped smoking and gaped at me.

'Impossible. You must have made a mistake.'

'No mistake. It's gone. Money and belt.'

'Come now. You've probably mislaid it. Forgotten to put it back—'

'No. It was there just before you all arrived. What's more the thief knew exactly where to go. Nothing else has been stolen.'

Mark bit hard on his pipe and sucked away in a fury.

'Then it was somebody here tonight.'

'It must be. Someone slipped upstairs unnoticed.'

'I didn't see anybody.'

'Neither did I, but we weren't in this room all the time. I went to the kitchen occasionally and so did you.'

'Then we'd better send for the constable.'

'No hope. He's gone back to Bridgend for Christmas. Anyway, what could he do? It's gone and that's that.'

'We must keep calm and think, John. Now who could have done it? Who do you suspect?'

'I don't know.' It was a miserable thought that one of my guests could have been responsible. They were all my friends and it seemed inconceivable that one of them could have done it. Then I had an idea.

'When I let the Mari Lwyd party in I thought I saw Ezekiel Meredith outside. I can't be sure but it looked like him.'

'But he didn't come in.'

'No, he didn't try. He knows he's not welcome here.'

'Perhaps he slipped in with all the fuss going on.'

'It's possible, I suppose.'

Mark looked round at the door leading to the staircase but before he could say anything more Mrs Treseder came in and we felt constrained to tell her. She gave a cry of disbelief and insisted on going to the bedroom again. This we did and looked in every nook and cranny, even searching the second bedroom and the landing. We then searched downstairs and the outside of the house, to no avail.

Then began forty-eight hours of misery, the like of which I hope never to experience again. The Treseders eventually left, fearful of leaving me alone in such a frame of mind, but I insisted that they went, taking little comfort from Mark's assurance that he would make it his duty to question my guests the following morning. I declined Mrs Treseder's invitation to join them for Christmas dinner and instead lunched alone on salted herring and what was left of the bread. I spent two sleepless nights, tossing and turning the whole time; and when not in bed sat in front of a cheerless, empty fireplace, thinking of the future. When Boxing Day dawned I was in no fit state for a marriage ceremony.

I went through the motions of dressing, wondering how and when I would tell Bethan. My misery was added to by the discomfort of my unaccustomed best suit, the cravat in particular giving me a choking sensation, for I was used to having my neck open to the fresh air. The new boots pinched at the toes and the bowler hat felt hard and constricting. It was almost a relief to hear a knock at the door and to know that Mark, who was acting as best man, had come to fetch me.

But when I opened the door I had a surprise. It was not Mark but Dafydd, also dressed in his Sunday best. His normally cheerful face was serious.

'Mark wants me to tell you that some business has detained him. He'll meet you at the church.'

'Business?' I replied. 'What business on Boxing Day.'

'It's something to do with the other night. You know—the money.'

'Oh! Did he tell you anything about it? What he's doing, I mean.'

'No. He just told me to come and get you. Right sorry I am to hear about it.'

'Not half as sorry as I am, Dafydd,' I said, trying to smile.

We spoke not a word after that. I locked up and we set off through the village. A frost had descended during the night making the ruts of Nottage hill hard and sharp. I felt the chill entering into my bones but we stepped out sharply and gradually warmed up. If it had been any other morning I would have had a sense of exhilaration, for I normally enjoy the air when it is sharp and frosty; but nothing on that occasion could revive my spirits and even when we saw small boys making a slide on the frozen water of Newton Pool I hardly glanced at them.

When we arrived at the church there were few people about. A group of children stood grinning by the lych gate, a ship's hawser in their hands with which they hoped to hold to ransom the three couples being married that day, of which Bethan and I were to be the first. In among the graves were old Ma Perkins and one or two of her old cronies. They waved and wished me luck as we passed.

We reached the porch. Standing there was Mark, dwarfed by the tall figure of the Rev. Edward Knight, the Lord of Pembroke Manor and Rector of Newton-Nottage, which surprised me somewhat, for I thought we were being married by the curate and not by such an important personage. Both of them looked very serious and, as my eyes became accustomed to the gloom, I could see that Mark's face was taut and anxious. I sensed that something was wrong.

'Good morning, sir,' I said to the Rev. Knight. 'Good morning, Mark. I'm glad to see you.'

Mark and the vicar glanced at each other and then it struck me: they were standing with their backs to the door which was tight closed as though they were barring entry; and the church, which by now should have been full of friends and well-wishers, was strangely silent.

'Is anything the matter?' I asked.

Again Mark and the vicar eyed each other.

'Where is everybody?' I added.

'They're inside,' said the vicar. 'Waiting for you.'

'Then shall I go and take up my position?'

'Not yet,' said the vicar hastily. 'Mr Treseder would like to have a word with you first.'

I turned my gaze on Mark who was the very picture of misery. He shuffled from one foot to the other, avoided my eyes, opened his mouth but said nothing.

'Come, Mr Treseder,' said the vicar. 'You'll have to tell him. Do not prevaricate.'

'I'm sorry, John,' said Mark at last. 'Believe me, I wouldn't have it like this for worlds, but I have some very bad news for you.'

'Come then,' I said, fear gnawing at my brain. 'I have had a surfeit of bad news recently. Let me hear the worst.'

'This morning,' said Mark in a quiet, throaty voice, 'I made enquiries to see if I could discover who had taken your money. I was given information which led me to a certain place. I went there and found the money. It was intact and still in your belt.'

I felt a load lift from my shoulders.

'You've found the money, Mark! Excellent. Now our worries are over. I am indeed indebted to you.'

'Your worries are not over,' said Mark lugubriously. 'Not when you hear where I found it.'

'Well!' I said, my fears returning. 'Where did you find it?'

'In the Rowland's hut. Under Mrs Rowland's bed.'

His words hit me like a punch between the eyes.

'You'd better be sure of your facts, Mr Treseder,' said the vicar sharply. 'What you say will have the most severe repercussions.'

'I am sure,' said Mark, 'and I have a witness. Guto Bach Dwl came with me. We entered the hut unknown to anybody and found the money. Under the bed, as I say.'

'You're lying,' I cried. 'This is a plot, Mark. You've always been against my marrying Bethan and this is your way of stopping me.'

'It's no plot,' said Mark wearily. 'Guto will bear me out.'

A sudden cheer from the children at the lych gate prevented further conversation. We heard the noise of carriage wheels and I knew that Bethan had arrived.

'You will soon hear the truth of what I say,' said Mark.

We turned to face the porch door. Bethan appeared first, dressed in white, the veil covering her face. Then came her father, walking with difficulty and supported by a man I did not know. Finally came Mrs Rowlands in a black organdie dress which I had paid for. They paused on the step, all four framed by the ancient arch.

For what seemed an interminable length of time no one spoke, then the vicar broke the silence.

'Mr Treseder! Say what you have to say, please.'

Mark cleared his throat.

'Mrs Rowlands, I accuse you of having stolen John Vaughan's money.'

I thought the woman was going to swoon. She stepped back a pace and her normally sallow complexion took on a yellowish tinge. She recovered instantly, however, but fear shone through her dark eyes.

'What did you say, Mark Treseder?'

'I accuse you of stealing John Vaughan's money,' repeated Mark. 'From his cottage.'

'This is nonsense,' cried Mrs Rowlands. 'Absolute nonsense. John! Are you going to stand there and allow this man to insult me?'

But I was looking at Bethan. Underneath her veil she was crying. Suddenly she swung round to her mother.

'I told you to put it back. Why didn't you listen to me?'

She gathered up her wedding dress and ran out of sight down the drive. Her poor father gaped after her, only half comprehending what was going on. The man with him was obviously discomforted, not knowing what to do. Mrs Rowlands remained facing us, breathing heavily.

'I'll have the law on you for this, Mark Treseder,' she said but in a strangled voice unlike her own. 'You've always been against my daughter, haven't you?'

For answer Mark reached into his jacket pocket and pulled out my body belt. In silence he handed it to me.

'Why?' I asked. 'Why Mrs Rowlands? Your daughter could have had anything from me without this.'

Then, showing her true colour for the first time the woman's face darkened and took on an appearance that I can only describe as tigerish. When she spoke next she almost snarled.

'You'll have to marry her, John Vaughan. She is with child. It is for the child that I took the money. I'll have none of your hair-brained schemes. You gave her the child and the child will need the money later on. You are not fit to be responsible for it.'

'Wrong ' said Mark. 'Your daughter is not with child. I know that too. You forget how thin the walls of your hut are.' He turned to me. 'I'm sorry, John, but it's the truth. It was part of the plot to get hold of you.'

'If all this is true ' said the vicar with obvious distaste, 'you must remember that I am also a magistrate. You must now consider, Mr Vaughan, whether you wish to press charges.'

Mrs Rowland gave a cry of fear.

'No, you must not do that! It was for your own good, I tell you.'

I eyed her with pity and loathing.

'Go now, Mrs Rowlands,' I said, trying to keep my voice steady. 'There can be no marriage after this. You have ruined two people's lives.'

She stared at me for a moment, her lips working silently, then she, too, gathered up her dress and hurried away. After her went Mr Rowlands, the stranger's arm around his shoulders. He said not a word, but I knew that the old man was weeping.

In the porch there was silence again. Mark stared at me, not knowing what to say. The vicar placed one hand on the door.

'I must release the congregation now, Mr Vaughan. I shall tell them nothing except that the marriage has been cancelled. Are you to press a charge?'

'No,' I said. 'And please allow me to get away before you open that door. I want to see no one.'

I left the porch and walked down the drive. The children were still by the gate, waiting expectantly. Mercifully there was no sign of Bethan's carriage. The belt was heavy in my hands and I could feel the hard outlines of the sovereigns in their small pockets.

But I felt little joy at the return of my money and hurried off home to conceal my grief.

CHAPTER FIFTEEN

To MY ENDURING gratitude the people of Porthcawl and the two villages were very gentle with me. No one said anything in my presence about the unfortunate affair and if they talked behind my back I cannot blame them, for an event of that magnitude was bound to cause a stir; and anyway there is little to do in the long winter evenings except gossip. That I had their sympathy I knew; but after many weeks of reflection I came to blame myself, for I had forced myself on Bethan and dazzled her with expectation of wealth. I had even shown her where my small hoard of gold was hidden, a temptation if ever there was one. Neither could I in all sincerity blame her mother, for she had so little in this world; and poverty drives people to do dishonourable things. I never saw either of them again but I heard later that Bethan had married a man from Wig Fach and is, to the best of my knowledge, still residing there today.

I was dry with Mark at first and for a long time we were uneasy in each other's company; but I knew that he had acted in my best interests, with no alternative but to do what he did. Our friendship became stronger than ever after a while and, although I kept my independence by continuing to reside at Tamarisk Cottage, I went regularly to the Treseders for my meals. After the fiasco at Newton Church I resolved to have nothing more to do with women but I found life lonely in the cottage and continued to harbour a sneaking wish that one day I would find the right person.

At first, to forget my sorrow, I plunged myself into my work, but that did not last long for in January the storms began and all activity on the breakwater ceased. We were employed on lining the eastern causeway with limestone blocks, but this required no specialised knowledge such as mine and for the most part I was merely a helper to Owain. I went several times to the breakwater at the height of the gales to see how our workmanship was standing up to the pounding. It now extended a hundred yards or more, a vast improvement on the stubby edifice I had seen when I returned from India. I was pleased to note that, except for one frightening moment when a huge block was prised loose and used by the waves as a battering ram, all remained well, the tall wall doing its job of breaking the onrush of the water against the ramparts of the outer harbour.

Just before Easter, Mark, Dafydd and Guto went by collier to Appledore and returned with a small but sturdy brig, which required one more hand but was eminently suitable for our purpose. Mark began trading straight away, taking limestone and flannel to the North Devon ports and bringing back cider and butter. He soon found that there was a demand for Welsh beer and Bridgend stockings, which latter lasted a lifetime, for our Glamorgan sheep grow much better wool than the Exmoor variety. He often sold direct from the quaysides but there was always sufficient to take to Bridgend market where Mark had a stall looked after by a hired man. Mark also made a connection with a lace manufacturer from Ilminster who brought his products across Exmoor by pack mule and we soon found that, weight for weight, we made more out of the lace than any other merchandise. Having learned to number satisfactorily I was entrusted with the book-keeping and was amazed to see how quickly our profits mounted, putting me in mind of my old Aunt Sarah's saying, that an ounce of business was worth more than a ton of labouring.

One day, when the weather was calmer (for I am not a good sailor) I took a day's holiday and accompanied Mark on a trip to Barnstaple. We started off the evening before and, guided by the new lighthouses that were then being set up all over the Bristol Channel, made a safe crossing. In the morning I left Mark to his business and explored the town, revelling in the sights and sounds of a new place. I imbibed at an inn, partook of a quayside lunch of lobster and cream and returned to the brig to find the cargo packed and everything ready for departure, which was being held up because Mark was somewhere in the town sealing a bargain. Dafydd asked me to coil a rope in the stern and this I did, little knowing what was about to occur.

I was first aware of a presence when I looked up from my chore and saw on the quayside, barely a yard from my eyes and on the same level as them, a dainty foot encased in the latest of satin shoes. I allowed my gaze to travel upwards along a gorgeous shot silk dress to the smiling blue-green eyes of Lady Catherine

Whitney-Browne. I straightened up in surprise, cracking my head on an iron pulley.

'Good morning, Mr Vaughan,' said Lady Catherine, smiling. 'I see by your expression that you are surprised to see me.'

'That I am, ma'am,' I said, touching my forehead. 'Very surprised I am, indeed.'

Lady Catherine laughed, a happy musical laugh which immediately brought a smile to my face.

'We are here on business, too,' she said. 'Sir Charles has a small estate near Bideford. We heard that one of Uncle James' ships would be here. We were hoping you could take us across to Porthcawl.'

'Mr Brogden's boat is there,' I said, pointing to a collier next door. This boat is Mr Treseder's—and mine. Partly, that is. We are in business together.'

Lady Catherine looked at the filthy craft in the next berth and her pretty nose wrinkled.

'We can hardly go across in that. It would ruin our clothes.'

'Then if you care to wait a moment I will see if it is possible for us to accommodate you.' I turned and shouted for Dafydd. He came in a moment, grinning broadly. 'Dafydd,' I said, 'is it possible for us to take Sir Charles and Lady Catherine with us across to Porthcawl?'

Dafydd pulled on his mop of hair.

'Don't see why not, m'lady. That is if Mark has no objections. I don't think he's bringing any more cargo aboard.'

'Oh! if you could it would help enormously,' said Lady Catherine. 'We are going to Porthcawl for the summer and it will take us a week to go round in a coach. We will pay you, of course.'

'No need for that,' said Dafydd. 'We're going there anyway and you are welcome. It all depends on Mark—he's the main owner and you never know what he'll bring aboard last minute. It may be an Exmoor bull for all I know.'

'I wouldn't like that! If it's a bull you can put him on the coal ship.'

We all laughed and at that moment Mark appeared. He doffed his hat to Lady Catherine and we appraised him of the position. He gave his consent immediately and within minutes the Whitney-

Browne's coach was alongside. Sir Charles clambered out, wheezing. I went up on the quayside to help him and he shook hands with me, although he could not remember my name.

'How are you, young fellow? Very pleased to see you. Glad you can take us over. Confounded nuisance goin' all the way round when you can almost see the damned place.'

We helped the driver and footmen with the baggage and when we had finished I was glad Mark had brought no extra cargo, for the deck was littered with cases and boxes. Even Sir Charles seemed surprised.

'Didn't know we had so much. You must have brought every dress you possess, Catherine. Will this affect the running of your ship, Mr—er Treseder?'

'Not at all,' said Mark cheerfully. 'Only too pleased to do you a favour, sir. We owe Mr Brogden a great deal for allowing us to use his quayside.'

The coach was then dismissed to begin its long detour through five counties and we helped our new passengers aboard. Mark gave a hand to Sir Charles and I guided Lady Catherine. I walked behind her on the gang plank, noticing again the strong, copper-coloured hair and the beautiful figure, its curves accentuated by the graceful outlines of the expensively tailored costume. In her wake she left the faint but heady perfume I had noticed before; and when I held her arm to steady her I experienced again the strange magnetism I had encoutered at Sker.

Mark busied himself about our small cabin, dusting down the only chair we possessed and tidying up the bunk bed for Sir Charles should he wish to lie down. Dafydd cast off and we moved out to open sea, there to find what we were hoping for, a steady south-westerly. The sails cracked open and in no time at all we were scudding past Bull Point, it being obvious that at this rate we would be home long before the coach got even as far as Porlock. We headed across open water where Dafydd entrusted the tiller to me, knowing full well that I could not hit anything, or endanger the ship, until we neared the Scarweathers.

After a further hour's sailing, when I was beginning to feel mesmerized by the hiss of the sea as it swept past on either side, I saw a movement in the cabin and shortly afterwards Lady Catherine appeared, her hair enveloped in a chiffon scarf. Swaying slightly with the movement of the ship she came towards me and sat down on the narrow gunwale plank. For a moment she said nothing, savouring the sight and sound of a sturdy craft doing its work. Then she turned to me.

'I am glad to see you again, John. Do you mind if I call you John?'

'Not at all, ma'am' I replied. 'I would esteem it an honour.'

'How is your leg, John?'

I felt a thrill of pleasure that she had remembered my leg.

'Very well, ma'am. As well as can be expected. I think it has improved in the last year.'

'I am very pleased to hear it. Your open air life has made you look very fit. I wish I could say the same. I have been cooped up in London for a whole year. The atmosphere plays havoc with one's complexion.'

'There's nothing wrong with your complexion,' I said without hesitation. 'You are as beautiful now as when I saw you last.'

'Thank you, John. That is very kind of you.'

I kept my eyes on the sea ahead, for I felt the blood rushing to my cheeks. I had not meant to be so forward. Lady Catherine studied the sea also, and for want of something to say I said:

'And how is *your* leg, ma'am? When I saw you last you were suffering as a result of a fall.'

'Oh that! Much better thank you. Do you know, I don't think I've ever thanked you for helping me on that occasion. Please allow me to do so now.'

'Oh! It was nothing,' I said, feeling light-headed from the perfume and her close presence.

'And so this boat is yours. You are in business, I hear.'

'Partners—with Mark and Dafydd. I am still employed by Mr Brogden, though.'

'That I know, too. I wrote asking about you and Uncle James keeps us well informed about all his undertakings. If you go on like this one day you will be rich and famous.'

'I don't know about being famous,' I said. 'But one day I would like to be better off than I am now.'

'And that you shall be without doubt. I was very sorry to hear about your unfortunate experience with—with a certain young lady.'

I winced, sorry that she had heard of the affair.

'Never mind,' said Lady Catherine quickly. 'Plenty more fish in the sea. One day you will meet a nice woman, not—not one like that. Then you will, be happy.'

'Perhaps. I am in no hurry to marry.'

She glanced curiously at me, her beautiful eyes reflecting the similar hue of the sea.

'We must find someone for you. We can't have a handsome man like you running around free. Are you courting anybody at the momemt?'

'No, ma'am.'

'Good. We must see what we can do. I also hear you've bought a cottage.'

'Rented, not bought. 'It's in Nottage.'

'I know. I would like to see it.'

'See it, ma'am?'

'Yes. Why not? Don't you want to show it to me?'

'Of course, if you wish. I—I didn't think you'd be interested.'

'I'm interested in all that goes on in Porthcawl, especially when it concerns Mr Brogden's ventures—it means so much to him and you are one of his key men. He told me so. Oh! I am looking forward so much again to being there. If you only knew how much I have yearned for sea air. I have been stifled—really stifled in the last eight months. Now I shall be able to hear the sea and the seagulls and fill my lungs with fresh air—and three months to do it in. You've no idea how much I'm looking forward to it, John.'

She took a deep breath as though to emphasize her future intentions and I warmed to her happy nature. Woman of the world she might be but she had a happy, youthful trait that I found most endearing. She leaned back against the gunwale, an action that drew up her dress slightly, revealing a degree of ankle which made me almost afraid to look.

'And John, I shall ride and go for walks and explore all the countryside. I want to see Margam Abbey and Candleston Castle —especially Candleston Castle, for they tell me it's haunted. Will you take me there, John?'

'Of course, ma'am if you wish. But will it be all right—I mean with—with—'

'With Sir Charles ? Of course it will be all right. He knows how you looked after me before. If it hadn't been for you I could have lain in that desolate spot for days. Anyway, he's always pleased when I'm enjoying myself. We shall go on horseback. Can you ride ?'

'Yes, ma'am. That is I'm used to horses, although I've never ridden a real thoroughbred.'

'Then that will be an experience for you. We will choose a fine day and I will see to it that Uncle James gives you time off.'

'That will be very nice, ma'am,' I muttered.

She fell silent then, contenting herself with staring at the blue, hazy Welsh hills which became clearer with every moment that passed. I said nothing also, trying to stifle the strange excitement I felt within me. It was as though the delectable creature by my side radiated unseen waves that kept me in a perpetual state of agitation, enjoyable but unnerving.

Then with a quick, sudden movement she placed her hand on mine. She took it away almost immediately and I only had time to notice how white it was compared with the mahogany of mine.

'I must go now, John, to see if Sir Charles is comfortable. But I warn you. I shall take you under my wing when we get to Porthcawl. I owe you a great deal.'

She stood up, smiled and made her way back to the cabin, her dress fluttering in the strong mid-channel breeze. I looked down at my hand. There was no mark where she had touched it but I could still feel its imprint. Surreptitiously, after first glancing around to see that I was unobserved, I raised my hand to my lips and kissed it.

CHAPTER SIXTEEN

I MUST NOW describe two events that affected me considerably, the first by making me something of a hero, a state of affairs I did not voluntarily seek, the second by saving my life, although how that transpired will not become apparent until later.

When news arrived that Parliament had at last passed the act approving the construction of the new dock there was no general rejoicing, for the act was a foregone conclusion and in any case the work was well under way. But to mark the occasion James Brogden held a garden party and financed a Sunday School outing for the children of the parish. This coincided with the visit of a circus and so an aura of festivity developed, greatly welcomed by the workpeople, for there was little in the way of entertainment in those days.

I cared little for the circus. It set up its tents in the hollow behind the dyke on which the intended promenade was to be built. It was an ideal spot, sheltered from the westerlies, but the stench of the poor animals in their cages offended me, and so I refused to go, although Mark and Dafydd parted with their money. I enjoyed the side shows, however. We laughed at the fat lady, were awe-struck by the two-headed dwarf and mystified by the conjuring tricks of the great Marvo. We tried to get Dafydd to take on the champion pugilist of Great Britain but he refused saying that he would be sorry if he knocked the man out, in which case the poor fellow would lose his job, and equally sorry if he got knocked out himself. Later Dafydd made amends at the Strength Machine. With this contraption a pivot was struck by a mallet which sent a block of wood up a scale-marked pole. If the block hit the bell at the top a small prize was given, but no one succeeded in winning until Dafydd had a go. He struck the pivot so hard that not only was the bell rung but the whole of the edifice collapsed, much to the annoyance of its proprietor.

On the day of the Sunday School outing the morning dawned bright but airless, a sign of great heat to come. The girls looked cool and sweet in their white pinafores but the boys were self conscious in their heavy jackets and knickerbockers. Some of the younger ones wore sailor suits, reminding us of our great navy, which is bigger than all the rest of the world's put together. They trooped from their various chapels until nigh on a hundred had collected on the Green at Iron Gate Point. There they sang and played games until the arrival of Mr and Mrs Brogden, the former gay and talkative to match the mood of the occasion, the latter still dour and forbidding. Mr Brogden then threw halfpennies and a right royal scramble followed, much to the amusement of the spectators.

After a picnic lunch of buns and ginger beer the children went for the second part of their treat, a trip to the Mumbles in one of Mr Brogden's iron-ore boats, specially scrubbed down for the occasion. We older people went with them to the outer dock to see them embark; and great was the excitement as they clambered aboard. There was much waving from both sides as the boat tacked out and we continued to watch as it rounded the breakwater and set off on a westerly course. Then Dafydd, Mark and I walked leisurely back to the Green where there was free tea for everybody. When we had drunk and eaten our fill we went on to Lock's common and there sat down to enjoy the sun and a day of freedom.

We had been there an hour when Mark remarked how hot it had become. It was not only hot but oppressive, the air being strangely still and quiet, unusual for that exposed place. I mopped my brow and looked out to sea, and was surprised to see how dark it was over the channel. We were bathed in bright sunlight but only a mile or two away there was a menacing blackness. Part of the Devon coast was completely obscured.

'Dafydd,' I said, 'take a look at that.'

Dafydd raised himself from the patch of heather on which he had been lying.

'Uffern! That's black. Looks like a storm to me. Oh, God! not with all those kids on board.'

'I don't like it,' I said, standing up. I scanned the expanse of water. There was no sign of the iron ore ship.

Then, chilling not only my over-heated body but also my heart, I felt a rush of cold air. It came from the west and when I looked seaward again I could see a turbulence among the blackness. Dafydd and Mark also got to their feet.

'It's a storm all right,' said Mark in a low voice. 'I wouldn't have thought it possible after such a morning. What can we do?'

'Nothing, said Dafydd, grimly. 'I hope Sam Evans has seen it and turned back. He should be somewhere off Aberafon now.'

We strained our eyes into the distance but could see nothing. The air around us began to eddy sharply, catching at our jackets and trousers. Within minutes we were being buffeted from all sides and I prayed that Sam Evans, the skipper of the ore ship, had spotted the danger in time. We ran to the edge of the common to get a better view down channel.

'There she is!' cried Dafydd. We stared in the direction of his pointing arm and there, sure enough, was the ship, wallowing in a sea that had suddenly become choppy. She seemed to be clear of the terrifying sand banks known as the Scarweathers but was perilously close to the jagged reef of Sker Point.

'He's hugging the coast,' breathed Dafydd, 'to get away from the storm. Don't get in too close, Sammy bach!'

We stood there watching as the ship, now running fast, came opposite us. Then, to my horror, I saw the dark mass beyond split up into several evil-looking funnels of swirling air and almost immediately one of them detached itself from the main mass and raced towards the ship, enveloping it completely. When the craft reappeared a few moments later it was bereft of its mainsail and most of its rigging, and was gyrating rapidly as though some giant finger was stirring the surrounding water. Finally it began to corkscrew its way up channel, but at a much reduced rate, its progress impeded by the expanse of canvas lying over its side.

'Come on,' I yelled. 'She'll clear the point. She'll come inshore further down.'

I set off at a great pace, followed by the others, our progress assisted by the wind at our backs. We reached the fairground and saw that we had gained on the ship, which was mercifully just clearing Iron Gate Point. A few horror-struck faces appeared above the dyke, so I cupped my hands over my mouth and shouted for all my worth.

'Follow us down to the breakwater. Pick up ropes on the way.'

They nodded and we set off again. The power of the wind was now so great that we were bowled along like hoops; and when we reached our destination it was almost impossible to stop. Indeed, if it had not been for an iron stanchion that I grabbed at the last moment I would have been lifted bodily into the seething water. But we all made it and cowered behind the sheltering upper wall of the breakwater. I paused only long enough to take three deep breaths then stuck my head over the parapet to ascertain the position of the ship. The screaming wind, now howling like a banshee, made my eyes water but I was able to make out that it was wallowing directly towards us, at about four knots, still impeded by the sail. I sized up the position as quickly as I could and withdrew my head.

'With luck she'll just clear the end of the breakwater. I'm going to swim out.'

'You'll never make it,' yelled Dafydd. 'You won't live two minutes in that!'

For answer I unlaced my boots, grabbed a coil of guide rope from its hook on the wall and knotted one end around my waist. Divining my intention two men brought up a hawser.

'Follow me, Dafydd,' I said. 'But stay under the wall. Pay out the rope as you come and make sure you put a good knot in it.'

For the first fifty yards or so I was safe, for the parapet protected me, but when I got to where the blocks descended into the water I began to wonder whether I was committing suicide, for there the sea was so tumultuous and the wind so ferocious that I doubted whether I would remain alive for two seconds, leave alone two minutes. But I tried to remain calm, as I had learned as a soldier, and made my way down the steps, clinging fast to each as the waves engulfed me, but all the time weighing up the position of the ship, which was now so close that I could see the huddled figures of the children on the deck. I took one glance at Dafydd far above me, saw that he had knotted the rope, waited for a moment between two waves and then took the plunge.

My intention had been to swim in a southerly direction, knowing that the current would drive me westward, in the hope that my line would pass in front of the prow of the ship and that I would then be dragged against the gunwales. It was a quick decision, made on the spur of the moment, but I had reckoned without the size and power of the waves, which is understandable, for I had never swum in those conditions before. The result was that, once I was in the water I lost all sense of direction and could not see the ship at all. I struck out as hard as I could, conserving my strength by going through the waves rather than over them, but within a very short time found myself fighting for breath.

When death is near, they say, people see the whole of their lives in one fleeting glimpse. That did not happen to me but I certainly began to commiserate over my past sins, wishing that I had been a better man and even got to the pitch of promising

God that, if only He would save me, I would mend my ways in future.

Then, just as I thought my end was near, I surfaced from a wave to find the ore carrier bearing down on me. I made a last despairing effort to get near and felt a grappling hook tear into my shirt. I was dragged to the wooden side where powerful arms seized me and hauled me aboard. I lay on the heaving planks among the sick of the children. Quickly and wordlessly the guide rope was loosened from my waist and two sailors began hauling on it with all their might. Soon the hawser came aboard and was promptly fastened to a bollard.

I have only a hazy recollection of what happened next, for I was exhausted after my endeavour. A sudden heaving of the deck sent me sliding across its slippery surface to the hold canopy which I clung to, listening to the crying of the smaller children who had been sent below. Groups of older children were lashed together in the stern and fo'c'sle, their faces white and terrified but staring at me in wonder. They little knew that the danger was not yet past for, unless the hawser quickly impeded our progress, we were heading for the Black Rocks; and once on that jagged reef nothing in the world could save us.

Then I felt the ship judder and swing round a half circle. Even above the roaring of the wind I heard the hawser crack tight then hiss as the strain went into it, but it held. We yawed and twisted, every timber stressed by the opposing forces of wind and rope, then we began to slide away from the cauldron of the open sea into the relatively calm water in the lee of the breakwater. On that structure, over which huge plumes of spray were rising, I could see men frantically working. They had looped the other end of the hawser around a huge stone bollard but, although twenty or more strained on it, they made not an inch of progress and so we remained suspended, at the mercy of a length of hemp.

Then I saw Dafydd leading a team of horses along the gangway, close in under the sheltering wall. I rubbed the salt away from my encrusted eyes and stared anxiously as they attached harnesses to a wooden drag and used marline-spikes and oars to lever the hawser around the drag. The horses took the sudden strain and were pulled back a yard or two, but they recovered and went forward a few paces. Anxious eyes on both ship and breakwater watched the hawser, which began to quiver alarmingly but still held. The horses stumbled forward again and each pace took us nearer to safety, for, although leaning over at a terrible angle, we were moving slowly towards the harbour wall. The whole process took barely ten minutes, although it seemed an age to me. I heard a distant cheer and saw what appeared to be the entire male population of Porthcawl hauling on the hawser, the horses standing by, their crucial job done. We were pulled in close to the slipway just in time to see the lifeboat come trundling down the steep slope on its big-wheeled carriage. Once afloat the crew rowed rapidly across the intervening gap, but before they could arrive Sam Evans came across the deck and put his arms around my shoulders.

'Thank God for you, John. The *Good Deliverance* would not have delivered us this time, as you can see.'

Then the hatch was opened and out came the little ones, yelling blue murder as well they might.

CHAPTER SEVENTEEN

LIKE THE SAILORS I refused to leave the ship until all the children had been transferred to the *Good Deliverance* and ferried to the slipway, by which time other ropes had been attached to us and we were slowly winched up to the breakwater and there made fast. I clambered up the snaking rope ladder and stood again on the gloriously solid rock; but was immediately seized and had my back made raw by slapping hands. Mr Brogden himself fought his way through the throng and praised me for my quick thinking, and from that moment on I became something of a hero. I found it gratifying in a way, for total strangers began to smile at me and call out hearty greetings; and the children themselves, although often shy, took to following me in droves, which was touching but occasionally inconvenient.

Later, when things became calmer, people talked of the event, some blaming the crew of the *Good Deliverance* for being tardy in getting to their posts, which was manifestly untrue, for the storm had risen so quickly. The older sailors told us that what we had experienced was no ordinary storm but a hurricane, which is rare in our parts but does occur, for legends have it that one such buried the ancient city of Kenfig and created the sandhills. When praised I thought it my duty to remind people that it was a team effort which saved the children and that I could never have done what I did without the help of Dafydd, Mark and the others, but it was I who continued to receive the adulation, and later folk collected money for me and handed me the princely sum of five guineas, which I promptly shared with the men who had helped me.

Having experienced the full frightening fury of a sea in those conditions I was in no mood to go into the water again for a while, even for a peaceful swim; but I was fated to do so, although in very different circumstances: and this episode I must relate for, although distasteful to me, it had an important bearing on my later life.

Truth to tell, although now a hero in the eyes of many I was still very much the villian as far as two men were concerned, namely Ezekiel Meredith and his son Jeremiah. They had never forgiven me for my earlier encounters with them, and indeed our mutual dislike stemmed back to childhood days. Our relations were made worse when Jeremiah was caught stealing a sledge hammer from the quarry and was promptly dismissed. He blamed me for informing upon him, which was untrue for I knew nothing of the incident until later. Then Ezekiel was demoted from his position as foreman to that of general labourer, a matter entirely his own fault for he frequently came to work drunk; but, of course, I was again accused of influencing Mr Brogden in his decision.

I knew from the attitude of both men that they would go for me one day, but that they would stoop to murder never crossed my mind. This they attempted, however, and it was the cause of my entering the water sooner than I intended. It happened one evening when I had gone to the breakwater to estimate work for the following day. I was standing at the end of the completed section marvelling at the sea which was now so calm that it seemed incredible that it could ever boil in a fury. It was almost dark, the moon was just appearing and there was no one about. Suddenly I heard a noise behind me and turned to see the tall bulk of Ezekiel Meredith, standing but a yard or two away.

'Good evening, Ezekiel,' I said civily.

Ezekiel said nothing, but without opening his mouth I could smell the strong odour of ale. As usual I prepared for danger, sizing up the position I was in. We were both standing on a part of the breakwater which was L shaped. To my left was the upright part of the L, a wall twelve feet high. To my right was a sheer drop into the sea, then half-way in. Ezekiel was blocking the passageway that led back to the promontory. Two men scuffling there would have little room for manoeuvre.

Ezekicl said nothing so, not looking for trouble, I made to go past on the wall-ward side, but he stepped in front of me.

'By the Old Nick himself, Vaughan,' he said. 'You've caused me some trouble since you came here. Now you're going to get some of it back.'

'Hold on, Meredith,' I said. 'I've caused you no trouble. Any trouble you've brought on yourself, and if you're thinking of the fight I had with your son that was a long way back. Do you harbour grudges that long?'

'I've had enough of your sneaking ways, Vaughan. Brogden's blue-eyed boy, that's what you are. Well, you know what happens to blue-eyed boys around these parts, don't you?'

'Just a minute,' I said, angry at his accusation, which I had heard before from other quarters. 'I've said nothing against you to Mr Brogden, but you can't act the way you do without it coming to his ears. He heard from other sources. You got what you deserved.'

'Did I now?' Ezekiel's snarl turned to a leer. 'And that's what you wanted, ain't it? You've been after my job ever since you arrived, Vaughan.'

'That I have not. I bid you good night, Meredith.'

I turned, intending to step past him on the seaward side, but again he blocked my way. Then, too quick for me to do anything about it, an arm came around my neck from behind and held me in a stranglehold. At the same time one of my arms was pinioned behind my back. I felt another ale-laden breath down the back of my neck.

'Good lad, Jeremiah!' said Ezekiel. 'Hold him fast. Now we'll deal with the bastard the way he's been asking for.'

I tried to swing away from the grip but the elbow tightened round my neck and my arm was forced upward until the bone made cracking noises. Close to my ear I heard Jeremiah's voice.

'I've got him, father. He won't get out of this one.'

I struggled again, the constriction around my throat making it difficult to breathe, but again the grip tightened and I allowed myself to go limp to save energy. At the same time I cursed myself for having been caught unawares. Jeremiah must have crept around the breakwater on the seaward escarpment and come up the blocks. A glimpse of his feet, encased in canvas slippers, told me why he had been so quiet.

'Now then, Vaughan,' said Ezekiel. 'We're going to give you what for.'

He swung back his fist and brought it crashing into my face. I tried to dodge the blow by moving my head but it caught me on the cheek and I felt the blood begin to flow.

'How'd you like that, Vaughan? Now here's one for what you gave my son.'

Again the fist went back only this time the blow was to my stomach. I doubled up with the pain, nearly sending Jeremiah over my shoulders, but he jerked me upright again.

'A few more like that, father.'

'No,' said Ezekiel. 'We don't want to beat him up too much. I don't want too many marks on him when he's found in the water.'

'Just one more,' pleaded Jeremiah. 'Then we'll do him in properly.'

Ezekiel stepped a little closer and measured his distance.

'One more then. A few marks will make it look as though he hit the rocks.'

I watched the fist rise and willed strength into my already taut muscles. When Ezekiel struck I wrenched myself sideways enough to dodge the blow which went over my shoulder. Meeting no resistance Ezekiel went off balance and stumbled forward This gave me my chance. I shot out my free hand and seized him around the throat.

'Get him off,' screamed Ezekiel, clawing at my wrist, but that was all he had breath for, for I squeezed so hard on his jugular vein and windpipe that my fingers almost met around them.

105

Within seconds Ezekiel's face went black and his eyes began to protrude.

Seeing what I was up to Jeremiah pulled me back, but I kept up the pressure and Ezekiel had to move with us. Jeremiah swung me from side to side, but it was like trying to dislodge a bulldog from its victim. Wherever Jeremiah and I went, Ezekiel had to go too, such was my grip on his throat.

Then Ezekiel collapsed and I could hold no more. He fell to the stones, frothing at the mouth. Jeremiah still tried to restrain me but his exertion had weakened his beer-filled body and it was a comparatively easy matter to tear myself away. I rounded on him and gave him one between the eyes with such force that he stumbled backwards against the wall. He rushed forward again but I stepped aside and sent in a wide, looping blow that caught him on the ear as he went past. His momentum carried him forward to the edge of the shelf and, before I could do anything about it he disappeared over the side. I heard the splash as he struck the water a few seconds later. I stood for a moment, breathing heavily, recovering my composure.

A wheezing, rattling sound made me look round. Ezekiel was still lying on the stonework but had dragged himself up on one elbow. With his other arm he pointed at the spot where his son had gone overboard. Incapable of further movement his lips jerked silently. Then came the rattling again and I could just make out his words.

'He can't swim.'

I went to the edge and looked down. There was Jeremiah bobbing up and down, trying to do a sort of dog-paddle for the breakwater. He reached the side and clutched at the stonework, but Owain ap Owen had done his work too well. There was not a place to which even a limpet could cling. Jeremiah began to disappear under the water.

I heard the hoarse voice again.

'Save him! Save him!'

'Very well,' I said. 'I'll save your son. On one condition: that neither of you molest me again.'

Ezekiel nodded. Not hurrying too much I kicked off my boots and undid my jerkin. I wanted Jeremiah to suffer a little longer before rescuing him. When I was good and ready I dived in, hitting the water cleanly, and surfaced to find Jeremiah's hand scrabbling against the wall. I seized it, pulled his arm around me in a way that reminded me of what he had done to me, and struck out for the slipway.

It was a very subdued Jeremiah that I put ashore. Half full of water he merely gasped and glowered at me, proffering not a word of thanks.

'I saved you,' I said, still slightly out of breath myself, 'on your father's promise that neither of you will bother me again. See that you don't.'

He said nothing, so I left him and went to retrieve my jerkin and boots. Ezekiel was still lying there, head and shoulders propped against the wall.

'Your son is safe,' I said. 'Remember your promise.'

Ezekiel nodded. I had squeezed his throat so tight that he was unable to speak for a fortnight.

CHAPTER EIGHTEEN

JAMES BROGDEN held his garden party in a field not far from Sea Bank House. A large marquee was set up there, together with several smaller tents, and I was invited to attend along with Owain ap Owen, who was teetotal only when it came to paying for his own drinks.

The marquee reminded me of my army days, for there is something about the smell of grass when it is encompassed by canvas that is unforgettable. It is as though all the odours of plantains, weeds and the grass itself have been trapped to mix freely, which does not happen in the open air.

I felt uneasy at the thought of going to the function, and even more so when I got there. The band of the Royal Welch Fusiliers played outside and the officers of the Regiment were much in evidence, handsome in their dress uniforms. I again envied them their easy nonchalance but now felt a little more equal to them because of my position in the town. This did not save me from being intimidated by the array of dignitaries and county families who were there and, although not ashamed of my suit, which was the best I could afford, I could not help comparing myself with the opulence that surrounded me.

I was ashamed of Owain, however, who offended me with the speed with which he put away delicacies and drinks; and so I moved away from him, to be met by Mr Brogden who introduced me to a man who had come to measure the future dock gates. But he was an Englishman, very full of himself and with no great love for the Welsh; and so I escaped from him also. At that moment the hubbub of conversation died down and I looked round to see what had caused its cessation. Mrs Brogden had arrived with a party of ladies. Immediately all eyes focused on one person in that group: Lady Catherine Whitney-Browne. She looked so ravishing in a dress that matched the colour of her eyes, drawn up tight into a bustle in a way that accentuated every gracious curve, that there was not a man present, young or old, waiter or guest, who did not eye her with admiration. She was immediately surrounded by a cluster of gallants; and I was put in mind of my original thoughts about her: that she could make a man happy and miserable all at the same time.

I watched her for a while, hoping for some small acknowledgement, but she was so busy in conversation and so obviously enjoying herself as the centre of attraction that there was little hope of that; and so I armed myself with a punch and went outside. There I listened to the band and watched a group of dockworkers kept well back on the other side of the field by a long rope on four foot high posts. I was of an inclination to go and join them for, position of trust or not, I knew I would be more at home with them than with the company I had just left. Still busy with my thoughts I felt a tap on the arm and looked round to see Lady Catherine by my side. She snapped open the parasol she had used to attract my attention, shielded her face from the sun and smiled at me.

'Hullo, John. You look miserable.'

'Not miserable, ma'am. I'm not used to these things, that's all.'

'I don't care for them either. I've had enough in London.'

'Can I get you something? A drink or a sandwich?'

'No thank you. I just want to enjoy the fresh air. Oh, how stuffy it is there! You can hardly move for people.'

'That's why I came outside.'

'I saw you there. I thought perhaps you were avoiding me.'

'Avoiding you, ma'am? I would never do that.'

My tone made her laugh, which attracted a group of officers who had come to the marquee entrance. They came towards us but Lady Catherine placed an arm under mine.

'Let us walk. I don't want to see those men.'

Gratified, I walked her round to the side of the tent to escape the admirers. Lady Catherine glanced at the band and the on-lookers and sniffed.

'John, take me away from here. Take me to see your cottage.'

I nearly spilled the punch over my suit.

'The cottage? Now?'

'Yes. Why not? I told you I wanted to see it.'

'I know, ma'am, but I didn't think—'

'Now's as good a time as any. Then we can escape from these people. You said you didn't like it here.'

'No more I do, ma'am. But—'

'If you're worried about Sir Charles, don't. He's in bed, indisposed.'

'I'm sorry to hear that, but won't you be missed—?'

'Fiddlesticks! There are plenty of women there. Yes, we'll go now! Come round to the rear of the house in ten minutes. I'll have a carriage waiting.'

She left me without more ado. I waited ten minutes or so as I was bid then went to the back of the house. A phaeton was there, with Lady Catherine already seated, her parasol held primly aloft. She motioned me to climb in beside her.

'Nottage, Edwards,' she ordered and off we went. We bowled up South Lane and I just sat there quietly looking at the curious faces of the people we passed. In no time at all we were outside Tamarisk Cottage.

'Come back in one hour, Edwards,' said Lady Catherine.

I helped her down and fumbled for the key.

'I'm not sure it's fit to be seen,' I mumbled. 'I live alone and only sleep here.'

'You want a woman,' said Lady Catherine briefly.

I opened the gate for her and then the front door. The cottage smelt musty for want of fresh air. Hastily I threw open a window.

Lady Catherine inspected the kitchen and the big room, her dress rustling against the walls of the passages.

'It could be made comfortable. It has the makings.'

'It has the makings,' I agreed.

Lady Catherine pointed to the stone staircase.

'What's up there?'

'The bedrooms.'

'May I see them?'

That was something I was afraid of. If the downstairs was untidy I dreaded her seeing my bedroom, for I have the habit of leaving my clothes all over the place. I demurred.

'The steps are dangerous.'

'Then you can help me.'

I did as directed, going behind her to make sure she did not slip on the uneven flags.

'Those two rooms are empty,' I said when we reached the top, but to no avail for Lady Catherine insisted on inspecting them. Then we came to my room.

'I don't know what it's like,' I said in desperation. 'I had to hurry to go to the garden party and it may be—'

'Let me see. I want to see if you are comfortable. I told you I was taking you under my wing.'

I pushed open the door and my worst fears were realised. My working trousers were on a chair, my shirt and jerkin on the floorboards. The bed had not been done and a chamber pot was visible underneath it, mercifully empty.

Lady Catherine smiled. 'I see what you mean.' She went to the window and peered out. 'You have a big garden.'

'It is big. I shall grow lots of vegetables.'

'What are these bushes?'

I stood immediately behind her.

'Tamarisks. That's what gives the cottage its name.'

'Of course.'

I remained standing behind her and suddenly felt a mad urge to put my arms round the slim waist and kiss the nape of her neck. Only a vision of an admonishing Mr Brogden prevented me.

Lady Catherine moved back a little and I felt her bustle brush up against me making my throat go dry. Then she turned

110

and walked over to the bed. She examined it closely before sitting down on its edge.

'It's comfortable, John.'

'It ought to be. I paid a good price for it.'

She regarded me quizzically for a moment then beckoned with her finger.

'Come here John.'

I went and stood in front of her.

'You seem very nervous. Is it because I am here alone with you?'

'Well, yes, it could be that. No other woman has been here with me. I mean—'

'I know what you mean. I have told you. Do not worry about my husband. He places no restrictions on my movements. You've noticed how much older he is than I?'

'Yes ma'am.' And then before I could prevent it I blurted out, 'Why did you marry him?'

This seemed to take Lady Catherine by surprise. She answered in a low voice.

'Because I had to, John. To save my family. My father was a poor clergyman who died leaving an invalid mother and eight children. By my marriage I have been able to help them. Does that explain the situation?'

'Yes, ma'am, it does. I thought it would be something like that.'

'And John, I am tired of being called "ma'am". I want you to call me Catherine, at least in private. Do you understand?'

'Yes, ma'am.'

'Catherine!'

'Yes, Catherine.' I had difficulty getting the name out.

Catherine stood up and faced me, so close that I could feel the hem of her dress touch my shoes.

'And now, John, you may do what you've been wanting to do ever since we came here.'

'Do? Do what?'

'Kiss me, of course.'

I felt the strength drain out of my legs.

'Kiss you?'

111

'Of course! Admit it. You've given every indication of wanting to do so ever since we came in this room. If you deny it you are a liar.'

'I'm no liar. I would dearly like to kiss you—but I cannot.'

Catherine's eyes opened wide in surprise.

'Why not? Most men I know would require no second bidding. Is it because I am married and the bible forbids it?'

'Not that.'

'Why, then? Am I not attractive enough?'

'Attractive! You are the most beautiful woman I have ever seen.'

'Well, then?'

I tried to seek the words I wanted to say. They came out slowly and stiffly, sounding bumptious and stilted, but it was the only way I could express my thoughts.

'I can think of nothing in the world I would rather do than kiss you. But it would not stop there. I would not be satisfied with that. I would want to make love to you. And if I made love to you I should fall in love also And than cannot happen.'

Catherine's surprise turned to puzzlement.

'Would it be so dreadful to fall in love with me?'

'More than dreadful. I would know no peace. For you it would be one more conquest. For me it would be like glimpsing heaven and then having it torn away. I could never possess you—and so I must not kiss you.'

Catherine raised her hands and placed them on the lapels of my jacket.

'That is an honest speech, John. But you cannot really think that one kiss would lead to that!'

'For me it would.'

She stared thoughtfully at me. I felt the pressure of her hands on my chest but remained stock still. Faced with a beautiful, passionate woman with a husband too old for her and my own bed but a yard away I could not trust myself to do otherwise.

'Very well, John. Then I shall kiss you.'

She lifted her hands to my cheeks. Their texture was soft but I felt them burn into me. She pulled my head down, raised herself on tip toe and kissed me full on the mouth.

'There, John! I have rewarded you for all you have done for me.'

112

Suddenly she laughed and went to the door.

'Come! Now you shall show me your garden. Tomorrow you shall take me to Candleston Castle. I must think very carefully about what to do with a man like you.'

She took my hand and led me out to inspect the tamarisk bushes.

CHAPTER NINETEEN

LADY CATHERINE rode the horse that had thrown her on Kenfig Moor. It was a beautiful, docile creature and I remarked how much better behaved it seemed after the lapse of a year. Catherine smiled at me.

'You'll be saying next, John, that I allowed myself to be thrown on purpose so that you could rescue me. Would you believe that possible ?'

Without thinking I began to say no, but something in her merry expression checked me. I merely returned the smile but thought about it for a long time afterwards, although not deeply for my horse was a stallion of seventeen hands with power in its legs that reminded me of a steam engine. The merest touch of the rein would sent it shooting ahead of the mare and I had all my work cut out to keep it in check.

We went first to Tŷ Coch and rode along the spur to Tythegston then struck out across the sandhills to our destination. The morning was fine and the scents of the countryside made me realise how good it was to be alive; especially with such a companion. She was dressed in a superbly-cut black riding habit and a small hat adorned with a feather, making the few yokels we met stare in awe. We walked the horses most of the time, occasionally breaking into a canter; but for the most part it was a leisurely journey, and we arrived at Candleston in good spirits. I tethered the horses to a tree and Catherine stared at the ruin with its eerie background of sand-encroached trees.

'It's not very big. I expected something larger.'

'It's not really a castle,' I said. 'It was a manor house belonging to the Cantelupes family.'

'Where are they now?'

'Disappeared. Died out.'

'Let's go inside. I want to see it properly.'

We entered the roofless ruin and stood in what must have been the banqueting hall. Ivy and lichen adorned the crumbling walls, which in places appeared in danger of collapse.

'It wasn't built to last, was it?' sniffed Catherine. 'I've seen old places in a much better condition than this. Uncle James say it's not worth building anything unless it stays up for ever and a day.'

'That's what he told me, too. But around here the sand is the enemy. It erodes everything.'

'Talking of buildings, did you know that my uncle is appointing an overseer—a man who will look after all his interests, the docks, the mines and the iron works?'

'No. I have not heard that.'

'It will be a position of great importance. I heard him say something about liaising between all the various activities. Do you know who has been appointed?'

I shook my head. Catherine slashed at a clump of nettles with her riding crop.

'Can't you guess?'

'No.'

'Then perhaps I should have told you before. You have.'

I gaped at her, but she merely threw me a mischievous glance and went through an archway. I heard her voice from the other side of the wall.

'I told him you were the best man for the job and he agreed. He will be informing you tomorrow. Now you will be a real gentleman.'

I went after her, stumbling out some incoherent words of thanks, but she kept her back towards me.

'Don't thank me, John. He had already made up his mind. I merely helped him. Now, then, tell me: where is this ghost of yours?'

She swung round, her face radiant. The news she had imparted had given her as much joy as I felt, but I knew better than to dwell on the subject. I pointed in the direction of the sandhills.

'Over there somewhere. It's near where some old stones are lying.'

'Show me.'

I led the way out of the ruins to the foot of an enormous hill.

'I don't know exactly where. These sandhills are constantly changing position. I could get my bearings from the top of this one.'

'Come on, then! I'll race you.'

We went full pelt at the sandhill but were soon slowed down by its treacherous surface. We struggled on, however, and eventually arrived, breathless, at the top. In front of us was a vast expanse of sandhills, even bigger that the one we were on.

'Where now?' asked Catherine.

'I don't know,' I said, gazing about me. 'It's some years since I was here. I think it's down there at the end of that path.'

'Then let's go there.'

We set off down the slope, slithering as our feet sank deep in the sand. Half way down Catherine suddenly gave me a push that sent me sprawling. In an unladylike voice she yelled:

'Silly John! Doesn't know where he is.'

Recovering from my surprise at the unprovoked attack I was immediately put in mind of my chase after Arabella Dinwiddy. I was further reminded of that episode when Catherine went careering past me.

'Silly old John Vaughan! Silly old John Vaughan! Lost and doesn't know where he is.'

There was no mistaking the challenge and I went after her, but was careful not to get within striking distance until she was at the bottom of the hill and had entered a small copse. I let her dodge a few trees then grabbed her round the waist. Laughing, she slipped from my grasp and went further into the thicket. I caught her again but she collapsed, breathless, on the leafy floor. I sank down beside her.

For a moment I just looked down at the blue-green eyes; then, without a further word we were in each other's arms. I knew from her expression that I must kiss her, and did so. She responded with an eagerness that surprised me.

When I had recovered my breath from running and kissing I raised me head and studied the beautiful face. It was as though I

115

was dreaming and yet I knew it to be true. This was the woman I held in awe, and a married one at that, but I was kissing her without qualms. Moreover I knew that she was as hungry for my love as I was for hers. I threw caution to the winds and began opening first her jacket and then her blouse.

Catherine allowed me to nearly complete my task then placed a restraining hand on mine.

'Wait, John, I must tell you something. You are honest and I must be honest with you. I cannot promise to love you for always. Perhaps it will be only for a short time. I don't know. I want you to understand that for I do not wish to hurt you. Will that be sufficient for you?'

I nodded jerkily. All I knew was that I was about to glimpse heaven on earth and wanted nothing to rob me of it.

'If you give yourself to me only once,' I whispered, 'it will be a memory I shall treasure always. I will expect no more.'

'Then kiss me again.'

I did so and felt her tongue search the inner confines of my mouth. Overcome with passion I undid the last button on her blouse and started on the ones on her skirt. Then, with a shock, I discovered that she wore not a stitch of clothing underneath. I was so surprised I wrenched away my lips and stared questioningly at her.

Catherine's expression was shy and yet challenging.

'I knew you would make love to me, John. I wanted you to. I came prepared.'

She sighed and settled back more comfortably into her leafy bed. I made love to her then, not once, but three times before riding back to Porthcawl.

CHAPTER TWENTY

CATHERINE CAME to Tamarisk Cottage many times that summer; more, indeed, than was good for her, or for me, for tongues began to wag. Sometimes she came openly, riding regally in her carriage, as though she was paying me a social visit: at other times she arrived on horseback, in which case we tethered the animal in the garden and hoped that no one would notice; but the best times were when she came secretly at night, for then she could stay for several hours.

My conscience sometimes troubled me, for I liked Sir Charles, but I was too captivated to really care. What I feared came about also, for I became jealous when I saw her in other male company. Well-to-do admirers called from far and wide at Sea Bank House and she received many invitations to attend balls and banquets. Many she refused but etiquette demanded that occasionally she went and then I became miserable. One evening I saw her arrive at Nottage Court with Mr and Mrs Brogden and a clutch of dandies; and I felt it keenly that I was not invited to attend such functions.

Catherine was aware of my feelings and, after such affairs, was always especially gentle and affectionate. When she had me in a good mood again she would debunk these social occasions, laughing and making jokes about the people she had met; and if I was longer than usual in recovering my complacency would lead me to the bedroom and give me such ecstasy that I invariably recovered my good spirits, thus becoming more deeply in love with her than ever.

The best times were when she could spend several hours with me. Then I would light a fire and she would cook a meal. It used to amuse me how a lady of quality could be so happy in the kitchen and her excuse was that it was such a change from her normal activities. She would sing away happily and sometimes appear with charcoal streaks on her face, which made me laugh and was often detrimental to the meal, for sometimes I chased her back into the kitchen and kissed her; which action often led to more amorous activities. Catherine also turned her energies on the cottage, making it into a real home. New curtains appeared, cushions, tablecloths and always there were vases of fresh flowers. She delighted in mending my clothes, darning my socks and sweeping the rooms. Indeed, there were times when I imagined us to be husband and wife, an illusion quickly shattered when the inevitable time came for her to return to Sea Bank House.

Now if I had been of a cynical disposition I would have accepted my good fortune without worrying about the future, enjoying the favours bestowed on me without expecting them to be permanent, as Catherine had warned me at Candleston. But Catherine had come to me at every possible opportunity and seemed so happy in my company that I began to wonder about the possibilities for the future. Accordingly, one evening when we were sitting on either side of the fireplace, with Catherine happily sewing a button on my shirt, I began a conversation with the object of sounding out her real intentions.

'Mr Brogden has confirmed my new post,' I said. 'I shall start in the autumn.'

'I am so glad. You will do well at it.'

'The work on the foundations must be completed first, then I shall be free to start my new job.'

'I am delighted you are finishing with explosives. It's dangerous.'

'It will require another three months' work before I finish on the breakwater. In the meantime something else is finishing soon.'

'What's that?'

'Your stay here. In two weeks you will be returning to London.'

'I know. I hate the thought of it.'

'When shall I see you again?'

'Next summer.'

'That means nine months at least without you.'

Catherine put down the shirt.

'Work hard at your new position, John, then the time will soon go.'

'Then next summer you will come for a month of two and go away again. What hope is there for me?'

I expected Catherine to remind me of our conversation at Candleston; instead she surprised me by saying:

'Every hope, John. My husband is old as you well know. He will not live for ever.'

Hardly daring to hope for more I asked:

'Does that mean if something happens to him—if he dies—you will come to me?'

'Of course. Who else?'

'I have no title.'

'Pooh! Who want a title?'

'Nor position—and not much money.'

'Very soon you will have both. Then I shall come and spend every penny you possess.'

118

'You may have every farthing as long as you love me. But be honest with me, Catherine. Why have you come to me? You can have any man you wish. Why?'

Catherine flung the shirt on the table, came over to me and sat in my lap.

'Don't you know?'

'No, I don't know.'

She regarded me with dancing eyes for a moment, then stopped and lightly brushed her lips on mine.

'Now do you know?'

I pretended to be simple and shook my head.

'Oh!' laughed Catherine. 'You are a fool!' She kissed me again.

'Ah!' I said. I am beginning to understand. Could it be this?' With a quick, deft action I lifted her skirt and thrust my hand deep between her thighs. Catherine squealed, wriggled then bit my ear.

'Yes, that's why. Partly anyway. I am very happy with you, John. I knew that the moment—the moment you made love to me at Candleston. But I must be honest with you. I could not live in poverty, but I do not require great wealth. I would willingly exchange my life in that dirty city for the fresh air of Porthcawl.'

'Which do you prefer? The fresh air or me?'

'You.'

'Then I will work hard and become rich and provide you with everything you want. But tell me one thing, Catherine. Will you be sorry if—if something happens to Sir Charles?'

'Of course! He has been kind to me. But so have I to him. I have done everything he has asked of me—I have acted as hostess on his estates and looked after him in his infirmity. It has been an arrangement beneficial to both sides, but there has never been any love between us. So I will not be upset when he dies.'

A feeling of happiness came over me, although still tempered with doubt. The thought that Catherine might one day be mine was heady and awe-inspiring. I could think of no better answer than to delve deeper into her multitudinous underclothes and touch the delectable spot that makes women different from men. Having found it, and in spite of a token show of resistance, I caressed it for a time then broached a subject I had set my heart on.

'Catherine! There is one thing I regret very deeply.'

'What's that?'

'That you and I have never spent a night together. Making love like this is all very well but now I want to sleep with you properly. Just one night—and then perhaps I can last out until next summer. Can you arrange it?'

Catherine's brows puckered.

'I'd like that, too, John! Oh yes, let's do it! I could say that I'm going to Swansea to buy porcelain. Edward can take me but I'll arrange for him to stay the night in Pyle. He can come back for me next morning. Yes! I'll see to it right away.'

And so it was arranged. Catherine made a pretence of going to Swansea by coach and Edwards, her personal footman, had a room booked for him at a coaching inn in Pyle, with instructions to return next day at noon. I bought a leg of mutton and a litre of wine and we had a right royal feast in front of the fire, with every morsel made more enjoyable by the knowledge that Catherine did not have to rush off, and that greater delights were to follow.

Yet when the time came to go to bed we were both strangely hesitant. For myself I was as nervous as a groom on his wedding night, and Catherine, too, seemed apprehensive. It was left to me to make the first move.

'Will you go to the bedroom first?' I asked.

Catherine nodded and left me. I undressed in front of the fire, my fingers awkward and clumsy. By now I knew Catherine's body intimately but the thought of actually sleeping with her for a whole night made my heart pump like a piston. I put my night shirt on the wrong way round and had to take it off again. Then I waited until I thought Catherine was ready and went upstairs. I knocked on the bedroom door.

'Come in!'

I opened the door to find Catherine still dressed.

'I'm sorry, John, but this hook has twisted itself. Will you help me?'

My fingers, already ineffective, had the sensitivity of marline-spikes, but I managed to get the hook undone. Catherine stepped out of the dress to reveal a mass of frothy undergarments. She divested herself of these and only the corset remained.

'Help me with this, too. It will be quicker.'

She turned her back on me and I had to heave on the strings to unloosened the first knot. I pulled so hard that Catherine was nearly dragged across the room.

'Why do you wear these things?' I muttered. 'Your figure doesn't require one.'

'Oh, yes it does! All the men admire narrow waists. Anyway this one's the latest from Paris. Don't you think it's attractive. I wore it specially for you.'

'Very nice,' I said, nearly cross-eyed from struggling with the knot. 'I think I'll get a knife.'

'You'll do nothing of the sort! Here! Let me try.'

Catherine reached behind her back and, with the dexterity of which all women are capable, succeeded eventually in divesting herself of her restricting garment. She stood naked in front of me.

'Are you going to wear that night shirt?'

'I thought to. It was bought specially for tonight—like your corset.'

'Let's sleep with nothing on at all! It's our only night together.'

Without more ado Catherine flung herself into bed. I peeled off my night shirt, blew out the candle and tumbled in beside her. Recovering from the shock of the cold sheets I put my arm around her and held her tight.

Catherine sighed.

'I'm glad we did this.'

'Me, too.'

'And to think we have until the morning!'

But it was not to be. No sooner had we warmed each other than there was a stentorian knocking on the front door. I felt Catherine's body stiffen.

'Who can that be?'

'I don't know, I said. 'I'll go and see.'

I went to the window and looked out. In the darkness below I could just make out the shadowy form of Edwards, the footman.

'What do you want, Edwards?' I called.

'Is Lady Catherine with you?'

'She is.'

'Will you tell her I must speak to her. I have bad news.'

I turned but Catherine had joined me at the window, dressed in a negligee.

'What is it, Edwards ?'

'I'm sorry, ma'am, but you have been sent for. I was lucky to meet the messenger in Pyle. It's Sir Charles, ma'am. He's dead. Died at the dinner table at eight o'clock.'

CHAPTER TWENTY ONE

THE DEATH OF Sir Charles upset me a great deal and, coming when it did, made my conscience uneasy. But there was little time to discuss the matter with Catherine for Sir Charles was placed in his coffin, taken to Bridgend by coach and conveyed from thence in a railway carriage to his ancestral home near London. In the entourage were Catherine and the servants and Mr Brogden as well, who went with them as far as Bath.

A few days later I received a letter from Catherine couched in affectionate terms but informing me that Sir Charles' affairs would take longer than expected to clear up as the will was being contested by the children of a previous marriage, and there was talk of lengthy litigation. I therefore resigned myself to a long wait throughout the winter before Catherine's return, but resolved to take her advice and busy myself in my new job, determined to make a success of it.

But first I had to finish my task on the breakwater. This became more difficult as the edifice neared its final extremity, for at the furthermost point of the foundation a deep layer of sand covered the rock. This had to be shovelled and blasted away each day, the work being limited to only an hour or two because of the tides. The weather did not help either, for first there were autumnal gales and then heavy neap-tide swells, which impelled us to wear ropes tied around our waists. There were rogue waves, too, which rose suddenly out of nothing, sending water cascading along the escarpment and over the unfinished wall. So menacing were some of these that a special look-out was posted to warn us of their presence, although that did not save us from regular and thorough dousings.

We were hampered, too, by hordes of spectators who came to watch the final stages, making Owain ap Owen's temper, already brittle, verge on breaking point: a state of affairs made worse by the knowledge that we had reached the crucial point of construction, where the waves would be unimpeded in their battering of the vulnerable apex. Owain personally supervised the laying of each stone, not merely those at the surface but the inner-core blocks as well; and heaven help those of his workmen who were slow with a plumb-rule, hammer or trowel.

Although uncompleted the breakwater had already become the predominant feature in the area. As there were (unlike now) barely a hundred habitations in the town, it could be viewed from almost every angle, and was evident from vantage points as far as Newton and Nottage. From Tŷ Coch ridge it had the appearance of a mighty serpent, but a benign one, although nearer at hand it seemed to possess a sort of brooding presence which deeply impressed those who saw it for the first time.

The breakwater seemed to affect me, too, for I had spent so many countless hours on its construction that it had become almost a way of life. For nearly three years I had laboured on it, thought about it, talked about it, even dreamed of it; and if the amount of salt water I had swallowed was anything to go by, even eaten it. It was as though I had become part of it, and it of me; and so there were times when I viewed my cessation of work there with something less than equanimity.

Keeping pace with the breakwater's development was the progress on the new basin. An area of seven and a half acres, it had already been lined on three sides with stout stone blocks, with arrangements well in hand to receive the immense iron gates. The northern shore had been levelled off with the intention of creating a boat-building yard there, and from the whole extended a network of new railway lines, ready to be linked with the wharves and chutes. It was not difficult to imagine what it would be like when operations commenced and the basin was full of ships.

All too soon the time came for me to take up my new appointment, which I found called for a different type of endeavour. Under Mr Brogden's personal direction I had to see to it that the trucks of iron and coal were dispatched at the correct time, with ships ready to receive the cargoes. This entailed frequent visits to the iron works at Tondu and the coal mines of Ogmore and Maesteg; and to carry out these tasks I was given a horse, with a carriage on call should I so desire. I enjoyed the new responsibility and the feeling of importance it gave me, for I frequently had to make decisions on my own. It was also good training for the future, for it was planned that the big new dock would be ready within a year, in which case my responsibility would become commensurately greater.

Having to consult so frequently with Mr Brogden I was in a position to enquire occasionally about Catherine, only to find that he knew little more about her affairs than I did, for she wrote to me regularly. I suspect he realised the reason for my inquisitiveness, but if he did he made no remark about it. I was also able to ask his advice about money, for my greatly increased salary had put me in a position of relative wealth, and I had no desire to repeat my experience with the body belt. Mr Brogden was good enough to introduce me to his banker in Bridgend and advised me to put any surplus money into the family concern, John Brogden and Company, which I did, thus tying me very closely to the development of the docks.

My affluence was also increased by the success of our trading venture, for Mark had an astute nose for business. He traded in everything from laverbread to limestone and our profits mounted steadily, so much so that we were constrained to erect a warehouse near the dock. This in turn branched out into ship chandlery, for which we had to employ extra men. I kept up my work as book-keeper, although I did these chores in the evening, and was glad of the opportunity to take my mind off the long wait for Catherine. In spite of our expenditure, because we had no middle men to deal with, I estimated that the return on my original investment was in the region of twenty per cent, which pleased me a great deal, for I knew that if ever I married Catherine I would be in a position of being able to maintain her in some at least of the luxury to which she had been accustomed.

My final piece of good fortune came when Mr Brogden offered me a company house on Pilot Row. This was a great step up for only the ships' captains and the port officials were allowed to live there. I gave up the lease of Tamarisk Cottage and moved into the new abode, very conscious of my important position in the town. I purchased a large quantity of furniture of a type suitable to my new status and solicited the help of Mrs Treseder in the important task of choosing curtains and fabrics. Soon I had the place fit for a queen and, my queen being Catherine, I aimed only for the best. From every front window there was a view of the sea and the distant coast of Ogmore; and so I could visualise Catherine waking up in the morning to the murmur of the surf and the cry of seagulls; and if she leaned out she could also see and hear the multifarious activities of the dock, interesting at all times. For one who loved the area, I adjudged, there could be no better place in which to live and I was sure Catherine would like it there.

I expected some people to be jealous of my new-found position, for I had come far in the relatively short time since arriving in Porthcawl, but this was not so. Except for the two Merediths, whom I occasionally saw with their normal churlish expressions, everyone treated me with kindness and respect, due in no small measure to the part I had played in saving the children, and also I think, to my own demeanour. For I was happy in myself, largely due to my expectation of one day possessing Catherine, and when a man is happy he generates the same commodity, with the result that those he meets become affected by his good humour. All I can say is that I was looked up to and treated as one of the foremost men of the town.

Being in such a fortunate position, and with such happy prospects, I was in a mood to partake to the full in the life of the community, and one such occasion was the taming of Owain ap Owen's termagant wife. This episode was humorous, a subject for talk in the town and helped me in my wait for Catherine; and so requires a chapter to itself.

CHAPTER TWENTY TWO

IT HAD BEEN KNOWN for a long time that Owain's wife was unkind to him. She was one of those women, unhappily too prevalent, who are morose and vindictive by nature, and the more ill-natured she became the more she took it out on her husband, blaming him and not herself for their predicament. One of the wags of the town said that Mrs Owen could never forgive her spouse for the wrongs she had done him which, if you think of it, is a very clever way of putting it. As a result, in spite of Owain's intransigent North Wales attitude to us inferior beings of the south, most people were secretly sorry for him.

One day Mark and I were walking near the docks when we saw Owain sitting on a bollard, his chin cupped in his hands. His face, lugubrious at the best of times, was as long as a fiddle. Mark nudged me in the ribs.

'Look at Owain. Doomsday's arrived.' Out loud he added: 'What's the matter, Owain? Breakwater fallen down or something?

Owain gave us a surly stare.

'What's it to you how I look, Mark Treseder?'

'Oh, come!' said Mark. 'We can't have people going around with faces like that. Life's too short. Can we help in any way?'

'You can't help,' said Owain. 'It's Marged as usual. She won't let me back in the house.'

'What have you done to deserve that?' asked Mark, winking at me.

'Nothing. I never do nothing.'

'It must be something. Have you been beating her?'

Owain laughed sardonically.

'Beating her? It's she that beats me. She's got a temper fel yr hen diawl. I've a good mind to go back to Llanberis and leave her here. I haven't eaten since last night.'

'Why not?' I asked.

'Because she won't cook for me, that's why not. Just because I complained about the bacon this morning she threw it at me, frying pan and all.'

'We must do something about this,' said Mark. 'Otherwise Owain won't have the strength to wield a trowel. What was wrong with the bacon?'

'It was all fat, the cheapest cut—and her having plenty of housekeeping money to buy the best.'

Knowing Owain's meanness I doubted that, but thought it best to say nothing. At that moment Dafydd appeared and we appraised him of the position. Dafydd scratched his head.

126

'How often does she go for you, Mr. Owen?'

'All the time. I don't get a moment's peace these days.'

'Must be something wrong then. You should show her who wears the breeches.'

'You come and do it. Big though you are she'd have you out of the house in ten seconds flat. Small she may be but she can punch like a dockside mule. I tell you straight, I'm scared of her.'

'If it's as bad as that,' said Dafydd, 'you ought to do something about it. Why don't you go and see Albert Rhys?'

'What can he do about it?'

'He's the chief elder of Nottage. He knows all about some treatment they used to give to wives like yours. I heard tell about it when I was younger. Cwltrin I think they called it. It stops women bullying their husbands.'

Owain looked interested.

'Is that true?'

'As true as I'm standing here. Go and see Albert Rhys. He'll advise you.'

'I don't want my predicament made known,' said Owain. 'This is a private matter, you understand. I don't want my name bandied about the village.'

'You'll have all the men's sympathy,' said Dafydd. 'And Albert Rhys is very wise. He'll help you.'

'I'll think about it,' said Owain dubiously. But he took Dafydd's advice and went to see Albert Rhys, who organised a Cwltrin ceremony to help the North Walian in his difficulties. There was certainly no privacy about the affair, for on the appointed day nearly all the men of the parish attended, along with a goodly number from outside the area, who came out of curiosity. By the time the ceremony started, in a wooded dell called the Rhyll, nigh on a hundred men and youths had gathered to witness the ritual.

First Albert Rhys appeared, adorned in a quilt and carrying a wand. He was attended by four of the chief elders, Abel Jones, Iwan Hughes, Caradoc Crocombe and Eurig Roberts. The venerable gentlemen sat down on a log, Owain was placed in front of them and all the rest of us formed a closely packed semi-circle.

Albert Rhys waited for the talking to die down then stood up and cleared his throat.

'Are there any women present?'

Everybody looked around and there was a chorus of 'No'.

'Make sure,' said Albert. 'This is a ceremony against women—a certain woman, that is; and there must be no woman present. You can tell by looking for breasts. Look around please and see if you can see anyone with breasts.'

We studied each other but could find no tell-tale swellings.

'Good!' said Albert. 'Now we can begin. This is a serious occasion. One of our brothers has been intimidated by his wife and we must support him. If we do not we will be in the same boat one day. The women of Nottage must be shown that it is we men who are the masters. Once women are given the opportunity to lord it over us there is no knowing where the end lies. We must stop the rot before it starts. We have one before us today who, through no fault of his own, is in a parlous state and we must give him aid as our fore-fathers did before us. Owain ap Owen is a stranger here—he is from North Wales—but we must rally round him for the sake of our manhood. Now then, Owain ap Owen, are you ready to be questioned?'

'Yes-s,' said Owain, hissing the sibilant more than usual.

'Does your wife scold you without cause?'

'Yes. All the time.'

'Do you quarrel frequently?'

'All the time.'

'Does she strike you?'

'Yes.'

'How often?'

'When the mood takes her—and that's often enough.'

'What is her reason for striking you?'

'If I complain about anything she goes for me.'

'Give the court an example of that.'

'Only this morning I complained that there were holes in my socks. I asked her to darn them but instead she threw the scissors at me.'

'Why the scissors?'

'She told me to cut my bloody toe nails, then I wouldn't have any holes.'

Albert Rhys blinked.

'I will now pass over the interrogation to Caradoc Crocombe. Caradoc!'

Caradoc Crocombe stood up, holding his wand in front of him.

'Have you those socks on now?'

'I have,' said Owain.

'Show us.'

Owain unlaced his boots and displayed his socks. The holes were so big that it was impossible to darn them. His toenails stuck out like scythes and to me it seemed impossible for any sock, unless it was made of Tondu iron, to withstand their onslaught. I began to understand Mrs Owen's difficulties, but it was obvious the elders thought otherwise.

'The scissors could have killed you,' said Caradoc soothingly. 'How did you escape injury?'

'I ducked just in time.'

'Has your wife thrown anything else at you?'

'She throws anything that's handy. Rolling pins, saucepans, books—you name it she's thrown it.'

'Is her aim good?'

'I have been struck frequently.'

'What causes her to throw these things?'

'She has no cause. She is in a perpetual state of temper.'

'You are not a big man, Owain ap Owen. Is your wife bigger than you?'

'The same size,' lied Owain. Mrs Owen was a good three inches shorter than he, and most men present knew it. To forestall any possible comment on this subject he added, 'She's not really big, sir, it's that she's very wiry and strong. She could throw most men here across the room.'

'And she has thrown you across the room?'

'Very often.'

Caradoc nodded understandingly and resumed his seat on the log. Eurig Roberts took his place.

'Owain ap Owen! Have you never retaliated against your wife and shown her that you will not stand such nonsense?'

'I have, but I always come off worst. I have told you. She is unbelievably strong, especially when she's in her tantrums.'

'Do you sleep together in the same bed?'

'We do.'

'Do you act in bed as man and wife should?'

'Not for many years. That side of things has never appealed to her. At least that's what she says.'

'Are you a good husband to her?'

'I try to be. I work hard and go to chapel I do not waste my money on drink. I am a law-abiding person and never been in trouble. Most women would appreciate a man like me, but not Marged.'

'Mr Owen, we have now heard a great deal about your married life, but only from your own mouth. Have you a witness you can call to verify your complaints?'

'I have. Nicholas John is my neighbour. He will testify on my behalf.'

'Call Nicholas John.'

Nicholas John stepped forward, grinning. He was a slouching, gangling man, a notorious poacher.

'Nicholas John,' said Eurig, 'are you prepared to answer questions on behalf of the plaintiff?'

'That I am!' said Nicholas. 'Right sorry for him I am, too.'

'Sorry? Why are you sorry?'

'I hear them at it night and day. There's no stopping to it—at least not to Mrs Owen. She goes on continuous. Always screeching at the top of her voice.'

'Have you ever seen her strike him?'

'Not actually seen her, but I've heard things flying about—and I've heard Owain call out as though he's been hit. Sometimes he runs out and hides from her.'

'Where does he go?'

'Down the tŷ bach. Many's the time I've found him there, sheltering, afraid to go in. We share the same one, see.'

'How long does he remain there?'

'Hours on end. One night she locked him out and he had to stay sitting there all night. He could hardly straighten up next morning, and there was a round mark on his arse for days afterwards.'

'Does Mr Owen give his wife any cause for these outbursts of temper?'

130

'None that I can see.'

'Then you think it's a plain case of a wife bullying her husband without cause ?'

'I do. He should have laid down the law in the beginning. It's too late now. Mind you, he's right when he says she's strong. I wouldn't like to tangle with her.'

Eurig nodded then conferred with his fellow elders. They were not long at it. Albert Rhys stood up.

'You have made out a case, Owain ap Owen. We are unanimous in our decision to allow cwltrin to proceed. Roger Pugh and Joseph Leison step forward.'

The two men named entered the semi-circle. Roger Pugh was dressed in his normal working clothes but Joseph Leison was attired as a woman, complete with be-ribboned bonnet. Pugh produced a broom and Leison a ladle. Before my astonished gaze they began fighting with their implements. Amid great laughter they laid upon each other but it was soon over, for Pugh and his broom were felled by a blow from the ladle. The victorious 'woman' stood over him waving her weapon in the air.

'That is enough!' cried Albert Rhys. 'The case has been proved. We will now proceed to the next stage of the ceremony. Bring forward the horse.'

A crude wooden horse was dragged forward on a small carriage. Joseph Leison gathered up his skirts and sat on it, still brandishing his ladle. Twenty or thirty men seized ropes and began pulling horse and Leison to the nearby lane. There we all formed up: first the horse pulled by the men, next the elders carrying their wands and the rest of us in a procession at the rear. Two stalwart men hoisted long poles. On one was a man's breeches; on the other a woman's petticoat. We then wended our way to the village.

Once in the village pandemonium broke loose. Some of the men had drums which they beat loudly, accompanied by others who blew on posting horns. Some of the youths pretended to beat Joseph Leison with sticks, he giving out simulated screams of anguish. Three times around the narrow streets we went, our loud fury bringing people to their windows and garden gates. Most of these spectators were women and children and they regarded us with differing expressions, depending on their attitude to the cwltrin ceremony. The majority laughed and cried

131

out ribald remarks, but a few women glowered and pulled their curtains, obviously regarding the proceedings as an affront to their sex.

After the third circuit we made for Owain's house and formed up outside the gate. I fancied I caught a glimpse of Mrs Owen's face at a window, but it disappeared so quickly I was not sure. The men carrying the poles entered the garden and stuck the base ends into the well-dug soil, thus displaying aloft the garments. As soon as this was done everyone present began pelting the petticoat with stones and clods, to which some eggs and rotten fruit were added for good measure. Soon the petticoat was a filthy, bedraggled mess; and after ten minutes of this treatment it was pulled down and torn to shreds by willing hands. This left the triumphant breeches, still in their pristine condition, a token of male supremacy.

Albert Rhys then advanced into the garden. He stood in a position half way up the path and addressed the still firmly shut front door.

'Wife of Owain ap Owen,' he thundered, 'know this: we, the elders and men, have held a cwltrin against you. We order you henceforth to treat your husband respectfully, to cease beating and bullying him. In default of this order we will return and deal more harshly with you. Come to the door and indicate your presence.'

The door remained shut, making Albert shuffle uneasily, but it eventually opened and Mrs Owen appeared. She smiled brightly at the elder.

'Why, if it isn't Mr Rhys. And what might you be wanting Mr Rhys? And all these people! What are they doing here?'

'We have just held a cwltrin court,' repeated Albert. 'Called for by your husband because of your treatment of him. We have heard the evidence and now adjure you to mend your ways. You must promise to treat him civilly or we must take further steps for his protection. Do you promise?'

Mrs Owen's smile became even brighter, but behind it the eyes were hard. They darted momentarily in the direction of Owain, who was standing by the gate, his mouth wide open.

'Called for by my husband?' said Mrs Owen sweetly. 'Just because we have our arguments like any other married couple? The silly man has been exaggerating to you.'

'We have evidence besides his,' said Albert. 'We know that you have not treated him well. I ask you again, will you promise to treat him civilly?'

'Well, now, Mr Rhys, you men have all been listening to men. You have not heard a woman's point of view. But whilst we're at it could you get my husband to give me more money to live on? You could also ask him to wash more often and cut his toenails. And has he told you he snores like a bull and keeps me awake half the night? See this dress I've got on? I made it myself ten years ago and I haven't had another since. Get my husband to change some of his ways, Mr Rhys, and we would live together civilly enough.'

Albert nodded and turned to Owain.

'Your wife has said certain things about you. How say you to that?'

Owain gulped.

'I'll give her more money. Just stop her thumping me, that's all.'

'Well, Mrs Owen,' said Albert, 'will you stop thumping him if he—er—does the things you request?'

'Certainly,' said Mrs Owen. 'Come inside, Owain, and let's talk things over privately, not for all the world to hear like this.'

Owain looked round helplessly and Mark gave him a shove.

'Go on, Owain. Now's your chance to put things right.'

'She'll eat me,' breathed Owain. 'She'll bloody well eat me alive after this.'

'Come along, Owain ap Owen,' called Albert. 'You have both made promises in public. It is now up to you both to better your marriage. But, Mrs Owen, we want to hear of no more bullying, otherwise the court will have to sit again.'

Mrs Owen smiled coyly at him.

'Just send my husband inside. We'll come to an arrangement.'

Mark pushed Owain again and the poor fellow went up the path looking like one of the unfortunates going to the guillotine. He paused by the doorway to glance helplessly around at the silent throng, then quickly disappeared as Marged yanked him out of sight. The door slammed shut and, after a few minutes, the men began to disperse. Dafydd, Mark and I remained until last, listening to detect any loud noises, but the house remained silent and so we went too.

But we had gone only a few yards when there was a piercing shriek which stopped us dead in our tracks. The elders and the other men came racing back. There was a bumping and banging and Owain came tearing out of the house, his face wild with fear. He did not stop until he was outside the garden gate, where he collapsed, petrified with fear.

Albert Rhys strode majestically through the crowd and confronted the quivering figure.

'What is the matter, Owain ap Owen? Has the cwltrin not acted?'

'Acted!' screamed Owain. 'Acted! You and your bloody cwltrin! She nearly half murdered me then.'

To the best of my knowledge that was the last cwltrin ever he'd in Nottage.

CHAPTER TWENTY THREE

WITH THE COMING of spring excitement mounted as the great new inner dock neared completion. The breakwater was not yet finished but Owain was confident that all would be ready by opening day. New jetties were set up for the expected increase in trade, particularly the export of coal; and on one of the wharves a large-scale drawing of the steam ship, *The John Brogden*, was displayed, a vessel destined to be the queen of the company's fleet. For me the excitement was added to by the thought of Catherine's return; and to this end I made sure that the new house in Pilot Row was furnished, polished and painted to perfection. Next to Sea Bank House and Colonel Knight's large cottage it was the most desirable residence in Porthcawl and I looked forward to showing it off to Catherine.

But the spring also brought trouble. I had been aware for some time that something was amiss for there had been a gradual influx of strangers into the area throughout the winter. These people, poor, hungry and penniless, intsead of going to Wig Fach, where such people usually went, had set up home on the surrounding common land, where they erected ramshackle hovels without sanitation of any kind. They were much resented by our workers, who had to pay rent for their cottages, but the greatest bone of contention was that the itinerants were a constant source of danger to the livelihood of those already employed, for they offered themselves for work at a rate below that already prevailing. Indeed, there was talk of some of our foremen accepting bribes to employ the strangers, pocketing the difference between the regular rates and the cash actually handed over at the end of each fortnight; and some of the men had confided to me their fears of becoming ill. The moment a man fell sick, they said, his place was taken by an itinerant, with little chance of ever obtaining re-employment.

It was to get to the bottom of these rumours that I decided to visit Ezra Probert, the licencee of the Ship Aground, a public house near the docks. A licencee is a good source of information at any time, but Ezra was a veritable fount of knowledge about local conditions, and had been useful to me on previous occasions. I went there on a Saturday night, not the best time for a social call, but effective in helping me to ascertain the true facts of the case: for the area bounded by the four public houses known as the Knight's Arms, the Ship and Castle, the Anchor and the Ship Aground was a teeming mass of humanity at that time, and any serious trouble was likely to be fermented there. I took Dafydd as a second pair of ears and also as a helpmate should we run into trouble.

First we approached the Knight's Arms, which emitted a strong odour of ale-drenched sawdust. From its open door came a cacophony of voices raised in song or argument, and from the brogue we knew it to be filled with Irishmen, who were putting the finishing touches to the broad-gauge railway which was to serve the port. The Irish themselves, with their love of fighting had been a source of friction in the past, but they were about to move on to the west, to complete their navigating there, and so we did not think it necessary to remain but moved on to the Ship and Castle. Here there was already a fight in progress, a vicious affair between some of our own men and a dozen or so strangers. The battle was turning against the newcomers when we arrived, for in their undernourished state they were no match for our brawny stalwarts. It ended in a shout of victory and our men returned to the public house to complete their drinking. I stopped one of them, whom I knew as Dick, and inquired as to the cause of the fracas.

'It's them buggers again Mr Vaughan,' he said. 'They come and takes our work and then they think they can swig our beer.'

I studied the strangers carefully. They were, without exception, dressed in rags, and filthy with it: but it was their demeanour that impressed me. They seemed proud and their faces, instead of having the pallor associated with poverty, were ruddy complexioned. I pointed to one of them, a young man of about twenty.

'You, lad,' I said in a voice intended to be friendly. 'What's your name?'

'What's that to you?'

'I would like to help you—to help you all. It's not to my liking to see you men fighting like this.'

Something about my attitude must have affected him for he replied with less surliness.

'It's not us who started it. It's them louts. They won't let us in the pub.'

I turned to Dick, who was standing by my side.

'Is that true, Dick? Why won't you let them in?'

Dick stared at me in amazement.

'You know why, Mr Vaughan. Those are the bastards who are undercutting us. They hang about each day waiting to jump into our jobs. They'll work for two shillings a week less if you let them—and we're only getting sufficient now.'

I studied the glowering strangers again.

'Where do you come from?'

'From near Court Colman,' replied the youth.

'What are you doing here? Why do you not return to Court Colman?'

The lad gave a sardonic laugh.

'Return there? To what? We are as welcome there as we are here.'

'Why? What crime have you committed?'

'No crime except improving our farms or having a different religion from our masters.'

'I do not understand you,' I said, genuinely puzzled. 'What has religion got to do with it?'

The lad looked pityingly at me.

'Do you mean to tell me you don't know what's going on around here? We had our farms once, but we're chapel, see. The land-owners don't hold with that for they're church. That's why they've thrown us out—and hundreds like us.'

'Not just because of religion, surely?'

'Oh no. That's only the excuse. You improve your farm, like what we've done, and what happens? The agent comes round and increases the rent. Then, when you can't pay no more, out you go, and somebody who can moves in. If we've been undercut we've every right to do the same to others. That's why we're here, mister, to get work, to feed our women and children. If it means taking less than your men, it's better than nothing.'

'That's true,' shouted another man, 'and the Church is as bad as any. You can't live for the tithes.'

A second fellow brandished a small book.

'If you don't believe it, it's all here. Read what Samuel Roberts says—then you'll see.'

'I don't dispute you,' I said. 'Are you all from Court Colman?'

'Not all,' said the youth. 'We're from every part of the Vale, and from the valleys, too.'

'Then bloody well go back there,' cried Dick. 'Or go the Patagonia. There's plenty of Welshmen going there, I'm told.'

There was an ominous muttering from the strangers.

'You fat-bellied bastard,' shouted one. 'How would you like to be driven from your home and go three thousand miles away?'

'Quiet, Dick,' I said. 'Don't make things worse.'

'But Mr Vaughan,' said Dick, 'it's our livelihood they're after, not yours. We've got wives and children to look after.'

'I'm well aware of that,' I said, 'but fighting won't do any good. I will consult with Mr Brogden over this.'

I stared again at the dispossessed countrymen. It took little imagination to understand the plight they were in, and the effect it had upon their families; and I was moved to pity. But what I could do to help I knew not. James Brogden was already employing as many men as he could and had promised to keep on the majority as stevedores. It was difficult to see how he could help any more men find work.

'I will consult Mr Brogden,' I repeated lamely. 'In the meantime I adjure you not to fight but try to live together as Christian men should.'

The words were futile but I knew not what else to say. I bade good evening to the men, ours and the strangers, and moved off towards the Ship Aground, Dafydd beside me.

'This problem must be resolved,' I said. 'It's wrong that men should be made to suffer like that.'

'I don't know what you can do about it,' replied Dafydd. 'I hear tell this is going on all over Wales.'

'I don't know what can be done either, but if we don't look out there'll be trouble. These people are living in conditions not fit for pigs.'

We approached the Ship Aground to find the crowds there even greater, although not abnormal for a Saturday night. There were drunks in abundance, and several ladies of doubtful morals soliciting their attention. The air was alive with singing, shouting and the calls of beggars and costermongers. Ragged children ran everywhere, some carrying earthenware jugs of ale to parents who lived nearby. At first everything appeared normal, just another night of hard-earned revelry on pay day; but then I spotted a gang of fifty or more men grouped together near the wharves. Some were leaning against a fence, but the majority were squatting down on their heels in a way that miners do. For the most part they were small, thin, gaunt men, and they remained quite silent with not a conversation going on between the lot of them. They merely stared at the door of the inn, from which came the usual sounds of drunken animation. I approached them and bade them good evening. To my surprise one or two of them answered civilly. Thus encouraged I started a conversation with those nearest to me.

'I see you are strangers. Might I enquire what you are doing here?'

They eyed my suit, which was now of better quality than I had ever had before.

'Looking for work,' replied one shortly.

'There is little of that here. We are already employing all the men we can. Where have you come from?'

'All over. Maesteg and Tondu mostly.'

138

'Then you are miners.'

'Not all. Some of us are iron workers.'

'Is there nothing in the smelting shops for you?'

'Not now. They're bringing in ores from Spain and the works are moving elsewhere.'

'Well, then, cannot you go where the new works are?'

'We've tried it, Mister,' shouted an old man. 'They're using new methods. They don't want us.'

'That's right,' cried another. 'The Bessemer process, that's what's put paid to us. Steel they want now, not iron.'

'I am sorry,' I said. 'But when I was up in the valleys last week the mines at Maesteg and Ogmore were working to full capacity Surely there must be work there.'

'There is,' said the first man, 'and for every miner there's one waiting to step into his place.'

'I will speak to the managers when I am next there and see what can be done.' My words sounded insincere and the men sensed it. One of them got up off his heels.

'I can see you mean well, mister, but I tell you this: before the end of the year you won't just have us down here. They'll be coming down in droves—and from further afield, too.'

'Aye,' shouted somebody. 'And not by the end of the year either! Next month more likely.'

'Anyway', said another, 'who wants to risk their neck down those bloody mines? The coal owners don't care a damn as long as they get their coal. Remember what happened at Risca—one hundred and forty six men that took, my father included.'

'Aye, and Cymmer got over a hundred.'

'And Margam! Bloody death trap that was.'

'What about Maesteg? Fourteen men there on Christmas Eve!'

Suddenly they lapsed into silence and stared at me. If I could have given them work on the spot I would have done so. Instead I merely nodded.

'I can promise nothing but I will see what I can do.'

I turned and, with the faithful Dafydd on my heels, was glad to leave the reproachful eyes. We fought our way through the packed mass of bodies in the passage of the Ship Aground until we reached a hatch. I knocked and Ezra Probert's face appeared.

'Be with you now, Mr Vaughan. Go into the kitchen.'

We gained the calm of the kitchen and Probert quickly arrived with two tankards of ale.

'Sit yourself down, Mr Vaughan, and you, too, Dafydd. This is on the house. Well, now, to what do I owe the honour of this visit?'

'Ezra,' I said, 'we have come to you for advice and information. I hear of things going on and wish to know more. You are well informed and no doubt you can help me.'

Ezra jerked his head in the direction of the door.

'You mean them outside. There's trouble there, Mr Vaughan.'

'I know. I've seen some for myself—and the effect it's having on our own men. But I hear rumours of something deeper.'

'You're right. There is something deeper. I hear tell some of our lads are going to form gangs to deal with them. It's the Scotch Cattle all over again.'

I felt a chill of apprehension when I heard this, for in my childhood I had heard of the Scotch Cattle. They were groups of men who took the law into their own hands, forming secret societies to deal with others who tried to take men's jobs by accepting less pay. The Cattle stopped short of nothing to intimidate their victims, murder, torture and arson being common-place. Their activities had died out in recent years, especially in Merthyr where they had been most active; but I had heard stories of isolated assaults. I took the threat of their revival with the utmost seriousness.

'We must stop this, Ezra,' I said, 'before it damn well starts.'

'I hope you can,' said Ezra doubtfully and something about his expression made me press him further.

'Have you heard anything more then?'

'Well, yes, Mr Vaughan. I was thinking of coming to tell you, but it's only rumours. There may be nothing in it, you see—'

'Tell me all the same.'

'Now don't let on I've told you. I don't want this place burned down about my ears. But I've heard there's been a man around here stirring up the strangers. He's got red hair and wears a red cap so they call him Cap Coch, like the old brigand who used to live in Merthyr Mawr, only nobody knows where this one comes from.'

140

'What sort of trouble has he been stirring?'

Ezra glanced uneasily at the door, then came closer.

'There is a story that he's going to bring a lot more men down. If they don't get work they're going to attack the docks and do Mr Brogden in.'

'Are they now?'

'It won't take many to do much damage,' said Dafydd thoughtfully. 'They could fire the ships and bring down the derricks in no time. The coal chutes are on wooden legs, too.'

'And don't forget the breakwater,' added Ezra. 'They'll go for that as well.'

'They couldn't do much damage to the breakwater,' I said. 'It's solid stone. They'd need gunpowder.'

'Plenty of that in the mines and quarries.'

I drained the tankard and set it down on the table.

'Thank you, Ezra. Between Cap Coch and the Scotch Cattle it seems we're in for a time of it. Sorry though I am for those men it's time to draw the line.'

CHAPTER TWENTY FOUR

WHEN I INFORMED James Brogden of the rumours he was, as might be expected, more concerned for the men than for his own safety. He did not under-rate the threat, however, and instructed me to take whatever steps I thought expedient to prevent industrial strife; and to this end I decided to enquire closely into the working of the whole of the Brogden enterprise, which ran like an artery from the colliery at Maesteg, via the iron works of Tondu, to the sea-outlet at Porthcawl.

I took the shortest route to my starting point, going on horseback across the forbidding Llangynwyd Common, and descending into the Maesteg valley a mile or two from the drift mine. It was pleasant riding along the wooded glens, then unspoiled by later developments, and so peaceful was it that thoughts of anarchy were temporarily banished from my mind. But the sight of the great gaping hole of the drift quickly brought me back to reality and I was lucky to catch the mine manager as he emerged from the darkness. He was helpful and cooperative but his answers to my carefully worded questions added little to the knowledge I already possessed. Yes, the men were working steadily. There was no sign of unrest, at least not as far as he could see. No, there had been no bad accidents: one or two injuries caused by trams on the steep incline, but nothing serious. No, there was no ring-leader that he knew of, and there were no explosives missing from the store. He warned me against thinking of raising rates of pay, saying that the more the miners got the more they would want; and intimated instead that wages could be cut slightly with the object of employing more men at the same cost. I listened carefully to his replies, made notes in my notebook, then entered the mine and talked to the men. I found them a cheerful lot, enduring their hardship and danger with a humorous stoicism that evoked my admiration. I found no indication of a plot or even bitterness, except over the question of injury. Every man there, like the soldiers I had known years previously, was less afraid of death than of injury, which would make them a liability to their loved ones, then denied wages or compensation of any kind. But I saw not a sign of mutinous unrest and began to wonder if the dangers I had heard of had been magnified.

I spent the rest of the morning at the colliery and in the surrounding village, still without hint of anything sinister afoot, and then rode down to Tondu, following the track that ran alongside the railway. Tondu was very different from Maesteg, for whereas a mine is a comparatively quiet place, with all the activity going on below ground, an iron works is nothing but a conglomeration of noise and heat. I picked my way over a network of rails, my ears assailed by the hissing of steam, the roar of furnaces and the thudding of enormous hammers. Smoke and fumes menaced me from all sides, giving the appearance of a hell on earth, made worse at night when tongues of flame lit up the surrounding countryside. Men working in such an environment would, I concluded, be susceptible to unrest, especially when fermented by clever agitators, and I decided to take time over my investigations.

I found the works foreman in his office and questioned him closely, discovering immediately that he himself was of low morale, largely because of the uncertain future of the works.

Several furnaces had closed down, and the books showed a gradual but definite loss of trade, principally to the newer works of Aberafon, Briton Ferry and Landore, all better placed to receive the purer ores from Spain. I obtained a picture of a declining industry, the final demise of which was not too far distant, with a resultant stultifying effect on the men engaged, all of whom eyed the future with apprehension. But, as at Maesteg, I could find no overt sign of violence or deep plotting, although one or two of the men struck me as being evasive when I asked them about the identity of Cap Coch. On the whole they were surly and uncommunicative, and if I deduced any feeling at all it was one of envy for a Porthcawlian who came from a pleasant place where the employment was steady and certain.

Thwarted in my endeavour to discover anything material I eventually took leave of Tondu, to find that most of the ride home would to have to be in darkness, for I had lost count of the time. I urged my horse into a canter and at first made good progress, passing many farms which on the face of it seemed prosperous. But as I rode I remembered the dispossessed agricultural workers I had met. It was one thing to lose one's livelihood through the introduction of new methods or the closing of an unproductive mine, but quite another to face starvation because of the whim or caprice of an absentee landlord, probably at that moment enjoying himself in London or some other fleshpot. It made my blood boil to think that the main threat to Brogden's endeavours might come, not from his own employees, but from a source entirely unconnected with him. The more I thought about it the more certain I was that Cap Coch would turn out to be a countryman.

It was almost completely dark when I came abreast of Cefn Ridge at a place named Bryn-du and I was on more than one occasion non-plussed as to which path to take. It was with relief that I saw a light ahead and, thinking it to emanate from a farmhouse, where I could obtain directions, I spurred my horse towards it. To my surprise I discovered that the light came from an old furnace, which I knew to have been derelict long since, and when I got nearer I saw that a fire was burning inside the decrepit ruin. I tethered the horse to a tree and, stooping low, entered the furnace. There I saw a scene reminiscent of *Macbeth*.

Seated around a fire of considerable proportions, their shadows dancing on the surrounding walls, were three hideous old women, obviously gipsies. With their dirt-engrained countenances, hooked noses and black, verminous robes, they gave the appearance of witches, especially as they were all stirring a huge cauldron, from which protruded the skinned heads of rabbits. They stared at me, startled, then one of them gave a toothless leer and struggled to her feet.

'Want your fortune told, mister?'

'Thank you, no, I said, backing towards the entrance.

The hag gave me a spiteful look.

'Then what you want?'

'I have lost my bearings. I am travelling to Porthcawl.'

The crones glanced at each other.

'Tell your fortune, mister,' repeated the one who had risen. 'You won't regret it. Old Meg is always right.'

'No doubt,' I said, smiling. 'Another time. I have to get back as soon as possible.' Truth to tell I have always been a little afraid of gipsies, principally because I believe them to possess powers beyond the scope of normal people, and I have never had a desire to know the future. Face things as they come has always been my motto, and in any case the stench of the place was turning my stomach. I bowed my way out through the entrance, but Old Meg followed.

'Cross my palm with silver,' she cried. 'I can tell you how to avoid dangers.'

'No doubt you can,' I said, mounting my horse. 'I will visit you another time.'

Old Meg's scrawny hand came up and seized the bridle. With her other she groped for my wrist and held it tight.

'You are in danger now. I can tell by looking at you. Old Meg has helped many in the past. Let me help you now.'

I tried to release her grip, but the talons cut into my flesh.

'I will cross your palm with silver,' I said, 'but I want no reading of my future. Perhaps I would not like what I hear.'

I searched for my purse and handed her sixpence. She dropped it into her apron but still kept hold of the bridle.

'Bless you, mister. But let me see your hand. I tell you truly I can help you. I felt it the moment I saw you. You have the colour of red about you.'

144

'Red!' I was intrigued in spite of my eagerness to get away. 'What do you mean by that?'

'Let me see your lines and I will tell you.'

Against my better judgement I lowered my hand. The old crone seized it and peered closely at its palm, now grimy, for I had not washed since morning.

'I fear you will not see much,' I said. 'You cannot see properly in this light.'

Old Meg merely grunted and peered more closely. Behind her I spotted her two companions grimacing from the flickering entrance of the furnace. I waited impatiently for the first utterance about my future.

At last the hag looked up.

'There is a woman in your life.'

'There is in most men's.'

'But this one is special to you. You love her very much. She is of the nobility.'

I stared down at the swarthy face, astonished. I could think of no way in which the gipsy could have known such a fact other than by knowing me well, and that was out of the question. Before I could recover from my surprise she went on:

'She loves you, too, but her love is not as deep as yours. You will never possess her. You will see her but once more and then she will disappear from your life for ever.'

I felt suddenly cold with fear. The thought of losing Catherine had always been at the back of my mind, but I had refused to face it. Now I was hearing it from a source I had always feared, a gipsy with the power to see into the future. I tried to withdraw my hand, without success.

'Do not be saddened,' said Meg. 'It is for the best. You will recover, but it will take some time. There is something of greater importance here. Let me see!'

Impatiently she rubbed at my hand, trying to loosen the dirt that impeded her art. She stared at it closely for a long time, then gave a sudden hiss and threw it away from her.

'There is nothing. I cannot see in this light.'

But her expression told me she was lying.

'There is something,' I said, 'I can see it in your face.'

'Nothing I tell you.'

'There is,' I persisted. 'And previously you told me I had the colour of red about me. Do the lines convey anything about that? I may as well know the truth of the matter.'

She stared at me, undecided.

'Come!' I said. 'I have been a soldier. All soldiers learn how to face death. I may as well know my fate.'

She nodded and drew my hand towards her again.

'The future can be changed if steps are taken. I will advise you. The red I see is blood. Yours and many other people's. You will be involved in much strife. You yourself will come near to death. Whether you live or not depends on you—your will to live. The lines are confused. I cannot tell you more than that.'

'And I cannot avoid this?'

'You can but you will not. I see more red—a man with red hair. Your paths cross. I advise you to keep clear of him, but you will not. You will fight before the moon is full again.'

'Cap Coch,' I said.

Meg looked at me without understanding.

'No matter,' I said. 'I thank you for your pains, although you have not exactly cheered me. I am to lose the woman I desire and then come close to losing my life, if I do not lose it altogether. Not a happy prospect, Meg, you must admit.'

The old crone retreated to the furnace door.

'I did not wish to tell you all.'

'I know. Still, I thank you.'

I turned the horse to retrace my way down the track but had gone but a pace or two when the bridle was seized again. This time it was not Old Meg but a man, swarthy and ear-ringed. My natural reaction was to kick him in the chest and spur the horse but something about his grinning face deterred me.

'Has my mother dealt fairly with you?' he leered.

I looked around for Old Meg, but she had disappeared inside the furnace.

'She has,' I said.

'Did you cross her palm?'

'I did.'

'Then you can cross mine. I can tell you more than she did. Only it will cost you more than silver. Gold is what I want.'

'Do you, now? And do you propose to tell my fortune as well?'

'More than that. My mother doesn't know who you are, but I do. I move around. I was in Tondu this afternoon. I know why you were there, Mr Vaughan.'

'All I would desire of you,' I said drily, 'is that you put me on the right track for Porthcawl.'

'In good time. I can tell you where the man you are looking for lives. And when the attack on the dock is coming. You don't need palmistry for that, Mr Vaughan, just eyes and ears in the right place. What is information like that worth?'

'A great deal if it is true. How will I know if you are speaking the truth?'

'Give me a sovereign now and another when events prove me right.'

I pondered. I had been empowered to give sums of money to elicit information, but only to reliable sources. After some moments I made up my mind.

'I will trust you. A sovereign now, another later. First, tell me where Cap Coch lives.'

'The money first, Mr Vaughan.'

I handed over the coin. The gipsy bit at it before pocketing it.

'He's an Irishman living in Cefn, two miles from here, in a hut near the cross roads. You can't miss it. His brood swarms all over the place, all red headed like himself. He was dispossessed last year and has been swearing vengeance ever since. Twenty five ricks he burned last autumn, and the house of the agent.'

'And the attack?'

'In two weeks time, unless Brogden gives in to his demands. He's got some guns stached away and gunpowder. He's boasting of an army of two hundred men he can call on—miners, foundry men and farm workers. If he was a Welshman or an Englishman I'd say you could buy him off with a bribe or an offer of a job, but you won't do that: he's a Fenian.'

'A Fenian!'

'And a rabid one. His family left Ireland during the famine and now that he's dispossessed again he's mad against the English— the ruling class, that is. I hear tell he's in league with the boyos across the water. You've got your work cut out with that one, Mr Vaughan.'

'And you think he's behind all this unrest?'

'Not behind it. Making the most of it more like.'

'Anything else you can tell me?'

'That's worth a bit, ain't it?'

'If true, yes.'

'It's true all right. I'll be round for the rest of the money later.'

'You shall have it. Now you can put me on the right track to Porthcawl.'

'Willingly, Mr Vaughan. Follow the hedge until you come to a lane. Turn left there and in no time you'll be in Pyle. You'll know your way from there.'

I thanked the fellow and urged the horse forward. Once in the right direction I had no difficulty in reaching Pyle and the rest of the journey was uneventful. But my heart was heavy, and for the first time in my life I felt a dread of the future.

CHAPTER TWENTY FIVE

MR BROGDEN had no hesitation in sending for the constable, for the knowledge that Cap Coch might be a Fenian cast a new light on our problem. The Fenians were at that time active throughout the Empire, stopping short of nothing in their attempt to force the central government to yield independence to their oppressed country. The fact that their fellow Celts, the Welsh, were often as ground down in poverty as themselves seemed to matter little to them, for their prime target was the English ruling class; and Brogden and his co-directors were English to the core. The trouble was that, in their attempt to reach an aim laudable in their own eyes, many innocent people had to suffer, for their methods included intimidation and indiscriminate bombing. The news that one of their members was active in the area was serious indeed.

Unfortunately the constable was dubious about making an arrest, stating that intent to commit a crime was not enough. A misdemeanour had to be perpetrated first, and evidence obtained, all of which was of little use to Brogden who wanted to clap the man behind bars without delay. The constable was also hesitant at the thought of going to Cefn which, until only recently, had been the headquarters of the violent Riders, as nasty a gang of ruffians as ever blighted the fair name of Glamorgan. Safe on their high ridge, looking down on the world about them with contemptuous and predatory eyes, they had preyed on everybody rich and poor alike; and, although the people living there now were bandits no longer, they still eyed strangers with hostility and suspicion, often severely beating those who ventured into their barren eyrie.

I thought I detected a shade of fear and uncertainty in the constable, which was understandable, for he was young and newly appointed. He telegraphed his superiors in Bridgend and, receiving no clear instructions except to support Mr Brogden to the best of his ability, agreed to accompany us to Cefn with the object of warning the shadowy figure who seemed to be at the bottom of our troubles. We went on horseback but the journey was, as expected, like running a gauntlet, with resentful eyes watching us every yard of the way; and when we reached the hovel which was Cap Coch's home the bird had flown, no doubt warned of our approach. His wife was there and a dozen of his ragged, red-haired offspring, all of whom stared silently at us, refusing to answer any question. We had no alternative but to retreat down the ridge, once again watched by the uncooperative inhabitants. It was little wonder to me that Cap Coch had found support in the Cribbwr area, for the poverty we witnessed was harrowing.

In the absence of direct action by the law Brogden made his own plans. Men were selected as guards and look-outs and a general warning system set up. Staves and pick-helves were stacked in sheds at strategic points and every workman was given instruction to defend a specific area. There was willing cooperation on all sides, for the employees knew that their livelihood was at stake; and some even looked forward to an encounter, for fisticuffs were a way of life with many.

Ten days after my meeting with the gipsy tension began to mount, for there was an increased flow of strangers to the camping grounds on the common. One of our scouts reported that he had seen a few men carrying arms, and so Brogden issued a handful of pistols and muskets, with strict instructions not to use them unless fired upon first. A police inspector arrived from Bridgend with three additional constables, and the Swansea Yeomanry were put on the alert, which was of little use to us for it would take the fastest horseman two hours to reach Porthcawl. But of Cap Coch there was still no sign.

Then, on a Saturday morning, one of Brogden's infiltrators reported that the strangers were gathering en masse, preparatory to being harangued by their leader. There was no doubt who their leader would be, so Brogden issued instructions for our men to take up position. Staves were issued and the western perimeter of the docks guarded by a man stationed every ten yards, with a further force of fifty of our strongest men acting as a mobile reserve. Brogden placed himself on the higher ground at the base of the breakwater, from which vantage point he could view not only the two basins but the approach from the common. Behind him stood the inspector and the constables together with the port officials and runners, all of which put me in mind of Wellington and his staff before Waterloo. I myself was glad of the presence of Dafydd, who kept by my side the whole time.

At noon we saw a stirring on the common and then a small army of some two hundred men formed up and came marching towards us. They kept in good order along the sea wall, then fanned out as they reached the flat ground in front of the breakwater. There they halted, and for the first time I saw Cap Coch. He was indeed a formidable looking man, not tall but powerfully built, with a shock of red hair that intermingled with a similarly hued beard. He had cold, grey eyes just discernible under bushy eyebrows that met in the middle, the whole giving a ferocious and intimidating appearance. He detached himself from the main body but still kept a good thirty paces away from us. The snatch squad that Brogden had ready would have a lot of ground to cover to get him.

Then Cap Coch spoke.

'Brogden! There are two hundred men here, all unemployed or maimed in your service. You owe them livelihood or compensation. Either promise that in front of witnesses or take the consequences.'

'Who are you?' parried Brogden. 'Name yourself.'

'Never mind my name. I speak for all present.'

'If you speak for those present I must know your name. You have an Irish accent. Are you the man they call Cap Coch?'

'Some call me that.'

'Then what are you, an Irishman, doing leading Welshmen? Have they no spokesman of their own?'

'They have elected me, for Welsh and Irish are united by one thing alike—suffering at the hands of you English task masters.'

'I am no task master. Ask any of my men. I pay them well.'

'You pay yourself better. You and your shareholders are waxing fat on the blood and sweat of men.'

'If you are talking of dividends we need every penny to finance this dock. I am already providing work for a thousand men.'

'Aye, until it suits you. As soon as you make a loss you get out— as you are doing at Tondu.'

'What happened at Tondu is beyond my control. I cannot keep men on if there is no work. If I did all those at present in my employ would lose their livelihood as well. I cannot make money. It has to be earned.'

Cap Coch's brow puckered. Leader of men he might be but he had met his match in argument. I thought it a pity when the inspector decided to chip in.

'O'Connor, stop this shilly-shallying. We know who you are. You are stirring up discontent for your own ends. You are a Fenian.'

Cap Coch was too clever to fall into that trap. He knew that one word admitting membership of the illegal society would be enough to give the police the chance they were waiting for. He grinned.

'I don't know what the man is talking about, begorra. Here am I, been elected by the men to speak on their behalf, trying to be civil. Tell the police to stay out of this, Brogden.'

Brogden motioned to the inspector to keep quiet.

'Then tell me, O'Connor, what is it you want?'

'Employment for these men with a promise of half pay for everyone who is injured working for you.'

'I cannot do that. I am employing all that I can now, and no master in the country can afford to support those injured. You are asking for the impossible.'

'Then look to yourself, Brogden. These men are starving. They have nothing to lose.'

151

'Threats won't get you anywhere. I have five hundred men guarding the docks. If you start anything, so much the worse for you.'

'We'll blow your bloody breakwater, Brogden,' shouted somebody with an alliteration that would have been humorous if the position had not been so serious.

'Now wait,' cried Brogden, raising his arms. 'No violence. If you injure the docks you are only injuring your fellow men. Then there will be hundreds unemployed in addition to you. I promise you this: I will look into the matter and consult my fellow directors. I will see what can be done to increase the work force. Does that satisfy you?'

I could see Cap Coch pondering. To what extent he was genuinely championing his army of unfortunates I did not know and began to doubt his more ulterior motives; but at that moment an event occurred which I had long feared. Some of Cap Coch's men, in order to see and hear their leader better, had edged forward and were perilously close to our own men. I could see our fellows fingering their staves and knew that some were spoiling for a fight. Suddenly pandemonium broke out. There was a fierce shouting as a dozen or so dock workers rushed forward. Brogden shouted to them to get back, but to no avail. The skirmishing extended down the line and before we knew where we were, there was fighting everywhere. I looked to Brogden for leadership but the speed of events had numbed him. He stared helplessly as the melee developed with the alacrity of a forest fire.

Suddenly I was violently pushed sideways as the constables, led by the inspector, made a rush at Cap Coch. They disappeared into the throng and I knew then that nothing could restore order. Cap Coch himself had melted into the mass of swaying bodies, and I myself was undecided what to do. Never afraid of a fight, I did not relish tangling with the gaunt and dispirited men I had seen. Dafydd, too, seemed of like mind and remained by my side.

Then, out of the corner of my eye, I saw a small body of men emerge from the rear of Cap Coch's army and go running down to the foreshore. They disappeared from sight behind the rocks, so I grabbed Dafydd's arms and pulled him to the edge of the sea wall.

'There, Dafydd,' I shouted. 'Keep your eye on those rocks. They're up to something.'

No sooner had I uttered the words than we saw the men again, darting from cover to cover. They were a good hundred yards away but there was no mistaking them now. One of them was Cap Coch and another was carrying a small barrel.

'Gunpowder!' said Dafydd. 'They're going for the breakwater.'

'Come on! We'll head them off.' I yelled over my shoulder for others to follow, but no one seemed to hear, and it was only Dafydd and I who descended the breakwater steps.

'They'll go for the middle,' I said, leading the way along the steep escarpment. Just as we reached the base of the wall the men appeared, five of them, led by Cap Coch who was carrying an ancient blunderbuss. They hesitated when they saw us then came charging up the slope.

'Get back all of you,' I ordered.

For answer Cap Coch levelled the blunderbuss at me, at the same time motioning the others to go to the wall. I noticed that the keg they were carrying was small, so I tried subterfuge.

'You fools! You haven't enough powder there to shift a limpet, but try it on and you'll all get the rope.'

'Stand back,' snarled Cap Coch, 'or I'll blow your bloody head off.' He swivelled the gun quickly round at Dafydd who had moved some distance away, hoping to attack from the rear. Dafydd stopped and the Irishman backed away, keeping us both covered. The men reached the breakwater and began unsealing the keg.

'Not enough to shift a limpet, eh!' said Cap Coch. 'But we'll open a crack or two. The sea will do the rest.'

Dafydd made a dart forward but stopped again as the gun was brought to bear. This gave me my chance and I rushed at the fellow with all the speed I could muster. But just as I was on him he brought his weapon round and pressed the trigger. There was a thunderous explosion and I felt a hail of pellets tear into my face. Immediately one eye went blind and I felt excruciating pain deep down in my brain. A spurt of blood momentarily closed the other but I continued to stumble forward and succeeded in grappling with my adversary. At that moment Dafydd descended on the man and bore him to the ground. I stood back and looked for the accomplices, to see them running pell-mell down the slope. A tell-tale hiss told me that they had ignited the fuse.

With the strength ebbing from my legs I made for the base of the wall, but I had gone only a few paces when the gunpowder went off. There was a sheet of flame and a huge slab of rock came hurtling towards me, striking me full in the chest. I was thrown backwards and fell to the ground, the slab on top of me. With no breath in my body I was horrified to find that I could not take the shallowest breath. Relentlessly the slab began to crush the life out of me.

Just before I lost consciousness I could see Dafydd heaving on the stone. He was using every ounce of his formidable strength but the remorseless pressure continued. I had a brief, fleeting glimpse of Old Meg mouthing her words of warning and I knew that my end was near.

Then, just as the world began to go black, I heard Dafydd shouting.

'For Christ's sake, Jeremiah, give us a hand or he's a goner.'

I saw the blurred outline of Jeremiah Meredith's ugly face staring open-mouthed down at me, then he bent and seized the stone with Dafydd. The weight on my chest lifted.

But it was too late. I saw the kind, welcoming face of my mother, long since dead, and knew I was about to enter the next world.

CHAPTER TWENTY SIX

'EE-AWK, EE-AWK!' said the apparition, which I thought very strange coming from a heavenly body. 'Ee-awk, ee-awk!' Then the apparition disappeared and I heard a hissing sound, followed by a muted, regular thumping. The constancy of the rhythm bored into my brain, so I put my hands to my ears, but to no avail: the thumping went on unabated.

Suddenly it ceased, to be replaced by a rushing, roaring noise which seemed to carry me along with it, as though I was being transported to a bottomless abyss. Then silence, a long, profound silence broken only by the ticking of a watch.

154

I heard a sob.

'Oh, John, I am sorry—sorry—sorry—'

The words echoed into the distance and died away. I turned to find their source but could see only the blurred outline of a face. A scent wafted over me, a familiar, beautiful, subtle, scent coming to me from the past, now aeons ago.

'Catherine, is that you?'

'Oh, John—John—John—' Again that damned echo.

'Catherine!' I repeated. 'Where are you?'

More sobs. Infuriated because I could not see properly I tried to sit upright, but a weight pressed against my shoulders, forcing me back. Not that slab again! Anything but that!

'Oh, God!' I said. 'Where am I?'

'Ee-awk, ee-awk!'

I gave up and lay still.

Again the scent, now so strong that I became determined to solve the mystery. The shadowy face was still there, so I stared at it, willing it to materialise into a recognisable shape. At last it came: copper coloured hair, blue-green eyes, beautiful mouth. It was Catherine!

'Oh, Catherine!' I said. 'I have been looking for you.'

'Hush. You must not speak.'

'But I must! 'I've missed you so much.'

'Later, John. When you feel better.'

I felt a hand take mine, a soft, gentle hand which trembled violently. Then came that maddening, ridiculous noise again.

'Ee-awk, ee-awk!'

The raucous abomination drove the face away. It receded into the distance, as though I was looking through the wrong end of a telescope. In despair I reached out.

'Come back, Catherine. Don't leave me.'

In response to my plea the face returned, growing in size as it came nearer. But now it was not Catherine. It was another face, softer and more angelic, with golden tresses, pert nose and sad, moist, blue eyes. It was familiar and yet not familiar. I tried to place it but failed.

'You're not Catherine.'

The violet-blue eyes filled with tears; then, to my disgust, it also dissolved, to be replaced by a kaleidoscope of others,

155

frightening this time. I saw Old Meg grimacing, Matt O'Reilly bleeding, Sir Charles admonishing, and finally Cap Coch eyeing me along his blunderbuss.

That blunderbuss! He had shot me in the face at point blank range. Was there anything left of it? Not that it mattered if I was in heaven and among the angels. There everything could be made to look nice again. But to be ugly for even a little while was not a happy thought. I wondered if there were mirrors in heaven.

'Let me see myself,' I said, starting up again. 'Am I ugly?'

'No, of course you're not.' The voice was a new one, but I seemed to recognise it.

'Who are you?'

I heard the sound of a curtain being pulled and began to see a little better. The apparition I had noticed before floated over to me and stooped low.

'Why!' I said, 'if it isn't Mrs Treseder.'

Mrs Treseder sobbed and giggled at the same time.

'Oh, Mr Vaughan! You're better. I can tell by your face you're better. Oh, thank God for that.'

'Where am I?'

'In your house. You've been here since the—the accident. Mr Brogden's doctor has been here nearly every day. He will be pleased when he calls tomorrow.'

'How long have I been here?'

'A long time, Mr Vaughan. Nearly four months. You had fluid on the lung caused by that stone.'

'Four months! Who's been looking after me all that time?'

'Me mostly. Me and Mark moved in to look after you. The doctor thought it best you stay here.'

'I thought I was in heaven, Mrs Treseder, and then in hell. I must have been feverish most of the time.'

'You were. We could see you tossing and turning, but there was nothing we could do except make you comfortable. Doctor said it was deliriums caused by the fluid. But he said you'd pull through, and now you have. Oh, Mr Vaughan! Wait until Mark sees you— and Dafydd. They've been to see you every day—and all the people of Porthcawl have been calling to ask how you are. Now I can tell them you're better.'

I eased myself up in the bed. Every muscle felt stiff and sore. Mrs Treseder helped me and then I heard a hissing followed by the roaring sound that had irritated me before.

'That noise, Mrs Treseder. What is it?'

'The docks, Mr Vaughan. Coal going down the chutes, and engines. There's engines all over the place now with the inner harbour working.'

'Is it open, then?'

'Open and working to full capacity I'm told. Mr Brogden is very pleased. We were all sorry you missed opening day.'

'So I missed that, did I?'

'Never mind. You'll be able to see it all now that you're better.'

'Ee-awk, ee-awk!'

I looked at the window. My sight was still hazy but what I saw made me smile. A huge seagull was perched on the sill.

'Why, you're laughing, too Mr Vaughan. You must be a lot better.'

'I am,' I said. 'I couldn't make out a sound I kept hearing. Now I know it was a seagull.'

'That dratted thing has been on the window ledge all day. I'll drive it away.'

'No, leave it. I like seagulls, especially that one. It's nice to know I'm not in heaven, delightful though that place may be.'

'Then rest now, Mr Vaughan, and I'll bring you some hot soup to build you up. Oh, how lovely it will be to see you eating of your own free will.'

'Mrs Treseder, bring me a mirror.'

Mrs Treseder froze into immobility.

'A mirror? What d'you want a mirror for?'

'You know why. To see my face.'

'Oh, Mr Vaughan! Later. All in good time.'

'Now, if you please. I want a mirror.'

Mrs Treseder burst into tears.

'Please, Mrs Treseder,' I repeated. 'I must know what I look like. I order you to bring me a mirror.'

She fled from the room. I thought she would not return but she did, carrying a small hand mirror.

'Give it to me. Draw the curtains wider.'

I took the mirror and stared at it. The face that looked back at me was mercifully still recognisable, but one side was deeply scarred and pitted. Worst of all, where my left eye had been was now nothing but a jagged, weeping hollow. If I was not ugly I had certainly lost my beauty. I put the mirror down.

'So that's it! Thank you Mrs Treseder!'

'Don't worry about it, Mr Vaughan,' she cried, trying to smile. 'Look, we've got one of these for you. If you wear it people won't notice.'

She rushed to the dressing table and took out a black eye patch.

'There! This will make it look better. Let me put it on for you.'

She placed the patch over my eye and tied the black ribbon around my head.

'See! Now you'll look distinguished, like Lord Nelson. What does an eye matter if your life's been saved.'

'Very becoming, but I would sooner not have to wear one. What happened to Cap Coch?'

'He got away. The police looked everywhere for him but he disappeared. I wish I could lay my hands on him! I could murder him!'

'Don't be too hard on him, Mrs Treseder. He was doing what he thought was just.'

'Just! Nearly killing you like that. How can you say such a thing?'

I was too weak to argue. Even in good health I could never hold my own with Mrs Treseder. The loss of my eye had been a shock and I wanted breathing space to recover. Instead I said:

'And how's Mark?'

'Very well. He told me to tell you—as soon as you got better that is—that the business is doing fine. You've no worries on that score.'

'Good. And Dafydd?'

'He's fine, too. He brought you some ale the other day, thinking you were about to wake up. When you didn't he drank it himself. But he'll bring you some more now you're better. Wait until they know!'

I smiled at Mrs Treseder's infectious gaiety, but there was only one matter uppermost in my mind.

'Has Lady Catherine been to see me?'

Mrs Treseder stopped tidying a cushion. She did not answer immediately.

'Yes, this morning. I didn't let her stay long, like the others.'

'How often has she been here?'

'Once before. Last week.'

'Have you any idea where she is now?'

'In Sea Bank House, I expect. Would you like your soup now?'

Something about Mrs Treseder's demeanour puzzled me. She had become uneasy at the mention of Catherine, but I was not strong enough to delve further.

'Yes, please. Soup would be very nice.'

Mrs Treseder was soon back, but with more than soup. Into the room behind her trooped Mark, Dafydd and Owain. They stood in a row at the bottom of the bed grinning delightedly.

'I had to send to tell them,' said Mrs Treseder apologetically, 'and they came running. Only for a minute though, and then they must go.'

'You're looking better,' said Mark. 'you've got some colour in your cheeks.'

'Now you'll be able to drink some ale,' said Dafydd. 'It will help to build you up.'

'The breakwater's finished,' added Owain. 'Wait until you see it!'

Mrs Treseder tucked a bib around my neck.

'That's enough. Off you three go.'

'Listen to her,' said Mark. 'Real bully she's turned out to be. She's been guarding you like a dragon, John.'

'Good thing too!' said Dafydd. 'It's because of her you've pulled round, not because of the bloody doctor.'

Mrs Treseder waved a spoon at them.

'Come along! Just a peep like I told you. You shall come again later.'

'The business is doing fine,' said Mark, ignoring her. 'We made a record profit last month. I've paid your share into the bank.'

'They'll be putting up the lighthouse soon,' said Owain. 'I've made a good, even platform for it. Solid it is, all round. That gunpowder hardly touched it.'

'It's easy entering the harbour now,' grinned Dafydd. 'Child's play it is.'

'Off!' said Mrs Treseder, putting her hands on her hips.

'Better do as she says, 'said Mark. 'You others don't have to live with her like I do.'

'I'll bring you the ale tomorrow,' said Dafydd.

'And I'll bring you some honey,' said Owain. 'Marged's very good at honey when she's in the mood.'

They shuffled from the room, still grinning. I tucked into my soup with relish, needing no second bidding. Then I slept and woke an hour or two later, refreshed. To my surprise Mr Brogden was standing by the bedside.

'Mrs Treseder let me in to see you,' he whispered. 'I was going to call tomorrow but I heard you were better. I've promised not to tire you.'

'You won't tire me,' I said, delighted to see him. 'Please sit down.'

Brogden drew up a chair.

'You are better then. You look so.'

'I am, indeed. Mrs Treseder is feeding me up and looking after me better than any nurse.'

'Good woman that! She needed no second bidding to come here. Another month or two and you'll be really well. Your salary has been paid direct to the bank, by the way; and Mrs Treseder can draw on me for anything she requires. We'll settle it all later.'

'Thank you, sir. That's very kind of you.'

'That patch quite suits you. You will be a commanding figure in the docks now.'

'More like a pirate I'd say.'

'You'll be a hero—second time over. Everyone knows what you did to save the breakwater.'

'I was a fool. They couldn't have harmed it much with the gunpowder they had.'

'They could have split it, which would have been serious. Anyway, the breakwater's fine, and the docks are working smoothly. We shipped a thousand ton of coal yesterday.'

'No iron?'

'Very little. Iron is on its way out as you know, so I'm concentrating on coal. We can sell every ton we mine. We're expanding in Ogmore and Maesteg and developing Park Slip and Caedu. There will be plenty for you to do when you get well.'

Brogden paused to draw his chair nearer. This gave me the chance I was looking for.

'How is Lady Catherine?'

To my consternation Brogden, like Mrs Treseder, looked uneasy. The kindly eyes wavered and avoided my gaze.

'She's well, John. She was here to see you this morning.'

'I know. I wish I'd been in a fit state to receive her. Where is she now?'

'She left for London on the noon train.'

'London! Then I won't be seeing her for a while.'

'Not for a long while, John. In fact, I doubt if she'll ever return.'

I felt my new-found strength evaporate like spindrift.

'Why not?'

Brogden studied the quilt with earnest concentration then cleared his throat.

'You loved her, didn't you?'

'Yes.'

'Most men did. She had that effect. She also loved you. She told me so. Do not judge her too harshly.'

'Then why—'

'Why has she gone? She couldn't face seeing you, John, lying here a cripple and apparently blind. You looked pretty ill and Catherine has a horror of illness. She loves life and gaiety as you know. Sickness and poverty are the two things she dreads most in life. So please do not be bitter.'

'I'm not bitter.' I tried to sound genuine.

Brogden pulled an envelope out of his pocket. It had a familiar sweet, evasive scent.

'She gave me this for you.'

'Read it, please. I still can't see properly.'

Brogden broke open the envelope and took out a single sheet of notepaper.

' "Dearest John" ,' he read. ' "Forgive me. I did love you. I still do, but I am a coward and not worthy of you. I shall remember you always—Catherine." That's all, John.'

I reached out and took the letter. We remained silent for a long while then Brogden said:

'I don't suppose it will make you feel better but I'm in the same boat myself. My wife is leaving me.'

'Leaving you! That's impossible!'

'Oh, no! We have come to the parting of the ways also, only with this difference: we've never really been happy together. She took no interest in my work and all she desired was to get away from here. We've never seen eye to eye.'

'I'm sorry. I didn't know.'

'Very few people did. We kept it to ourselves. So do not be distressed. When you marry it must be to the right woman. The wrong one is purgatory. You would not have been happy with Catherine. For a while, perhaps, but not in the long run. You'd have ended up like me.'

'I shall not marry,' I said moodily. 'I have been unlucky with women.'

'Nonsense! Your body will heal and then you will feel better. You won't want for feminine company, believe me. Anyway I have tired you and must go. I am sorry to have brought you bad news but I thought it best for you to know now rather than go on lying here wondering.'

He patted me on the shoulder and rose to go. At the door he paused.

'There is one other thing I must tell you. Shortly I shall be leaving for New Zealand.'

'New Zealand!'

'Don't let that worry you. My brother, Alexander, will take over from me here. He knows all about you. Your job is safe and you may stay here as long as you wish. I shall be away three years. The firm has undertaken a contract to build a railway there.

'When do you leave?'

'In a week's time. I shall come and see you before I go. Don't forget, I shall need you when I return. We must go on with the building of the town. The plans are merely in abeyance. We will start as soon as I return.'

He waved and was gone. I stared at the ceiling, watching it shimmer with the reflection of the sea. Everything Old Meg had prophesied had come true. I had seen blood flow, come near to death and lost Catherine. Now James Brogden, my friend and benefactor, was in trouble and about to go to the other end of the world. But Old Meg had also said that I would recover if I had a mind to. The question was: did I have a mind to?

162

At that moment the gull alighted again on the sill and uttered its raucous cry. I studied it, noticing for the first time how battle-scarred it was. One leg was dragging, half its feathers were missing and there was a deep gash on the top of its head. An old campaigner like me.

There being nothing like other creatures' adversities to put our own troubles in perspective, and being not yet ready to enter the next world, I decided to emulate the gull and battle on, whatever fate had in store.

CHAPTER TWENTY SEVEN

WHEN I HAD sufficiently recovered my strength Mrs Treseder allowed me out for a short walk. I went as far as the breakwater and studied the now completed structure. The slimness of the upper level, barely four feet wide, gave no indication of the massive strength that had been built into its base; but that it would withstand the onslaught of the elements I had no doubt. It was indeed a fitting memorial to James Brogden, his engineers and the men who built it; and I was pleased that I had a hand in it myself.

I went first to the end of the upper catwalk, which ran along a third of its length, and there paused to look down at the place where Cap Coch's men had exploded the gunpowder. They had chosen the spot well, for it was there that the breakwater crooked slightly to the left to give better shelter to the harbour, and Owain himself had expressed doubt as to its strength at that point But now all was repaired, with not a mark to be seen, not a scratch indicating that the attempt had been made.

Pausing only to glance briefly at the place where Cap Coch had shot me, I resumed my walk to the end of the breakwater. There a flat, circular platform had been constructed ready for the beacon, with a low, surrounding wall for the protection of its base. I sat on the parapet and surveyed the scene.

The tide was full in and it was a pleasing experience to sit there, almost as though one was aboard ship. A light breeze played, the sun shone and the seagulls hovered, making me glad that I had decided to remain alive. From my vantage point I could see both the inner and outer docks, almost buried beneath a dark forest of swaying masts, indicating that every berth was occupied. Across the water came the roar of derricks, cranes and coal chutes, frequently interspersed by the shouts of men and the shrill whistle of locomotives. Over all lay a hazy cloud of coal dust, thankfully dispersed to sea by the prevailing westerly wind.

Seeing and hearing all this activity it seemed foolish to have doubts about the future of the port, but doubts I had. The inner dock was geared to ship five thousand tons of coal a day, but now all Brogden's eggs were in one basket. The failure of the iron trade meant that we had no second string to our bow, and most ships were still returning in ballast, which immediately halved their earning capacity. But Brogden had faith in an expanding and permanent market for coal and would not have sunk a quarter of a million pounds into the enterprise without expectation of a substantial return, so I had no choice but to trust in his judgement and hope that my now considerable investment in the firm would remain safe.

As though to cheer me up and dispel the dark thoughts about the financial future, I heard a stentorian hooting and looked round to see the steam ship *The John Brogden* come hustling across the bay. Without hesitation she made straight for the harbour entrance, slowing down only at the last minute. Then she hove to, dwarfing all the coastal sailing ships alongside her. The speed with which the manoeuvre was executed amazed me, for a canvassed vessel would have taken half an hour tacking her way in, sometimes resorting to oars for the last few hundred yards. With more ships like that, I reasoned, my fears about the future were surely groundless.

For a few minutes I watched the black smoke from *The John Brogden* spiralling lazily into the air, then my thoughts returned to my own predicament. I did not relish the thought of Alexander Brogden taking over from his brother, for it was a well-known fact that the two were not well disposed to each other. Indeed, there had been rumours of frequent quarrels at Tondu House, with hints of a break-up in the partnership. James had recommended me to his brother but whether that was in my favour was a matter about which I had misgivings. Handicapped as I now was, with an aching body, a leg aggravated by a long stay in bed and a constant throbbing where my eye had been, I felt in no state to do justice to my job. Alexander was not the kind, approachable man his brother was and would no doubt look with disfavour at a man who failed to be diligent; but diligent I would have to be to hold my position, and so I took deep gulps of the salt-laden, health-giving air, intending to speed up my recuperation.

The biggest ache within me was, of course, the loss of Catherine. Looking back I knew how foolish I had been, and yet I could not blame her. Although in different walks of life we had been drawn to each other like magnets, but the gulf between us had been too great. She herself had warned me that she could not face poverty, and the sight of my battered body must have intimidated and frightened her. Nevertheless the hurt was deep within me, one that it would take some time, if ever, to heal; and I resolved that, come what may, I would never allow myself to fall in love again, for the misery of a broken heart is worse than any physical pain.

All the time I was sitting there, deep in my thoughts, no one had come near me. Most men were busy at their work and the novelty of the breakwater had already worn off as far as the children were concerned. So I had the place to myself, which suited my pessimistic mood, and I was glad not to have to converse with anyone, even a friend.

Then I heard a sound that made me look up. Coming towards me was a young girl of about nineteen. Because of her slow, unhurried pace and with the wind slightly ruffling her long hair she appeared to glide rather than walk. She came up to me and smiled.

'Hullo, Mr Vaughan. I am glad to see you out.'

I must have looked foolish, for I gawked in surprise. I could see her face clearly now: red, smiling mouth, humorous, turned-up nose, violet-blue eyes, all framed by hair the colour of ripe corn. It was the face I had seen in one of my delirious dreams, the angelic face that had supplanted Catherine's.

'You don't remember me, do you, Mr Vaughan?'

To hide my confusion I prevaricated.

'I do know you but I am sorry: I cannot recall your name at the moment. I—I saw you a couple of weeks ago, I believe.'

165

'You did, but you didn't recognise me then. At least I don't think so, for you were asleep—or half so.'

'You saw me?'

'Yes. Mrs Treseder allowed me into your room for a moment. I'd brought you a present to cheer you up. I have it with me now.'

She held out a small parcel bound with a blue ribbon.

'It's nothing, really. I merely hoped it would—would take your mind off things.'

Still in a turmoil I took the parcel. The girl's face was still a mystery to me, although I knew now how it had got mixed up in my dreams. But why she, a perfect stranger, had visited me was something I could not comprehend.

The girl's eye glinted with merriment.

'Oh, Mr Vaughan! You still don't remember me, do you?'

'I'm afraid not.'

'I'm Sally Martin!'

I stared at her.

'But Sally Martin was a—a—'

'A thin, little, freckled girl with pig-tails? Don't worry, Mr Vaughan, you're not the first who's failed to recognise me. I have been back in Porthcawl a month now and very few seem to remember me. I must have changed a lot in four years.'

'Changed! I wouldn't have known you.'

Sally laughed.

'I must have been terrible-looking in those days.'

I did not know what to say. In four years the skinny, frightened little girl who had helped me in my first lessons at the Lias Road school had transformed herself into a delectable, poised young woman. I could hardly believe the evidence of my own eyes so I fumbled with the parcel.

'Thank you for this. May I open it now?'

'If you wish.'

I unravelled the parcel to reveal a brand-new dictionary. I opened the cover and looked at the fly leaf.

'To Mr Vaughan,' I read. 'Hoping that you will be better soon. Sally Martin.'

'I hope it will be of use to you,' said Sally shyly.

'You couldn't have given me a better present,' I said, and meant every word.

166

'And now you must return home,' said Sally. 'Mrs Treseder told me where to find you and gave me strict instructions to bring you back. She doesn't want you taxing your strength.'

'Then I had better do so. Mrs Treseder must be obeyed, or I shall be for it.'

We walked together back along the breakwater, but after only a few yards my leg gave out and I started to limp. Without hesitation Sally placed an arm under mine and helped me along. I did not know whether to feel annoyed at my infirmity or pleasure at being aided by such a charming companion. I decided eventually on the latter and we walked along steadily, reminiscing over our days together at Mr Thomas's school.

When we reached Pilot Row Mrs Treseder was at the door, wiping her hands in an apron.

'So you found him, Sally. Did he come when you told him?'

'Yes, Mrs Treseder. Mr Vaughan knows that he has to obey you in all things to get better.'

Mrs Treseder laughed.

'Come in, Sally and have tea with us.' She looked knowingly at me. 'You will do him good. It's time he had a bit of young company to cheer him up.'

CHAPTER TWENTY EIGHT

OBSERVATION HAS led me to believe that the smaller the woman the greater her determination; and when two such make up their minds to do something it is a case of an irresistable force meeting an immovable object—with dire consequences for the immovable object, which is often a man. Unfortunately for the egoes of us men the women are invariably right, which is a good argument for giving in to them in the first place.

It did not take me long to perceive that such a force was building up against me. During tea Mrs Treseder suggested that I took up lessons again, and who better to instruct me than Sally Martin, who had previously been my teacher? I fell in readily with this for, although my numbering was now excellent, my vocabulary and spelling still left much to be desired. Sally accepted with alacrity. She was now a full-time teacher at the Newton Church of England School, having accepted an appointment there although she herself was Presbyterian. She readily consented to visit me every other evening armed with the latest tracts and novels.

This meant her staying for supper, after which it was only polite and proper for me to see her home to her parents' house in Philadelphia Road; and so in this way we began to see a great deal of each other. I was not averse to her company for she was a charming, gentle, good-natured young lady, a skilful tutor and blessed with a great fund of common sense: but because of the disparity in our ages (Sally was nineteen and I approaching thirty) I merely regarded it as an amicable arrangement and nothing more.

But Mrs Treseder had other ideas. During the long winter evenings when Sally and I would be poring over our books at the table sitting fairly close together because of the indifferent light of the oil lamp, Mrs Treseder always found some pretext for visiting a friend for an hour or so. Then, after I had taken Sally home, she would drop hints as to what a good seamstress my tutor was, what an excellent cook, and how lucky some man would be to have her for a wife. I am not stupid and after a while I saw through her designs but said nothing, keeping my thoughts to myself.

Then Mark started on me. He arrived at the house one afternoon after seeing that his own cottage was in order and, seeing the books on the table, made a joke about marrying one's tutor in order to save money. I was able to counter his snide suggestion easily.

'I don't pay Sally. She won't accept anything.'

'Won't accept anything! Well, well!'

'I shall give her a present at Christmas instead—a good one.'

'A present, eh!' Mark grinned so much I felt like kicking him. 'Do you like her?'

'Of course I do.'

'She likes you, too.'

'Does she now?'

'I think she likes you enough to have designs on you.'

I glanced up from the book I was reading.

'Mark! You're as bad as your wife. Not a day goes by without Mrs Treseder trying to get me cornered. I know what you're up to. You're wasting your time.'

'I wouldn't need a second chance to marry a girl like that. You can't stay single all your life.'

'Can't I?'

Mark took out a pen-knife and began paring his nails.

'Remember what you used to tell me about the artillery?'

'What did I used to tell you?'

'About how you used to range on a target with them new breech-loaders. You know—the first shot would be too short, the next one too far, but the third would land smack on.'

'What the hell are you taking about?'

'Well! *Your* first shot was too short, wasn't it? Bethan Rowlands, I mean. Then you ranged a bit too far—aimed a bit high, as it were—'

I slammed down the book and glared at him.

'Sorry,' said Mark contritely. 'I thought you knew how to hit targets.'

How long this assault would have gone on I had no means of telling. I was still aching over the loss of Catherine and in no mood for futher entanglements, although the thought that a young girl should see anything in a one-eyed wreck like me was gratifying. I put it down to the fact that I was still something of a hero in the town and that Sally had a small dose of hero worship. So, once I was aware of the situation, I watched her closely and was alarmed by the look in her eyes. She never said anything untoward, for she was of a genteel disposition, but I knew. The answer to any question lies in the eyes, and there was no doubt about Sally's eyes. She was part of the force ranged against me. I pretended not to notice.

But my fate was sealed ultimately by, of all things, a game of bando, the visit to which was contrived by Mrs Treseder. Bando is a fierce game which has been played in Glamorgan for a century or more, still holding its own against the new-fangled rugby. The players use bent sticks of ash or oak to drive a wooden chock, called a colby, across the opposing team's lines. Often the colby is forgotten and the players concentrate on each other, but it is a good training for manhood. Our great enemies were the

Pyle boys, who thought themselves a cut or two above everyone else and needed pulling down a peg or two.

It was against Pyle we were playing on this particular occasion, and on the day hundreds of Porthcawlians walked to Sker beach, where the contest was to be held. Guto Bach Dwl was our principal hope in the scoring of goals and Dafydd, who had been chosen as rear guard because of his strength and bulk, had been regarded for years as a Rock of Gibraltar in defence. The match had been looked forward to for a long period of time, causing a great deal of interest for miles around, and was therefore not to be missed. Mark had been elected linesman so Mrs Treseder suggested we hire a carriage and make a day of it. Naturally she asked Sally to accompany us, who accepted and appeared in a pretty new dress, rabbit-wool cape and muff.

It was a bitterly cold January day so we went first to the *Prince of Wales* inn in order to fortify ourselves against the biting wind and the long walk to the beach. Our thirty players were changing at the hostelery, vocally encouraged by twice that number of supporters. The inn was therefore a seething mass of humanity, and Mark and I had to push and squeeze to clear a path for Sally and Mrs Treseder. All the rooms were full so we got no further than the bar counter, where we eventually succeeded in obtaining a hot punch of such quality that it set the blood racing through our veins. All the while I had to guard Sally against the press of the throng and Mark did likewise for his wife.

The Pyle supporters, who outnumbered us by two to one, were at their usual game of pre-match intimidation, one large fellow being particularly vociferous.

'We're going to slay these bloody Porthcawlians today. Then we'll feed 'em to the crows.'

'Aye,' shouted another. 'Hoity toity bastards these Porthcawlians! Stuck-up sods! We'll fix 'em!'

'They're just bloody seaweed, lads. Laverbread! We eats laverbread around here.'

These remarks, intended mainly for our team changing in a rear room, had an immediate and expected response.

'Listen to them Pyle piss pots. Like a lot of bloody grannies. All wind and no go.'

'Always were, always will be. Just wait! The buggers won't know where they are when we've finished with 'em.'

I glanced at Sally, alarmed that such language might harm delicate ears but to my surprise she was trying not to laugh.

'Did you hear that?' she said. 'They called us seaweed! Now we'll have to beat them.'

Her remark, allied to the feeling of well-being generated by the punch, warmed me towards her.

'It's a good name,' I said. 'Why shouldn't we be called seaweed?'

Some of the men nearest us grinned. There was no malice in the ribaldry and everyone knew it.

'Hear that?' shouted a Porthcawlian. 'We've got a new name, lads: The Seaweeds! Let's show these cow pats what the Seaweeds can do.'

Amid the resulting laughter the Pyle team emerged from their room. Dressed in breeches and white shirts they looked a powerful and purposeful lot. They were followed by our men, wearing blue and white banded jerseys which made them appear shorter and bulkier than they were. We pressed ourselves against the wall to let them pass, then finished our punches and followed them out.

It took over half an hour to reach the beach but I enjoyed every yard. The hot, fiery liquid had warmed out vitals and the gusting east wind seemed nothing. Even in the middle of winter the moorland grass was green and springy, giving zest to our strides. Sally kept her hands in her muff except when we came to a hillock, when she reached out for aid. Feeling her small hand in mine, and glancing occasionally at her happy face, I began to have my doubts about remaining free from entanglement. But there was no time for deep thought for there were too many distractions caused by the shouts and conversation of those around us, and when we reached the playing area there were already about a thousand spectators gathered around the pitch.

Mark disappeared to take up his appointment and I struggled to get Sally and Mrs Treseder to a vantage point. By luck we managed it and found ourselves near the halfway flag. Both women clung to me for dear life and were only saved by marshals who insisted that everyone stayed well back from the line, thus making many run to the sandhills, which eased the pressure slightly.

The teams appeared, glared at each other, and tried out their sticks. I saw Dafydd take some ferocious swipes at the air and adjust the padding in his breeches. Guto made a practice run across the glistening sand, twirling his stick dexterously with one hand. Then the referee called for order and the match began.

It was obvious from the start that the Pyle men intended trampling our lads into the sand, even as far as the lug worms underneath. They started with a concentrated rush, each man choosing a victim. Where the colby was I had no idea. It was a barbarous, determined, well-planned attempt to crush the opposition in the opening minute. There were sharp cracks as bando sticks fell upon heads, howls of anguish and groans from our supporters. A skirmish developed near us the like of which I have not seen since the Russkies charged us in the Crimea. It was Dafydd who saved the situation. He came up to the mass of bodies, stick flailing and in no time at all Pyle bodies were stretched out in all directions. Suddenly the colby appeared and was sent scudding across to Guto, who had miraculously kept out of trouble. He took it at speed and went up the pitch as though the Cwn Annyn were after him, the colby dangling at the end of his stick as though glued. At precisely the right moment he struck the colby with a graceful swinging action sending it across the Pyle line. The Pyle players stood stunned, their murderous plan thwarted.

Sally, like all the Porthcawl supporters near us, cheered. She took one hand out of her muff, thrust an arm under mine and hugged it tight. I looked down at her, saw the pretty, excited face and fell to wondering again.

Having survived such an onslaught our men gradually rallied, and a good game ensued in which the colby travelled from one end of the pitch to the other with incredible speed. The Pyle team favoured a tight, bunched formation, and when they advanced it was like a charge of Angus bulls; but always, somehow, our lads managed to stem the tide. Whenever possible the colby was shot out to Guto, who made many dazzling runs, evoking admiration from even our adversaries. But his brilliance paid the penalty, for no less than five Pyle players began to mark him, and it was only his great speed and agility that kept him from being clobbered into submission.

At half time the score was still one-nothing. Both teams conferred secretly as to tactics for the second half; and when the game recommenced it was obvious that the Pyle team was going to play a game of possession, for they began working their way down the right side-line, keeping the colby away from our match-winner.

In one of these rushes they came close to where we were standing. Suddenly, from one of the mauls, the colby popped out and went straight to the feet of Mrs Treseder. Without hesitation she stepped on it, hiding it from view beneath her long skirt. The Pyle team came to an untidy, bucking halt.

'Where's the bloody colby gone?'

'That thieving bitch's got it under her dress. I saw her.'

'Cough up, missus', said one with a face like a hooligan, 'or we'll up-end you.'

'You dare,' said Mrs Treseder, folding her arms.

Unknown to the Pyle players a Porthcawl supporter had already retrieved the colby from its hiding place and was making his way surreptitiously along the line to a waiting and unmarked Guto. Not knowing this, however, the Pyle men made a rush for Mrs Treseder. Immediately she was surrounded by Porthcawlians and a general melee ensued, in which players and spectators alike took part. I had time only to place my arms around Sally to protect her, and so we stood there, an oasis of calm amid the strife.

'You'll be all right,' I said. 'It won't last long.'

Sally pressed herself close to me.

'I'm not afraid.'

'Good! I'm not surprised Mrs Treseder thinks a geat deal of you.'

'Does she?'

'Enough to want me to marry you.'

'Oh!'

I kicked away a rolling body.

'And that's silly, isn't it? I'm ten years older than you.'

'Does that matter?'

'I don't know. I'm also a bit knocked about.'

'I hadn't noticed.'

A bando stick descended on my shoulder.

'Ooh!' said Sally. 'Did that hurt?'

'A bit. I wonder how Mrs Treseder is getting on.'

'I can't see her. She's surrounded by people.'

I looked around and through the milling throng had a brief glimpse of Mrs Treseder wielding her umbrella.

'She's holding her own—got plenty of support.' Then, still light-headed with punch, I added: 'By the way she tells me you love me. Do you?'

'Yes.'

'You only think so, Sally. You can't really.'

'But I do. I've always loved you.'

'Always?'

'Ever since you came to Lias School.'

'But Sally, you were a schoolgirl then. I can understand that but now—'

'I wish Mrs Treseder hadn't told you.'

'But she has and so I must be honest with you. It's not just physically I've been knocked about. There are other things as well—things you know nothing about.'

Sally buried her face deep in my lapels.

'Do you mean Lady Catherine?'

Non-plussed I muttered 'Yes', and was glad of a diversion caused by two wrestling bodies bumping into us. When we had recovered our equilibrium I added: 'So you know about her.'

Sally did not reply so I put a hand under her chin and raised her head. Her eyes showed what I can only describe as apprehensive tenderness, but before I could question her further there was a cheer and as though by magic the fighting around us stopped.

'What's happened?' asked Sally.

'Guto's scored. Then be patient with me, Sally. Give me time. Just give me time.'

Sally nodded, her eyes suddenly moist. We pushed our way through to Mrs Treseder to find that no harm had befallen her. The Pyle supporters around us were chagrined and dismayed, but there was nothing they could do about it. Stealing the colby was part of the game and they would have done the same to us had the chance presented itself. Thereafter the match proceeded normally, with the colby in play the whole time, and ended two-nothing in our favour. The bruised, bleeding players shook hands and trooped off the pitch, happy in the knowledge than an evening

174

drinking ale together would follow. The spectators began to disperse, their shadows long in the late winter sunlight.

Mrs Treseder adjusted her hat, which was still askew after the skirmish, and looked knowingly at Sally.

'There you are, Sally! I told you we'd win, didn't I?'

I knew by the tone of her voice that she was referring to something other than bando, and from that moment on my future was sealed.

CHAPTER TWENTY NINE

THERE WAS great rejoicing when the beacon was completed, especially among the sailors. Set on its own platform at the extremity of the breakwater it was squat and reassuring, in keeping with the feeling of strength engendered by the breakwater itself. There was no public ceremony to mark the occasion, for it was feared that a press of people on the walks would result in fatalities, or at the very least unwarranted dips into the briny. Alexander Brogden visited it with a handful of notabilities but that was all. This did not stop hundreds of sightseers visiting the place just before dusk, merely to see the light in operation; and then there occurred an event that moved me greatly. Spontaneously, without prompting of any kind, the entire throng began singing William Williams' great hymn, Dechrau Canu Dechrau Canmol, to the tune of Y Delyn Aur. They sang as only Welsh people can, with fervour and natural harmony. Other hymns followed and I was lucky enough to be standing by the Richards family, whose men are all basso profundos. Their deep, organ-like notes echoed from the walls and across the water, blending with the other voices in a way that was unforgettable. An hour the singing lasted; and came to an end only when a rising tide sent spray splashing over us, making us sorry that it was over.

Fortunately no mishap occurred and gradually the townsfolk became used to their new acquisition, which emitted a single beam of light, unlike the lesser edifices along the coast which merely blinked and winked intermittently.

The most pleased person on this occasion was Owain ap Owen, for the beacon (or lighthouse as some people were already calling it) was the crowning glory to his achievement. He could be seen for days afterwards walking on the breakwater or eyeing it from a distance, admiration oozing from every pore. Unfortunately his long sojourn in Porthcawl had done nothing to increase his liking for us southerners, and very soon he returned to North Wales where, no doubt, he regaled his fellow Snowdonians with tales of our barbarous activities. Marged went with him and I saw neither of them again.

Shortly after the completion of the beacon I met Ezekiel Meredith. This was the first time I had seen him since the attack on the breakwater and so I lost no time in conveying to him my thanks for the help afforded me by his son. To my surprise it was a very subdued Ezekiel that I met, quite unlike his usual pugnacious self: indeed he seemed to have shrunk in size, and when I enquired as to his health he admitted that he was not well, which made me feel sorry for him, enemy though he had been. I was even more sorry when he told me that Jeremiah had been killed in an accident at Cornelly quarry a fortnight previous. There was no doubt that the father was grieving deeply and, for myself, I felt a sudden sense of remorse, for there is something very frightening about the finality of death. Once it has interceded there is nothing one can do; we cannot apologise for our actions or retract angry words. Now there was no way in which I could personally thank Jeremiah for helping to save my life. If only we would remember this fact I am sure we would be more amicable in our relations with each other, and life would be a lot easier.

The hunt for Cap Coch went on until well into the autumn but he was never found, a fact that pleased me secretly, in spite of what he had done; for there was never any doubt in my mind that such a man could never have achieved such eminence, or led such a gathering of men, had he not been aided by the dreadful economic conditions then prevailing. Fortunately for us the trading climate improved and many of the unemployed found work in Walter Coffin's coal mines in the Rhondda, a fact that pleased me greatly, for the memory of the starving, downtrodden army that attacked the breakwater haunted me for a long time.

As far as I was concerned, in my own personal life, the start of the beacon also heralded what I had long sought; a period of happiness founded on the secure base of a woman's love. Ever since the bando game I had been growing more attached to Sally, even to the extent of feeling a sense of loss if she was away from me for any length of time. But I still hesitated about committing myself and was careful not to show, by word or deed, that I was in any hurry for deeper involvement. Looking back now I realise how patient Sally must have been with me, but one person was certainly not patient: Mrs Treseder. One day, when I had a few hours off work and was sitting by the fire, with Mrs Treseder opposite me, I noticed that she was sewing with more than her usual vigour. She was also sitting cross-legged, with the upper leg swinging up and down with monotonous regularity, which is a certain indication among women that they have something on their minds. She glanced at me a few times, no doubt trying to assess my mood, then began a short but pregnant conversation.

'What are you going to do about Sally Martin?'

'What should I do?'

'Marry her.'

'You know my luck in the past—'

'Neither of them others was right for you. Sally is. She'd make you a good wife. Mark my words.'

'I always do mark your words, Mrs Treseder. I've never known you wrong in anything.'

'Well, then! Marry her.'

'I'll think about it.'

'Don't think too long. She won't wait forever.'

'I fully realise that.'

'There's a dozen men after her now, but it's you she wants. But it's not fair—' Mrs Treseder snapped off the cotton with a finality that emphasised her words '—to keep her in suspense.'

I got to my feet and reached for my stick.

'I shall not do that, Mrs Treseder. I have too much regard for Sally to cause her unhappiness. Now please excuse me. I shall go for a walk.'

It was not merely to get away from Mrs Treseder's reproaches that I left. My friendship with Sally was now causing me concern, for it had reached a pitch when something had to be done, and

Mrs Treseder's words had merely underlined the fact. I wanted to get away to think, and there is no better place to think than a large empty beach, with nothing but the sound of the wind and waves to detract from one's mental processes.

I went first to Sand Bay, which is large enough to accommodate forty thousand bathers, assuming that such a number would ever visit there, which is unlikely; and walked across the glistening sand to the water's edge. Pausing only to look back at the long trail of footprints I then skirted the water until I came to the Black Rocks. There I sat down and began my thinking.

The first item I was sure about was my good fortune in being wanted by such a fine girl as Sally. But two other women had wanted me also, with unfortunate consequences both for them and for me. So what were my chances in the future? Would I find happiness with Sally and she with me? I stood up again and went to the furthermost point of the rocks, slipping and sliding on the limpet-studded surface. I remained there for a good twenty minutes, staring at the waves. Had Mark been right with his clever metaphor about ranging with breech-loaders? Had I reached too far on the one occasion and under-reached on the other?

Suddenly I made up my mind. The target was there for the hitting and I was a fool to hesitate. I glanced at my watch. It was half past three. If I hurried I would be at Newton School before closing bell. I clambered across the rocks and took a short cut across the dunes to the village.

But when I reached the Green I paused. Facing me was St John's Church and for a fleeting moment I saw again the scene that had been enacted in the porch: Bethan crying, her mother scowling, the vicar intoning, 'Are you to press a charge, Mr Vaughan?' I shuddered, the memory too painful to bear. Surely, I thought, fate would be more kind to me in the future.

Then the school bell rang and children poured from the door. Some of them ran past me, shouting a greeting as they went. I waited until the last was out of sight, then crossed the road and entered the vestibule. There another door confronted me. I took a deep breath and gingerly pushed it open. The smell of chalk and old books assailed me, and when I peered in I saw Sally seated at her desk, which was before a roaring fire.

Quietly I entered the room. Sally did not see me at first, for she was engrossed in marking a register. Then my foot creaked on a floor board and she looked up. Surprise and consternation flooded her face, as well they might, for it was my first visit to the place.

'Hullo, Sally,' I said.

'Hullo, John.' Sally got up from the desk and stood beside it, flustered and with her consternation growing. 'What are you doing here?'

'I've come to ask you,' I said in a voice unusually low for me, 'if you'll have me for a husband.'

Sally did not seem to believe me at first, then realisation dawned and she laughed and cried at the same time, which is a feminine attribute that always disconcerts me. So I just held out my arms and she ran into them, which was as good an answer as any.

CHAPTER THIRTY

SALLY AND I were married at Easter in Nottage Presbyterian chapel and have lived happily ever since, which is a good point to end this story. Thereafter my life became uneventful, without fights, mishaps or strife of any kind, an excellent state of affairs but uninteresting to all except me. All stories have loose ends, however, which must be tied up before a tale can be adjudged complete, and this I will now endeavour to do.

My love for Sally was not of the tempestuous variety, which is a good thing. It was slow to grow, like a shrub that starts hesitantly but ends with a multitude of blossom. Truth to tell, I did not realise how cynical I had become, for my armour had been pierced too deep and to often for comfort. But with gentle affection Sally healed the wounds and made the second half of my life as happy as the first had been unfortunate; so much so that I could not contemplate life without her. And for that I am also grateful to Mrs Treseder, who had a hand in it from the very beginning.

We intended making our marriage a quiet affair but the Treseders would have none of it, and I swear that half the population of

Porthcawl turned up to see us wed. Alexander Brogden insisted that I return to work the very next day and this I did, determined to give him no chance to find fault with me. He never took to me, or I to him so, when the opportunity arose to purchase my Aunt Sarah's old cottage in Newton, I did not hesitate, and we left Pilot Row. It was not the grand house I had envisaged in my earlier years but it was comfortable, had enough rooms for our requirements and, above all, was our own, which meant security of tenure.

Although I never liked Alexander Brogden, I must admit that he had a good eye for business, and under his forceful leadership the docks prospered exceedingly. In 1871 no less than 165,000 tons of coal were shipped, a record bettered on only one other occasion. But the men did not like him either and there was general rejoicing when James Brogden returned from New Zealand; so much so that a song was written in his honour, sung first at a dinner at Aberkenfig, which I attended.

With him he brought his new wife, Mary Caroline. His choice surprised us at first for Mary, like her predecessor, was of army stock: indeed she was related to the famous General Picton, of Waterloo fame, and had that illustrious man's martial attributes in no small measure. So formidable did she appear to some that there was talk of James Brogden having fallen into the same trap as before: but there was this difference—Mary Caroline loved her husband deeply, and came to love Porthcawl also, to such an extent that in later years it was she who became the main force in the building of the new town.

James Brogden welcomed me with great warmth and was delighted that I had made a happy marriage. He lost no time in appointing me as overseer of supplies, not only for the dock but for the town as well, and I soon found myself working eighteen hours a day; a state of affairs I did not mind for it was rewarding to see the long-laid plans come to fruition. A new promenade was constructed with three magnificent streets leading to it, John Street (named after the father) and Mary Street and Caroline Street (after Mrs Brogden). Soon a great new National School was built and when Florence Nightingale gave her support to the building of a Rest Home for poor people, Porthcawl became a town to be reckoned with.

180

But underneath the seeming prosperity all was not well. James, as might be expected, quarrelled again with his brother and they were foolish enough to take their differences to court. Expensive litigation followed and James, already financially weakened by the failure of the New Zealand venture, found himself in difficulties; and soon the partnership was dissolved. To add to these mishaps trade at the docks declined rapidly, chiefly due to the competition of other, greater ports, such as Swansea, Aberafon and Cardiff. The Brogden affairs were placed in the hand of the Official Receiver and, to raise money, Sea Bank House was mortgaged. This last attempt to stave off disaster failed, and James Brogden was adjudged bankrupt. I, too, lost all my money, for the shares were now worthless; but my chagrin at this was nothing compared with the distress I felt at seeing a great and gentle man brought low.

Fortunately for me Mark's trading venture continued to flourish, and this has been our main source of income in later years, for Sally stopped teaching when our first child was born. The Treseders are old now, but Dafydd's son has taken over the business; and the dividend we receive each half year is enough to keep us in tolerable comfort. Within a year of James Brogden's return I heard that Catherine had married an earl, and it is my fervent wish that she, also, is happy; although I often wonder if she thinks of me and misses the sea air of which she was so fond.

As the century draws to a close my leg is troubling me a great deal, and I am limited to walks as far as Newton beach, which is no penance for I never tire of the view along the coast to Nash. Sometimes, on summer evenings, I sit on the village green, regaling the children with tales of the dock in its hey-day. They have some awe of me still I believe, principally because of my stick and eye patch, but many of them are the children of the youngsters I helped to save; and so they have respect also, which pleases me and makes me think that I will be remembered for some little time yet.

Occasionally I take a carriage and visit Porthcawl, where I am saddened at the sight of the docks, now largely empty and in decay. Only a short while ago one could see hundreds of masts, but now only a few; and the silence there is oppressive. I cannot but feel how wasteful it is that so many men laboured for so long at a project so quickly brought to nought. Even the talk I hear that Porthcawl will become a fine seaside resort fails to dispel my gloom; and the sight of Sea Bank House, now a boarding school for boys, is particularly depressing.

But my most vivid memories return when I walk on the breakwater itself, for there I am constantly reminded of how this great wall of stone has affected my life. I see the place where Cap Coch unleashed his blast at me and marvel at the accuracy of Old Meg the gipsy's prognostications. I pass the spot where I fought Jeremiah and Ezekiel Meredith and shudder with horror at the memory of that vicious encounter. Then, at the end of the structure, where they have erected the beacon, I never cease to recall my plunge into the waves to save the iron-ore ship and its precious cargo. Even now I have nightmares about that rash act, dreaming that I am about to be drowned. Fortunately that spot also has the happiest memory of all, for it was there that Sally found me on my first day of recuperation and began the process by which I was finally restored, physically and mentally. I can see her now, walking towards me, smiling and with the dictionary in her hand.

As I look back I have many regrets, knowing full well that I have often lacked in generosity and compassion; although I suppose this is the lot of most men, for none of us is perfect. But I have one regret above all others and it is this: although the breakwater has a special significance for me I never cease to remember the men who laboured so long in danger and adversity to build it; but their names are now all forgotten. There is not even a plaque to commemorate them. Yet I know that in the distant future, when the docks have finally ceased to function and Porthcawl is a great and thriving town, the breakwater will still be in existence, possibly until the end of time, and if this brief account has gone some way to correcting such a grievous omission then I shall be well satisfied.